Much Ado about Nutmeg

Books by Sarah Fox

The Literary Pub Mystery Series
Wine and Punishment
An Ale of Two Cities

The Pancake House Mystery Series
Much Ado about Nutmeg
The Crêpes of Wrath
For Whom the Bread Rolls
Of Spice and Men
Yeast of Eden
Crêpe Expectations

The Music Lover's Mystery Series
Dead Ringer
Death in A Major
Deadly Overtures

Much Ado about Nutmeg

Sarah Fox

LYRICAL UNDERGROUND
Kensington Publishing Corp.
www.kensingtonbooks.com

LYRICAL UNDERGROUND BOOKS are published by

Kensington Publishing Corp.
119 West 40th Street
New York, NY 10018

All Kensington titles, imprints, and distributed lines are available at special quantity discounts for bulk purchases for sales promotion, premiums, fund-raising, educational, or institutional use.

Special book excerpts or customized printings can also be created to fit specific needs. For details, write or phone the office of the Kensington Sales Manager: Kensington Publishing Corp., 119 West 40th Street, New York, NY 10018. Attn. Sales Department. Phone: 1-800-221-2647.

Lyrical Underground and Lyrical Underground logo Reg. US Pat. & TM Off.

First Electronic Edition: January 2020
ISBN-13: 978-1-5161-0776-6 (ebook)
ISBN-10: 1-5161-0776-4 (ebook)

First Print Edition: January 2020
ISBN-13: 978-1-5161-0779-7
ISBN-10: 1-5161-0779-9

Printed in the United States of America

Chapter One

Wildwood Cove's population of senior citizens was about to double. The seaside town was already bustling with activity, thanks to all the tourists who'd arrived to enjoy the beautiful beach and the charming town now that the summer season was at its height. Over the next few days, it was expected to get even busier as seniors flocked to the town. The new arrivals wouldn't be frail old ladies or doddery men, though. In fact, these seniors would probably put plenty of young people to shame, because they were heading to Wildwood Cove to compete in the Golden Oldies Games, a statewide sporting event for athletes aged fifty and over.

As the owner of The Flip Side—the local pancake house—I was more than happy to welcome the visitors to my town. Business was always good during the tourist season, but I was expecting it to be even better over the next couple of weeks. The athletes wouldn't be the only new arrivals; coaches, family members, and spectators would also be coming to the games. Hopefully they'd bring their appetites with them.

The sporting events wouldn't get underway until the weekend—still a few days away—but I'd heard through the town grapevine that the organizers and even some athletes had already arrived in Wildwood Cove.

In anticipation of the increased business, I dug four extra tables out from the storage room. With the help of the doorstop, I left the front door of the pancake house open so I could move the tables outdoors. As I was dragging the first one across the floor, Leigh Hunter hurried into the restaurant, a few minutes early for her waitressing shift.

"Let me help you with that, Marley." She grabbed one side of the table, instantly lightening my load.

"Thanks," I said with a grateful smile as we tipped the table so it would fit through the door.

"We're going to need the extra seating over the coming days," Leigh said, backing out of the pancake house.

"That's what I'm hoping." We set the table down on the pavement outside The Flip Side's large front window and I took a moment to gaze out at the ocean. "And I'm sure some of our customers will want to make the most of this gorgeous weather."

"Who wouldn't?"

The Flip Side was located on the paved promenade that ran along the top of Wildwood Beach. It had the best view in town, especially on a day like this, with the early morning sunshine sparkling on the ocean waves and the blue sky clear except for a few puffy white clouds drifting along. It wasn't yet seven o'clock, but already the sun warmed my face.

I reminded myself that I still had work to do and headed back indoors. Leigh helped me move the other three tables and several chairs out onto the pavement. When that was done, I set out a large dish of water for any thirsty dogs that might need a drink while their owners enjoyed a meal of pancakes or crêpes.

I didn't bother to close the door once I was finished setting up outside. The fresh, salty breeze drifting in off the ocean was too pleasant to shut out. Later we'd probably need the door closed and the air-conditioning on, but for now the temperature was perfect inside and out.

The pancake house opened at seven and it didn't take long for the first customers to show up. By eight o'clock the place was hopping, and I donned my red apron and jumped in to help serve the customers.

"Talk about a full house!" Sienna Murray said as she passed by me on her way to deliver plates of crêpes and waffles to a table of four. Sienna would be starting her senior year of high school in a few weeks' time. During the year, she worked at The Flip Side on weekends, but at the moment she was working five days a week just like Leigh.

"It's a nice sight to see," I commented before Sienna was out of earshot.

Every table was occupied at the moment, indoors and out. Half a dozen people hovered outside the door, waiting for space to free up. It wasn't often that we had a line and the booming business brought a smile to my face.

An hour or so later, the rush of customers slowed slightly. Most of the tables were still occupied, but there were a couple of free ones inside and there was no longer a line at the door. I was about to untie my apron and head into my office to take care of some administrative tasks, when one of The Flip Side's regular customers arrived.

Leaving my apron on, I grabbed the coffeepot and headed across the restaurant as Marjorie Wells pulled out a chair at one of the free tables. She kept her gray hair cropped short and was usually dressed ready for a workout. Today was no exception. She wore sporty shorts and a tank top, with running shoes on her feet. As soon as she sat down, she removed her phone from her armband and set it on the table, off to one side.

"Morning, Marjorie," I greeted as I poured coffee into a mug, not needing to ask if she wanted any. "Will Eleanor be joining you?"

Eleanor Crosby was one of Marjorie's closest friends. They dined together at the pancake house at least once a week.

"She'll be here any moment," Marjorie replied.

I rested the coffeepot on the table. "Are you all set for the games?"

"You bet. I've been training every day for months now. I can't wait to get out there and race next week."

Although in her sixties, Marjorie was one of the most active people I knew. She swam in the ocean every day during the summer, she got around town either on foot or on her bicycle, and she played regular games of badminton and squash. She'd also taken up racewalking in the past year or so, and when she heard that the Golden Oldies Games would take place in Wildwood Cove, she'd wasted no time signing up to compete in that event.

"I'm hoping I can be there to cheer you on," I said.

"Thanks, Marley. Even if you can't make it, I appreciate the sentiment."

"I'll definitely do my best to be there," I assured her before continuing on my way around the restaurant, refilling mugs for anyone who wanted more coffee.

As I finished my rounds, Eleanor arrived. I waved to her before gathering up dirty dishes from a table that had recently freed up. I knew Leigh would take Marjorie's and Eleanor's orders, so I carried the dishes into the kitchen.

When I returned to the dining room, a group of four adults had just entered the pancake house. I directed them to an open table and made sure they each had a menu. Three of the new customers—two fair-haired women and a man with graying dark hair—appeared to be in their mid- to late fifties. Their clothes were fairly casual but looked expensive, as did the gold jewelry the two women wore.

The fourth member of their group didn't quite fit in, appearance-wise. He wore jeans and a form hugging T-shirt that showed off his muscular build. He was good-looking, with golden blond hair and blue eyes, and was probably in his late thirties, a few years older than me. As I filled coffee mugs, I noticed the woman sitting next to him place her hand on his knee.

"I'm Marley McKinney, The Flip Side's owner," I said as I filled the fourth mug. "Are you visitors to Wildwood Cove?"

"We are," the older man replied. "We're competing in the Golden Oldies Games. Well, three of us are, anyway. Levi's not a golden oldie yet." He smiled at the younger man.

The woman next to Levi gave his knee a squeeze. "Just golden."

Levi grinned at her and covered her hand with his own.

"Which sports?" I asked the group at large.

"Tennis," the older man said. He offered me his hand and I shook it. "I'm Easton Miller. My wife, Rowena, and I are competing in mixed doubles and Pippa here"—he nodded at the woman next to Levi—"is in the singles event."

"Is that how you all met?" I asked. "Through tennis?"

"No," Pippa replied. "Tennis just happens to be a shared interest. Rowena and I go way back, and she and Easton went to school together." Pippa smiled as her eyes met Levi's. "And Levi's my personal trainer."

Very personal, by the looks of things, but I kept that thought to myself.

"Good luck with the games," I said with a smile. "And welcome to Wildwood Cove. I hope you'll enjoy your stay here."

I left them to look over their menus, after assuring them that Leigh would be there to take their orders shortly. The pancake house was nearly full again, so I quickly gathered up dirty dishes from a table by the window, wanting to free it up as soon as possible.

"It should be cool," Tommy Park was saying to chef Ivan Kaminski as I entered the kitchen. "I get a press pass so I'll have up-close access to all the events."

Ivan acknowledged his assistant's statement with a nod as he flipped pancakes on the griddle.

"Press pass?" I echoed, setting my load down on the counter by the dishwasher.

Tommy paused in the midst of adding some crispy bacon to a plate of eggs Benedict and sausages. "I'll be doing some sports photography for the *Wildwood Cove Weekly,*" he explained, referring to the local newspaper. "I won't get paid for it, but I might get to see some of my photos in the paper."

"That's great," I said.

Tommy was a talented photographer and had recently landed a few paying jobs taking photos for local businesses to post on their websites. He'd also agreed to do the photography at my upcoming wedding.

I loaded the dishes into the dishwasher. "Speaking of photography..."

The door swung open and Sienna scurried into the kitchen. "Guess what!"

"Just tell me it's nothing bad," I said, although I was pretty sure it wasn't. Sienna wouldn't have been smiling if there was a disaster unfolding in the other room.

"Not bad, but definitely surprising."

"Don't leave us in suspense." Tommy returned from the pass-through window where he'd set the plate of eggs Benedict. It had disappeared almost immediately as Leigh grabbed it from the other side of the window.

"Ed's here," Sienna said.

"Ed Herman?" I asked.

"Yep."

Ivan added whipped cream and fresh strawberries to the stack of pancakes he'd set on a plate. "That's not surprising."

Ed showed up at The Flip Side at least twice every week with his buddy Gary.

"Sure," Sienna said, her grin widening. "But how often does he show up with a woman?"

"Seriously?" Tommy asked. "That's got to be a first."

I turned on the dishwasher before facing Sienna. "Just a woman? No Gary?"

"No Gary." Sienna's smile was lighting up the room. "I think he's on a date."

That was definitely unexpected. I'd lived in Wildwood Cove for more than a year now, and I'd never seen Ed in the sole company of a woman. I'd also never heard of him dating anyone.

Tommy peeked through the pass-through window. "She's got to be at least ten years younger than him."

I took a quick look myself before pulling Tommy away from the window. "We don't want to get caught staring." I could see that Leigh was busy at another table. "I'll go take their orders."

"Find out who she is," Sienna said as I headed for the door. "I've never seen her before."

I was as curious as Sienna and Tommy, but I didn't want to grill Ed. Hopefully he'd offer up some information without any prodding.

Grabbing the coffeepot on my way by, I headed straight for his table.

"Morning, Ed." I filled his mug, knowing he never went without at least one cup of coffee at the pancake house.

"Morning, Marley." Ed had a big smile on his face and a touch of red in his cheeks. "I'd like you to meet my friend Yvonne Pritchard."

I exchanged greetings with the woman. Her hair was the same honey-blond shade as Rowena Miller's, but with dark roots just beginning to show.

Tommy was right about the age difference. Ed was retired and Yvonne appeared to be in her early to mid-fifties.

"Are you new to town?" I asked her as I filled her mug, after checking that she wanted coffee.

"I'm here temporarily," she said. "I just arrived yesterday."

Ed beamed at her. "We met at the bakery. Yvonne's a reporter with the *Seattle Insider*. A sports reporter."

"You must be here to cover the Golden Oldies Games," I said.

"That's right," she confirmed. "But I'm enjoying a couple days of R-and-R first."

Ed took a sip of coffee, his grin returning immediately afterward. "I'm going to show her the sights."

"That's great." I smiled at him before addressing Yvonne. "I hope you'll enjoy your time in Wildwood Cove."

I took their orders—blueberry pancakes with bacon and sausages for Ed and banana nut pancakes for Yvonne—and returned to the kitchen.

Sienna had been wiping down a table, but she followed me through the swinging door.

"Well?" she asked as soon as we were in the kitchen.

"Her name's Yvonne Pritchard," I said. "She's a sports reporter from Seattle, here to cover the games. She and Ed just met yesterday, but he already seems smitten."

"That's so cute," Sienna said.

It was, but I wasn't exactly free of concerns. Yvonne wouldn't be in town for long. I'd grown fond of Ed over the past year and I was glad he was happy, but I had a niggling feeling that the sports reporter could end up breaking his heart.

Chapter Two

The next couple of days were so busy that they passed in a flash. Before I knew it, Friday had arrived, and along with it came even more hungry customers. Most—if not all—the athletes competing in the games had arrived in town, along with everyone else involved in the event. The opening ceremonies would take place that evening in Wildwood Park, and several customers told me that they hoped to take in the free festivities. I planned to go as well, after heading home first. I was comfortable in the pancake house in my jeans and a T-shirt, thanks to the air-conditioning, but with the sun beating down outside, I knew it would be a different story at the park.

After The Flip Side shut down at two o'clock, I spent time cleaning, paying invoices, and updating the pancake house's website. As I'd anticipated, the walk home along the beach left me hot and thirsty, and I was glad to reach my beachfront Victorian, where my cat and dog waited for me, along with an ice cold pitcher of sweet tea in the fridge.

I made a mental note to pack a pair of shorts in my tote bag the next morning so I could change before leaving the pancake house at the end of the workday. The first few weeks of summer had been relatively cool, but that was no longer the case.

The animals were as happy to see me as I was to see them, but I didn't stick around too long. I let them spend some time out in the yard while I changed into a cooler outfit and drank a tall glass of iced tea, and then I set off again, heading back into town on foot and making my way to Wildwood Park. Although the sun beat down on my shoulders, I didn't second-guess my decision to walk. If I'd driven, I could have enjoyed my car's air-conditioning, but I was glad for the chance to stretch my legs and enjoy the fresh air. Even if I did get too hot, I could always stop by Scoops Ice Cream after the opening ceremonies.

As I got closer to the park, I realized I'd made a good decision by leaving my car at home. Every parking spot was taken and a good crowd had already gathered. The limited shade offered by the trees had been claimed by people with blankets and lawn chairs, and the sunny areas were filling up too. At one end of the park, a small stage had been set up. A row of chairs on the stage stood empty, but upbeat music played from the large speakers set at either side of the platform.

I made my way around picnic blankets, chairs, and groups of people standing around chatting. I searched for familiar faces in the crowd, but so far I hadn't recognized anyone. Many of the people present were probably family members of the athletes, in town to cheer on their loved ones. I also noticed a photographer, snapping photos of people I assumed were athletes. He had a nose like a hawk and had plenty of gel in his brown hair to keep it spiked on top. As I passed him, he introduced himself to a group of three women as Jay Henkel. He didn't look familiar and his name didn't ring a bell, so I assumed he was from out of town. Our local paper had only two full-time employees and I knew both, at least by sight.

A moment later I finally caught sight of my best friend, Lisa Morales. She was lounging in a lawn chair, with Ivan in the seat next to her. A cooler sat on the grass in front of them.

Lisa shaded her eyes and waved as she saw me approaching. "Hey, Marley. Where's Brett?" she asked, referring to my fiancé.

"Still working," I said as I reached her. "But he's meeting me here later."

"You'll sit with us, right?"

"Sure, if you don't mind."

"Of course we don't," Ivan said.

Lisa frowned. "Too bad we didn't bring an extra chair."

Ivan moved to get up. "I can go home and get one."

"No," I said quickly. "That's okay. I'll sit on the grass."

He got up anyway. "Take my seat."

"Thanks, Ivan, but I'm fine. Really." I plunked myself down on the grass.

Ivan scowled at me, but that was his usual expression so it didn't worry me.

He lowered himself back into his chair. "You'll eat with us."

It sounded more like a command than an invitation, but Ivan's gruffness didn't bother me anymore. He looked intimidating with his large muscles, tattoos, and almost permanent scowl, and he sounded scary at times too, but I knew he was a good man with a big heart.

Lisa knew it too. She and Ivan had been dating for several months now. "Ivan packed us a picnic," Lisa said, nodding at the cooler. "I hope you'll help us eat it. He made all the food himself, and we've got plenty of it."

"Then I'd be a fool not to take you up on your offer," I said. "No one cooks better than you do, Ivan."

He accepted the compliment with a hint of a nod. Lisa took his hand and gave it a squeeze. I noticed that he returned the pressure and his typical scowl eased slightly. I smiled, loving the fact that they made each other so happy.

As I made myself more comfortable on the grass, I checked out the crowd around us. I spotted a woman with honey-blond hair and thought she was Ed's new lady friend, Yvonne, until I realized that Easton Miller was there too. The woman with him was his wife, Rowena, not Yvonne.

I waved to the Millers as they set up their folding lawn chairs on a free patch of grass nearby. They waved back and a moment later Pippa and Levi joined them, settling on a picnic blanket next to their friends.

"They're not locals, are they?" Lisa asked.

"No, they're here to compete. Well, three of them are," I amended.

Before I could say anything more, a man approached the microphone at center stage and announced that it was time for the ceremonies to begin. Speeches followed, luckily not lasting too long. Then a video played on a large screen, highlighting inspiring stories of athletes from past Golden Oldies Games. By that point, Ivan had opened the cooler, and we munched on delicious finger foods as we watched. Not long after the video finished, the main part of the opening ceremonies wrapped up.

A concert was scheduled to take place next. A Seattle band had been booked to play for the next couple of hours, and most people were sticking around to enjoy the music. I'd grown tired of sitting on the ground, so I decided to get up and stretch my legs while the band set up onstage. I walked around the edge of the park, smiling at a few people I recognized, including Pippa. She was in conversation with a dark-haired man I'd never seen before, but she smiled back as I passed by.

Food trucks had parked along one street at the edge of the park and had a steady stream of customers. I saw Ed in line at a taco truck and a second later I realized that Yvonne Pritchard was mere feet away from me, standing in the shade of a maple tree, another woman I didn't recognize chatting with her.

I was about to say hello to Yvonne when I caught what her companion was saying.

"Looks like you've got an admirer, Yvonne," the woman said, her eyes on Ed as he picked up his order at the taco truck.

The reporter smirked. "I figure it's worth putting up with him for a few days since he likes to pay for my meals."

I barely kept my jaw from dropping. Anger burned in my chest and rose up to heat my cheeks. I was about to turn on Yvonne and give her a piece of my mind when Ed passed in front of me.

"Hi, Marley," he said. He was carrying drinks and tacos on a cardboard tray and had a big smile on his face.

I forced myself to smile in return. "Hi, Ed."

"Beautiful day, isn't it?"

"It is," I managed to say, despite the fact that my jaw wanted to clench.

He'd reached Yvonne by then, so I kept walking. Anger continued to warm my cheeks far more than the summer sunshine. Ed was such a nice man, and he seemed so smitten with the sports reporter. The fact that she was using him to get free meals made me furious. It was probably a good thing Ed had spoken to me when he did, otherwise I might have let my anger get the best of me.

I wished I could tell Ed what I'd overheard, but I didn't want to be responsible for hurting him and wiping that big smile off his face. Besides, would he even believe me? I wanted to think he'd know I'd never make something like that up, but I also knew that feelings like the ones he had for Yvonne could be blinding.

But if I didn't say something, would I be setting him up to be crushed by Yvonne?

I was still angry and upset when I'd completed my circuit of the park. Marjorie called out, waving me over to her, and I welcomed the distraction. She stood near the park's drinking fountain and was talking with a slender woman with long, jet-black hair.

"Claudia," Marjorie said to the woman, "this is Marley McKinney, the owner of the local pancake house. Marley, this is Claudia Wu, one of my fellow competitors."

I exchanged greetings with the women, masking my surprise. Claudia had to be at least fifty to compete in the Golden Oldies Games, but she easily could have passed for being in her early forties.

"Have you competed in race walking before?" I asked her.

"Oh, yes. I've been involved in the sport for a few years now, and I compete in several events each year."

"She's too modest to add that she wins most of her competitions," Marjorie said. "She's the favorite to win here."

Claudia smiled. "I've been fortunate to do well in recent events, but you never know what will happen on race day."

"I think it's great that both of you are competing," I said. "It's inspiring to see so many people staying active over age fifty."

I noticed someone waving out of the corner of my eye. As I turned that way, I realized it was Tommy. He jogged over to us, a camera around his neck.

"Evening, ladies."

"Hi, Tommy." I introduced him to Claudia. "Taking some pictures for the paper?"

"Yep. I thought I'd get a few shots tonight. Do you mind if I take a couple of the two of you?" he asked Marjorie and Claudia.

They readily agreed and moved closer together, smiling as Tommy snapped a few shots.

"Perfect," he said as he lowered his camera. "Thanks. I'm going to track down a few more athletes for some photos. See you in the morning, Marley."

We bid him good-bye, and Claudia excused herself as well.

I shaded my eyes so I could get a look at the stage. Several musicians were up on the platform with guitars, a keyboard, a bass, and a drum kit.

"Looks like the concert's about to start," I commented.

"Excuse me," a sugary voice said.

Marjorie and I both turned toward its owner.

I gritted my teeth and forced my expression to remain neutral when I realized it was Yvonne who'd joined us.

"Are you one of the athletes?" she asked Marjorie.

"I am. I'm competing in the race walking event."

"And you're a local?"

"I sure am. I was born and raised here in Wildwood Cove."

"Fabulous." The reporter's tone was far different than when I'd overheard her earlier. "I'm Yvonne Pritchard with the *Seattle Insider*. I'd love to interview you."

She gave no indication that she'd met me before. She didn't so much as glance my way.

"Oh." Marjorie said, sounding pleased. "Sure. Why not?"

"I'll see you later," I said to Marjorie, wanting to get away from Yvonne. If I didn't, I might end up saying something scathing and I didn't want to cause a scene. I also didn't want to spoil Marjorie's moment.

"What's it like competing in your hometown?" I heard Yvonne ask as I walked away.

I had to take a quick step to the side to avoid two little kids running across the grass. I was about to continue along my intended path when I noticed a tanned, blond man standing in my way, glowering at something beyond my right shoulder.

"I can't believe she dared to show her face here," he said under his breath, his voice full of venom.

The intensity of the anger on his face startled me. I could practically feel the heat of it radiating off his body. Without ever noticing me, he turned on his heel and stormed off. I shot a glance over my shoulder, wondering who he'd been talking about.

My gaze landed on Yvonne Pritchard.

Chapter Three

Clearly I wasn't the only one who was less than impressed by Yvonne. I didn't know who the blond man was or why he had a problem with the sports reporter. The ferocity of his anger left me uneasy, but so did Yvonne. She obviously wasn't the nice woman she pretended to be with Ed, and she'd inspired such hatred in the blond man. That only left me all the more worried about Ed's relationship with her. But what could I do about it?

Not much, I decided. It would be best to mind my own business. Hopefully Yvonne would be gone once the games were over, if not before. It seemed that would be best for everyone, especially Ed, even if he didn't realize it.

That said, he was a grown man and had likely survived heartaches in the past. If Yvonne ended up hurting him, he'd have plenty of friends around to support him.

A man had approached the microphone onstage and was introducing the band. Before the music got started, I quickly returned to Lisa and Ivan and told them I was heading out. Although my original plan was to hang around for the concert, I no longer felt like staying at the park. All I really wanted to do was to spend some quiet time with Brett.

The band struck up the first song as I made my way out of the park. I paused at the edge of the audience to send a text message to Brett, asking if he wanted to meet me at Scoops Ice Cream. A delicious treat enjoyed while walking on the beach with my fiancé would be the perfect way to end the day.

Once I'd hit SEND, I glanced up and spotted Sienna's mom, Patricia Murray. She was heading my way and stopped to chat.

"Not staying for the concert?" she asked.

"No," I replied. "I've got a craving for ice cream and Brett's company."

"Let me guess—you're meeting him at Scoops."

"Got it in one," I said with a smile.

"Not long until the wedding now."

My smile brightened. "Less than a month." I felt like I'd been floating on a cloud of happiness ever since Brett had proposed to me back in the spring. I couldn't wait for our late-summer wedding.

"Have you got your dress?" Patricia asked.

"I've picked one out," I said, "but it hasn't arrived yet. I ordered it online. I'm not a big fan of shopping, so I thought this would be an easy way to go." I crossed my fingers. "I hope it wasn't a bad decision."

"I bet it'll be fine. If you need alterations, you can always get Sally North to help you out. She owns the tailoring shop here in town."

"That's good to know, thanks. I'll keep her in mind."

We chatted for another minute or two about the wedding plans before Patricia continued on her way into the park. I checked my phone and saw that I'd received a response from Brett. He'd arrived home from work and was about to have a quick shower, but he'd meet me at Scoops in twenty minutes. That sounded perfect.

I was about to leave the park behind when I ran into Tommy again. This time he had a young woman with him. She had long auburn hair and appeared to be in her early twenties, like Tommy. She held a sheaf of papers in one hand and was giggling at something he'd said.

"Leaving already?" Tommy asked when he saw me.

"I'm answering the siren call of ice cream," I said.

He grinned. "I already gave in to that temptation earlier today." He addressed the young woman at his side. "This is Marley, my boss at the pancake house."

"Avery Adair." She held out a hand to me. "I'm an event volunteer."

I shook her hand. "Nice to meet you. Are you from Wildwood Cove?"

"Port Angeles, actually. But I heard about the volunteer opportunity through my archery club and thought it would be fun to help out. Speaking of which…" She grabbed the top page off her pile of papers and offered it to me. "Are you interested in the event schedule?"

I glanced down at the paper. It listed all the days, times, and venues for the different sports. "Thanks. This is great. I definitely want to check out at least a few competitions."

"I hope you do. It should be fun." Avery took a step back. "Anyway, I should make the rounds and hand out more of these. Keep me company, Tommy?"

I half-expected her to bat her eyelashes at him. From the way she was looking at Tommy, it was clear that Ed wasn't the only one in town with a crush.

"Sure." He gave me a parting grin. "Enjoy your ice cream."

"I will," I assured him.

I thought I'd make it out of the park without further delays, but when I reached the sidewalk the sound of angry voices drew me to a halt. Near the end of the line of food trucks, Claudia Wu and Yvonne Pritchard were facing off. I couldn't hear much of what they were saying, but the snippets I caught weren't the least bit friendly.

I stayed put, not wanting to land in the middle of the heated argument.

"You're nothing but a pathetic troll." Claudia practically spat the words at Yvonne.

Before the reporter could respond, Claudia strode off, her head held high, her eyes flashing with fury.

Yvonne rolled her eyes with a sour expression on her face and pulled out her phone. She started texting as she walked back into the park as if nothing had happened.

The tension that had built up in my shoulders eased slightly. I shook my head and continued on my way, hoping I could make it to the ice cream shop without encountering any further drama.

* * * *

My evening with Brett was as relaxing as I'd hoped it would be, and it helped me to push all the drama at the park to the back of my mind. Brett and I both worked on Saturdays, so we were up early the next morning, and I set off for The Flip Side a few minutes before six o'clock. I made the trip on foot, as I usually did during nice weather, and followed the beach toward town.

It was a perfect summer morning. The blue sky was clear of clouds, and the rising sun was peeking over the horizon, its light glinting off the ocean waves. A heron waded through the shallows and an eagle soared overhead. The salty air and the rhythmic breaking of the waves brought me a sense of peace and I couldn't help but smile. I lived in a beautiful town, I was engaged to the love of my life, and I owned a business that I enjoyed. I didn't think life could get much better.

I was only a minute or so away from the pancake house when my smile faltered. I shaded my eyes to get a look at a boat traveling parallel to the shore, heading eastward. It wasn't too far out, and I was pretty sure it was a Coast Guard vessel. I paused, watching the boat for a moment before I continued on my way. Hopefully it was just a routine patrol and nothing bad had happened. As much as I wanted that to be the case, a nugget of unease had taken up residence among the peace and happiness I'd felt moments before.

When I arrived at The Flip Side, I made sure the restaurant would be ready to open at seven. That didn't take long and when everything was set, I had some time to spare, so I stopped by the kitchen to make myself a cup of tea.

Leigh showed up as I was fishing the tea bag out of my cup.

"How's the wedding planning going?" she asked me as she poured herself a cup of coffee.

"So far, so good. I've ordered my dress—hopefully it'll fit—but I still need to take care of the cake and flowers." I blew on my hot tea. "I wonder if Marielle does wedding cakes."

Marielle owned and operated the local bakery.

"I'll do the cake," Ivan said as he chopped up some asparagus.

"It's nice of you to offer, Ivan, but I don't want you to have to do any work for the wedding."

He glared at me over the island worktop. "I'll do it. Unless you'd rather Marielle did."

"No, no," I said quickly. "It's not that at all. Any cake you make will be amazing, but I don't want you to feel obligated."

He returned to chopping, his knife *thunk-thunk*ing rhythmically against the cutting board. "I don't feel obligated. I want to do it."

A big smile took over my face. "Thanks, Ivan. We'll have to talk about payment."

This time the glare he sent my way nearly turned me to stone. "You're not paying me."

"But—"

"Consider it my gift to you and Brett."

My smile returned. I set my cup on the counter as I made my way around the island. Ivan set down his knife just before I hugged him.

"You're the best, Ivan. Thank you."

He gave me a quick squeeze and then released me. Maybe I was imagining things, but when I stepped back I thought I spied the slightest smile on his face.

Tommy had been in the walk-in pantry and emerged at that moment with a big bag of flour. He began talking to Ivan about their prep work while Leigh and I left the kitchen with our drinks in hand. We finished up our tea and coffee, and Sienna arrived just before it was time to open the door to customers. We predicted another busy day and we weren't wrong. Within minutes of opening, several tables were occupied, and it only got busier from there.

I helped out Leigh and Sienna with taking orders and delivering meals as more customers arrived. Even with three of us working, we barely had a moment to rest. Shortly after eight o'clock, Lisa showed up with her seventy-something neighbor Joan, whom I now considered a friend. After a five-minute wait, a table by the window was free and they claimed it as soon as Sienna cleaned it up. I grabbed the coffeepot on my way to their table, knowing they'd both want some. Lisa never liked to start a day without at least one cup of coffee.

"Morning," I said as I filled their mugs. "How are you doing today?"

"I'm not fully awake yet, but otherwise good," Lisa said, pulling her mug of coffee closer to her.

"We're certainly doing better than some people this morning," Joan added.

"Which people?" I asked, wondering what she meant.

"You haven't heard the news?"

Apprehension skittered up my spine. "What news?"

"One of the athletes," Lisa started. "Dr. Miller, I think his name is."

"Miller," I echoed. "As in Easton Miller?"

"You've met him?" Lisa asked.

"Remember the people I waved to at the park yesterday? That was him and his wife. I met them here on Wednesday."

Lisa exchanged a glance with Joan.

"What is it?" I asked, my apprehension growing. "What happened to him?"

"Nobody seems to know quite *how* it happened," Joan said, "but he fell overboard while on his yacht. Now he's missing and presumed dead."

Chapter Four

If Joan hadn't told me about Easton Miller, I would have found out soon anyway. By midmorning it seemed as though the whole town had heard the news. It was the hot topic of conversation at The Flip Side for the rest of the morning. The locals didn't know the Millers, but some of the athletes and coaches who were dining at the pancake house were acquainted with the couple. Although it was the first day of competition for the Golden Oldies Games, very few diners were chatting about that. Easton Miller's death had overshadowed everything else.

"Poor Rowena," I heard one woman saying to the other three people at her table. "As if she hasn't suffered enough already."

I was curious to know what she meant by that, but I didn't catch her next words.

Patricia Murray and her husband, John, showed up for lunch around noon. Sienna waved to them, but she was in the midst of taking orders at another table so she stayed put. I greeted the couple and left them alone with their menus for a minute while I fetched them both glasses of iced coffee.

"I guess you've heard about the man who fell overboard," Patricia said once I'd returned with their drinks.

"It's terrible news," I said. "I met him and his wife here the other day. It's such a shock that he's gone." I bit down on my lower lip. "I don't suppose there's any chance he's alive?"

"Doubtful, unfortunately," John said. "From what we've heard, he never resurfaced once he went under. Search parties scoured the shoreline this morning and didn't find any sign of him."

"Such a shame," Patricia said. "The Coast Guard is still out looking for him. I hope they find him soon. At least that way his wife can have some closure."

I agreed that was the best outcome to hope for if Easton really had drowned, which he most likely had. It certainly sounded like there wasn't much chance of him surviving.

I swallowed down a lump of sadness. I'd only met the Millers briefly, but I still felt awful about what had happened. I knew too well how hard it was to lose a loved one in a tragic accident.

I took Patricia and John's orders and headed for the kitchen. When I returned to the dining room, I noticed Pippa and her personal trainer, Levi, standing at the front of the short line outside the open door. Two tables had just been vacated, so I hurried to clear them of dirty dishes and wipe them down. Sienna showed the couple to one of the free tables and got them settled with menus. She took their orders a few minutes later, and when I had a free moment, I stopped by their table.

"Hello," I said, reminding myself just in time not to wish them a good morning. It was clearly anything but for them. Pippa looked paler than the last time I'd seen her and she and Levi both wore somber expressions.

"Hello again," Pippa said, her voice subdued. "It's Marley, right?"

"That's right. I wanted to offer my condolences. You've been friends with the Millers for a long time, haven't you?"

"Yes," Pippa said, her voice cracking.

Levi reached across the table and covered one of her hands with his. "She's known them for decades."

"I'm so sorry," I said. "It must be terrible for Rowena."

Pippa nodded, her eyes watery. "She's been so distraught. I prescribed her something to help her rest, but Levi and I will check on her again after we've had some lunch."

Levi's thumb skimmed back and forth over her knuckles. "Pippa hasn't eaten anything yet today."

"I couldn't." One of her tears escaped and rolled down her cheek. She wiped it away with one finger. "I'm so heartbroken. Easton was a good man, and Rowena... Poor Rowena. She's already been through so much."

"I heard someone else mention that too," I said.

As soon as the words were out of my mouth, I wondered if I should have kept quiet, but Pippa didn't seem to think I was prying.

"She and Easton lost their son two years ago," she explained.

"He was only twenty-four," Levi added.

A fierce ache cut through my heart and nearly took my breath away. "That's terrible."

"It was. It all is." Pippa took a napkin from the dispenser and dabbed at her eyes.

Sarah Fox

"I'm so sorry." I hated to intrude on their grief any longer, so I took a step back. "Please let me or Sienna know if you need anything. Your meals will be ready soon."

They nodded their thanks and I left them alone. I retreated to the office and shut the door, needing a few moments alone to gain control of my emotions. I'd lost several family members in tragic circumstances—my stepfather and stepsiblings to a car accident on a mountain highway, and my cousin Jimmy to murder. Most of the time now I coped well, but every so often grief would rise up again and punch me in the stomach. This was one of those times.

I leaned against the edge of the desk and took some deep breaths until I was no longer fighting tears. I felt terrible for Pippa and Levi, and especially for Rowena. At least she had some close friends here in town with her. Hopefully she'd lean on them for support and not drown in her grief like her husband had most likely done in the ocean.

* * * *

When I heard Brett's truck pull into the driveway early that evening, I headed for the front porch to meet him. Bentley, our exuberant goldendoodle, charged out the door and down the steps, wriggling with happiness as Brett climbed out of his vehicle. I waited on the porch until Bentley had soaked in enough attention and trotted off to sniff at the bushes growing along the fence. As Brett headed my way, I descended the steps to meet him, leaning into him and putting my arms around him. I closed my eyes and held on tight, letting the sound of his heartbeat comfort me.

He wrapped one arm around me and ran a hand over my hair. "Hey. You okay?"

I didn't want to let go of him, but after another moment I stepped back. "I'm all right. Just sad about what happened this morning. Have you heard?"

"About the man who fell off his yacht and most likely drowned?"

I nodded. "I feel terrible for his wife. Her son died a couple of years ago, and now her husband…"

Brett took my hand and tugged me closer, wrapping one arm around my waist. "I didn't know about her son. Her husband was an athlete here for the games, right?"

"He and his wife were going to compete in the mixed doubles tennis match. I met them at the pancake house a few days ago."

Brett kissed the top my head. "I'm sorry, Marley."

I laced my fingers through his, and we walked slowly toward the house. Bentley bounded up the porch steps ahead of us and disappeared through the front door.

"I need to focus on something happy," I said as we climbed the steps.

Brett pulled me to a stop before we stepped through the door, giving me a kiss. "Like our wedding?"

"That's definitely a happy topic."

Still holding Brett's hand, I led the way into the house. Our orange tabby cat, Flapjack, was sitting in the middle of the foyer, his tail swishing. I picked him up and he settled into my arms.

"Ivan's going to make our wedding cake," I said as I headed for the family room at the back of the house. "I told him I didn't want him to feel like he had to, but he insisted that he wants to, as a gift to us."

"That's good of him." Brett followed me down the hall. "And now we know it'll taste fantastic."

"That's for sure. He's going to make a few different types of cake for us to try. Do you mind coming by The Flip Side next Sunday for a taste test?"

"Do I mind?"

"Okay, silly question. I'll tell Ivan we'll both be there."

I gave Flapjack a kiss on the top of his head and set him down on the couch. I'd left the French doors standing open, and while the air was still warm, a gentle breeze wafted into the family room, bringing with it the delicious scent of salty air.

"So what's left for us to do?" Brett asked.

"There's the flowers to deal with. I'll stop by the flower shop this week. And I'm still waiting for my dress to arrive."

"Right. The dress." He grinned as he tucked my hair behind my ear. "I can't wait to see you in it."

I smiled and kissed him. "You'll have to wait. You're not seeing it until our wedding day." I wasn't particularly superstitious, but I wanted the dress to be a surprise.

"It'll be worth it."

I hoped he was right about that. I was a bit nervous about the fact that I'd purchased the dress online. What if it wasn't as nice as it appeared in the photos?

"I booked our hotel today," Brett said, distracting me from my worries about the dress. "Three nights at the Empress, just like we planned."

Since the tourist season wouldn't yet be over when we had our wedding, we were keeping our honeymoon short. We'd take the ferry from Port Angeles to Victoria, Canada, and stay in the beautiful Empress Hotel while my mom helped out at the pancake house. In the winter, when The Flip Side wasn't so busy, we'd take a longer trip to somewhere farther afield.

"It's going to be perfect," I said.

"It is," Brett agreed.

I leaned my head against his shoulder. "But how about our more immediate plans?"

"You mean dinner?"

I nodded. "It's too hot to turn the oven on."

"How about we throw some veggie burgers on the grill?"

"That sounds like a good idea." My gaze wandered out through the open doors. The tide was slowly making its way out. "And how about a walk on the beach later?"

Bentley had been lying on the back porch, but he jumped up at the sound of the word "walk."

"Uh-oh," I said. "I shouldn't have used the magic word."

"We'll go out in a bit, Bentley," Brett told the dog, ruffling his fur. "First, let's get the grill fired up so we can eat."

* * * *

We took our time over dinner, eating out on the back porch while enjoying the view and each other's company. After we'd finished our meal and had put all the dishes in the dishwasher, we headed out for a walk, Bentley racing down the beach ahead of us. The tide was still working its way out, and several children were playing on the exposed sandbars, chasing each other and building sandcastles.

When Brett and I reached the wet sand, we set off toward the eastern end of the cove, away from town and the busiest part of the beach. Bentley ran back and forth between us and the shallows, where he splashed around. We walked at a leisurely pace, the sea breeze lifting my hair from my shoulders and ruffling Brett's blond curls. After we'd been walking for a few minutes, I spotted another couple at the far end of the cove, out by the rocky tidal pools that had been exposed by the receding tide.

"Is that Ivan and Lisa?" The couple was too far away to be sure, but I thought I was right.

"Could be," Brett said.

"I'm sure it is," I said a minute later, once we were a bit closer. "But what's that behind them?"

Ivan and Lisa were quickly moving inland, away from what looked like a heap of clothes on the seaweed-covered rocks. I waved to catch their attention. Ivan drew to a stop and put his cell phone to his ear while Lisa let go of his hand and hurried toward us.

I was going to call out a cheery greeting, but as Lisa drew closer to us, my smile slipped from my face. Her eyes were wide with shock, and her face was pale.

"Lisa, what's wrong?" I asked as soon as she reached us.

She wrapped her arms around herself as if she were cold, despite the warmth of the evening sunlight. "We were out walking and…" She swallowed hard before continuing. "We found a body."

My gaze snapped to what I'd thought was a heap of clothes.

"Dead?" I asked weakly, even though I already knew the answer. If the person was in need of help, Lisa and Ivan wouldn't be giving them such a wide berth.

Lisa nodded, more color draining from her face.

Brett quickly took her arm. "Are you going to be okay?"

"I think so."

I put my arm around her as she drew in a deep breath.

"Ivan's calling for help," she said with a glance his way.

"Is it Easton Miller?" I asked. I figured it must be.

"I don't know," Lisa said. "Thankfully, I didn't see much. Ivan took a closer look." She shuddered. "I've heard about what happens to bodies when they're in the water. I couldn't bring myself to get any closer."

"That's probably for the best," Brett said.

I agreed. I didn't want my friend to have such a terrible image imprinted on her memory forever.

Ivan ended his call and joined us a moment later. "We need to keep an eye on the body until Sheriff Georgeson gets here. And we need to make sure no one else gets too close."

Fortunately, it didn't seem like that would be too difficult. There were only private homes out at this end of the cove, and it was far quieter than it was closer to town. Locals came walking out this way sometimes, and so did the occasional tourist, but at the moment the four of us were on our own.

"Is it Easton Miller's body?" I asked Ivan. "He was in his late fifties with graying hair."

Ivan surprised me by giving a curt shake of his head.

"Are you sure? Who else would it be?"

"It's a woman," he said, surprising me again. "The press pass around her neck says her name is Yvonne Pritchard."

Chapter Five

Ivan's revelation left me so shocked that I couldn't speak for several seconds.

"Did you know her?" Brett asked, watching me with concern.

"I met her a few days ago," I finally managed to say. "She's a sports reporter from Seattle. She ate at The Flip Side with Ed Herman, and I saw her at the park last night." I shook my head as my mind struggled to come to grips with the news. "Poor Ed. He seemed to really like her."

Even though I thought Ed deserved far better than two-faced Yvonne, I knew the news of her death would hit him hard.

"Two drownings in one day?" Lisa said. "I don't think that's ever happened here before, not in unrelated incidents." She looked my way. "Or did she fall off the same boat?"

"Not that I know of." Surely people would have been talking about Yvonne going overboard as well as Easton if that had been the case. "I haven't heard anyone say she was missing."

"Maybe no one knew," Brett said, resting a hand at the small of my back. "If this was a completely separate incident and she wasn't a local, it could be that she wasn't missed."

"That's true." Several thoughts tumbled around in my head all at once. "She was at the opening ceremonies last night, so whatever happened for her to end up in the water must have taken place in the last twenty-four hours. Maybe she was out on a boat this afternoon and fell overboard."

My eyes searched the ocean. There were a couple of boats out on the water, but they both appeared to be heading back toward the marina.

"Here comes Ray," Brett said.

I followed his gaze toward the public access path that led between two private homes. Sheriff Ray Georgeson had one of his deputies with him, and they were making their way down the beach on foot. Ray was Brett's uncle and we'd all met Deputy Devereaux before, so there was no need for introductions when they arrived.

Once Ray had asked a few preliminary questions, he told us we could head home. He knew where to find all of us if he needed to ask us anything more. Not that Brett and I could offer any further information. Beyond telling Ray what little I knew about Yvonne Pritchard, there wasn't much I could do.

Leaving Ray and his deputy to their work, the four of us made our way up the beach while the sun sank slowly toward the western horizon.

* * * *

I didn't sleep well that night. Visions of Easton and Yvonne drowning in the ocean troubled my dreams, and I awoke with a start more than once. When my alarm finally went off, I was tired but relieved to escape any further disturbing dreams.

While I enjoyed my usual breakfast of a smoothie, I sat at the kitchen table, going over the notes and lists I'd made for the wedding. All the guests had been invited and had responded. Everyone was able to come, including two of Brett's closest friends who lived in California and Spain. Brett and I had decided early on that we wanted a small wedding, so we'd kept the guest list short. We had a marriage officiant lined up and a caterer booked to provide a spread of tea sandwiches and other finger foods. Brett had rented a canopy and folding tables so we could have the food outdoors. The actual wedding would take place down on the beach, with the reception in our yard.

As I'd told Brett, the only things left to take care of were the flowers and making sure my dress fit. And hoping the weather would cooperate. That was the one thing I had no control over. I promised myself I wouldn't get upset if things didn't unfold as planned on the big day. The only thing that really mattered to me and Brett was getting married. As long as that happened, we'd be happy. Even so, a rainy day would be far from ideal.

I pushed my notebook aside with a sigh before finishing off my smoothie. Brett dropped two slices of bread into the toaster before coming over to the table and kissing the top of my head.

"You're not stressing about the wedding, are you?" he asked.

"Not really. I'm sure glad we decided to keep it simple, though. It's still taking a lot of planning and I wouldn't want to lose focus of the real reason for it all."

He tugged me up from my chair and pulled me in close. "That won't happen, but I'm always happy to remind you anyway."

I wrapped my arms around his neck and smiled. "Same here."

He kissed me and then rested his forehead against mine. "You and me. That's what it's about."

"Best reason ever."

As my smile faded, I leaned against Brett.

He wrapped his arms around me, holding me close. "Are you thinking about the reporter?"

"Yes," I said. "And Ed. If he doesn't know about her death yet, he will soon."

I'd told Ray that Ed had spent time with Yvonne over the past few days. If Ed hadn't already been asked if he knew anything about what happened to Yvonne, he'd probably be questioned today. Unless Ray had somehow already figured out how the reporter had ended up in the ocean.

I'd probably find out soon if that were the case. News always spread quickly in Wildwood Cove, and The Flip Side was often where locals exchanged information about the latest events over coffee and pancakes. Although I was reluctant to leave Brett, I tore myself away from him and finished my morning routine before heading off to work.

As soon as I had The Flip Side ready to open, I made myself a cup of strong tea, stifling a big yawn as I fished the tea bag out of the hot water. The kitchen door swung open, and Sienna burst into the kitchen.

"You're early," I commented with a glance at the clock on the wall.

The pancake house wouldn't open for another half hour. Leigh and Sienna usually showed up closer to seven o'clock.

"I couldn't sleep," she said. "Not after what happened last night."

"You heard about the body on the beach?" I asked.

"That was quick," Tommy said.

I knew Ivan had already told him about the discovery, although probably not in much detail, knowing the chef.

Sienna tugged a stool over to the island and perched on it. "It was the body of that sports reporter from Seattle."

"Yvonne Pritchard," I said with a nod as I sat on another stool. "How did you hear about it?"

"From the sheriff, when he showed up at my place last night."

"Your place?" Thoughts clicked together in my head. "Was Yvonne staying there?"

Sienna's mom ran the Driftwood B&B, housed in a pretty yellow beachfront Victorian.

"Yep. She checked in a few days ago and was supposed to stay until the end of the Golden Oldies Games. Sheriff Georgeson showed up late last night, right when I was about to go to bed. He wanted any information my mom knew about her, and he took a look at her room."

"That makes sense," I said after blowing on my tea. "He's probably trying to track down her next of kin."

"That and her killer."

I nearly spat out the sip of tea I'd just taken. "I thought she'd accidentally drowned."

"Nope," Sienna said. "She was definitely murdered."

Chapter Six

"Sheriff Georgeson told you that?" I asked Sienna, still in shock.

The fact that Yvonne was dead was disconcerting enough, but murder? I really hadn't expected that.

"He didn't *exactly* tell me," Sienna hedged.

"What does that mean?" Ivan asked, staring at her from across the island.

Although Sienna averted her gaze from Ivan's, I was impressed that she didn't shrink beneath his intimidating glare. Plenty of people twice her age would have withered immediately.

"When he was looking through the reporter's room, he got a phone call," she said. "I overheard him mention that there was no sign of the murder weapon near the body."

"You were eavesdropping," Ivan accused.

"Not really." She bit down on her lower lip and seemed to reconsider what she'd said. "Okay, so I was. But can you blame me?"

Ivan directed his glower my way.

"I didn't tell her to eavesdrop," I defended myself. "I didn't even know Yvonne was staying at the B&B."

Ivan didn't respond. He slapped several slices of bacon on the griddle.

"I swear," I added.

Sienna came to my defense. "It's true. Marley had nothing to do with it. I just couldn't help myself. Don't be mad, Ivan."

When he glanced up from washing his hands, he got the full force of Sienna's version of sad puppy dog eyes. It was a look that was highly effective when directed at me. Apparently, I wasn't the only one it worked on. Ivan's expression lost some of its sternness.

"I'm not mad," he grumbled. "I just don't want you ending up in danger." He speared me with his dark gaze. "Either of you."

"We don't plan to do anything dangerous." I glanced at Sienna. "Right?"

"Of course not," she said with a smile.

I understood Ivan's concerns. I worried about Sienna's penchant for sleuthing myself. At the same time, I couldn't blame her for it without being a total hypocrite. I had much more of a history of sticking my nose into murder investigations and ending up in dicey situations than Sienna did.

"What else did you overhear?" I asked, hoping Ivan wouldn't disapprove of the question.

Fortunately, he continued his food prep without dishing out any reprimands.

"Not much," Sienna said with obvious disappointment. "My mom had Yvonne's home address and her cell number. She gave those to Sheriff Georgeson, but she didn't know much else about her, other than the fact that she's a reporter. The sheriff talked to our other guests. One of them said she'd seen Yvonne at other events over the years but hadn't ever said more than a few words to her. That's about all I heard."

"The other guests at the B&B are involved with the Golden Oldies Games?"

"Two of them are. They ate here the other day, with the guy who fell off his yacht. Pippa Hampshire is a tennis player. Her boyfriend is staying with her at the B&B, but he's too young to compete."

"Levi," I said with a nod. "He's her personal trainer."

"That's some *very* personal training," Sienna said with a grin.

Ivan shot her another glare, but she just shrugged. Behind Ivan, Tommy was grinning as he slid a tray of breakfast scones into the oven. I couldn't take issue with Sienna's comment since I'd had the same thought the other day.

"He must be something like thirty years younger than Pippa," she said.

"More like fifteen to twenty," I amended.

Ivan's scowl had returned full-force. "The age difference doesn't matter."

"Of course it doesn't," I said quickly, knowing there was a gap of about ten years between him and Lisa. "They're both adults and they seem to be happy together. That's all that matters." I addressed Sienna again. "Did the sheriff give any indication of how Yvonne died or when she was killed?"

"Not that I heard."

"When was the last time she was at the B&B?"

"Friday morning. She left after eating breakfast, around eight o'clock."

"So she didn't come back Friday night?"

"Nope. My mom gave her a key, and when she didn't come back before we all went to bed, we just figured she was staying out late. In the morning when she didn't show up for breakfast, my mom saw that her bed hadn't been slept in. I know my mom was a bit worried by then, but to be honest, I thought Yvonne had hooked up with some guy and spent the night with him. My mom tried calling her cell, but no one answered. She was going to call the sheriff if Yvonne didn't show up again last night, but then he came by and told us she was dead."

"When you found Yvonne, did you notice any clues as to how she was killed?" I asked Ivan.

He gave a noncommittal grunt as he sliced up some mushrooms.

I watched him closely as he set down his knife and wiped his hands on a towel. Ivan wasn't a very talkative man, but I was getting better and better at reading him.

"You already knew she was murdered," I said.

"Strongly suspected," he corrected.

Tommy paused as he was about to break an egg into a bowl. "You never said anything."

"If the sheriff hasn't said publicly that the woman was murdered, he might not want people to know yet." Ivan directed his piercing gaze at the three of us in turn. "So this information shouldn't leave this room."

"It won't," I assured him, before rethinking. "Well..." When Ivan scowled at me, I quickly explained. "I can't keep secrets from Brett, but I won't tell anyone else."

That seemed to satisfy him.

"But why did you suspect she was murdered?" Sienna's eyes widened. "Did you see a gunshot wound?"

"She was shot?" Tommy asked.

"I was just guessing," Sienna said.

Ivan slid two Belgian waffles onto a plate and set a small jug of strawberry syrup next to them. "There was a wound, but not from a gunshot."

"A wound on her head? Somewhere else?" I pressed.

Ivan passed the plate of waffles to Sienna, receiving a bright smile of thanks in exchange.

"An abdominal wound beneath a tear in her clothes," he said as Sienna began to eat. "A penetrating wound. It could have been caused accidentally, or after she was in the water."

"But you don't think so," I finished for him, knowing he wasn't convinced by those possibilities.

"I didn't think it was likely," he admitted. "And now that the sheriff's looking for a murder weapon…"

I nodded, trying to absorb all of this new information. Sienna remained quiet, too busy eating her strawberry-drenched waffles to speak.

"So there's a good chance she was stabbed," I said after a moment. "But where did the murder happen? And why did someone kill her?"

"Those questions are best left to the sheriff," Ivan advised.

"I'm not planning to investigate," I said.

The grunt he gave as he turned back to his work suggested that he didn't believe me.

* * * *

The same questions I'd posed in the kitchen continued to circle in my mind as I worked. It was clear from the conversations going on around the pancake house that it was now general knowledge that a body had been found on the beach. Not everyone knew the identity of the victim, but that information spread quickly from diner to diner.

From what I overheard, everyone assumed—as I had done—that Yvonne had accidentally drowned. I heeded Ivan's advice and kept quiet about the fact that Ray was investigating her death as a murder. Sienna did too, not that I'd expected anything different.

As interested as I was in Yvonne's murder, my curiosity took a sudden backseat when Gary Thornbrook arrived at The Flip Side with Ed in tow. My heart ached when I saw that Ed's usual happy expression had been replaced by a somber one.

The two men had arrived during a lull between the breakfast and lunch rushes, so they didn't have to wait for a table. They even managed to snag their favorite one, and I hurried over to fill their coffee mugs as they got settled.

"Ed, I'm so sorry about Yvonne," I said, resting a hand on his shoulder.

"Thanks, Marley. I appreciate that." He shook his head as I filled his mug with coffee. "She was a wonderful woman. I don't understand how this happened." He turned his head away, overcome by emotion.

"It's a terrible thing," Gary said.

I could see in his face that he was worried about his friend.

"Have you talked to the sheriff?" I asked Ed once he'd had a chance to compose himself. "He probably wants to talk to anyone who had contact with Yvonne while she was in Wildwood Cove."

Ed nodded and tugged his coffee mug closer to him. "I talked to him this morning. I wasn't much help. He wanted to know when I'd last seen Yvonne and what I knew about her plans for Friday night. All I could tell him was that I'd last seen her at the park in the evening. She was interviewing some athletes when I left." He stared into his coffee. "That was the last time I saw her. She never said what she planned to do later that evening."

"I'm so sorry," I said again.

"Not knowing how she drowned makes it even harder."

I didn't correct him about the cause of death. Clearly, Ray hadn't shared that with him and I wouldn't break the promise I'd made to Ivan. Besides, I didn't want to be the one to tell Ed that someone had killed Yvonne.

"Sheriff Georgeson will figure it out," Gary said in an attempt to reassure his friend.

"Maybe," Ed said without much conviction. He looked up at me, a spark of hope appearing in his eyes. "Or Marley will."

"Um…" I wasn't sure what to say to that.

"How Yvonne drowned is a mystery," Ed said. "You're good at solving mysteries. I bet you could figure out what happened."

"I'm flattered by your confidence in me," I said, "but Sheriff Georgeson will probably have answers for you soon."

And at least some of what Ray knew would hurt Ed even more.

"But if he *doesn't* figure it out soon, will you try?" he pressed.

I hesitated, remembering Ivan's warnings to leave the matter to the authorities.

"Please, Marley?" Ed asked. "I don't think I can handle never knowing what happened."

I glanced at Gary, only to have my heart ache even more. His eyes were almost as beseeching as Ed's.

There was really only one thing I could bring myself to say to them in that moment.

"If Sheriff Georgeson doesn't figure it out soon, I'll do my best."

Ed reached out and squeezed my hand. "Thank you, Marley."

The gratitude in his voice almost brought tears to my eyes. As soon as I'd confirmed that both men wanted their usual orders, I hurried off to the kitchen, desperately hoping Ray would solve Yvonne's murder quickly.

Chapter Seven

By the time I closed The Flip Side later that day, my mind was still spinning. I couldn't stop wondering why someone had killed Yvonne and why they'd done so here in Wildwood Cove. Despite how highly Ed had thought of Yvonne, I knew she wasn't the nice woman she'd pretended to be when she was around him, but I was still shocked by her murder.

Did that not-so-nice side of her have something to do with why she was killed? Maybe what I'd witnessed while Ed was out of earshot was merely a hint of what she was truly like. Or maybe it was just a bad moment. I didn't really believe that, though. Yvonne had argued with Claudia Wu at the park on Friday evening, and there was that blond man who definitely wasn't glad to see her. I hardly knew the woman, but it struck me as though there were more people who disliked her than those who liked her.

Was that simply because she was rude and unkind? Or was there more to it? Did the fact that she was a reporter have something to do with her death?

I shook my head as I swept the floor of the pancake house. So many questions. They rattled around in my head, making it hard to think of anything else, but no matter how much I mulled them over, I didn't come up with any answers.

When I arrived home that afternoon, I spent some time with Flapjack and Bentley. My preoccupation had caused my mood to slump in the middle of the day. Hanging out with my animals cheered me up, but my mind was still a muddle of questions. The hot weather only seemed to make matters worse. It was the hottest day of the summer so far and I felt sluggish, like my limbs and my brain were struggling to work properly.

I didn't know how to answer all the questions lingering in my mind, but I did know how to make myself feel better.

After changing into my swimsuit, I headed down to the water. The tide was working its way in, just one sandbar left to cover before the ocean would creep over a swath of pebbles to reach the high-water mark. The sun beat down on my bare shoulders as I crossed the sandbar, leaving a trail of footprints behind me. In the shallows, the water was as warm as a bath, thanks to the sun-heated sand. As I waded deeper, the temperature dropped until it was nice and cool, and even a bit chilly.

I dove into an oncoming wave, feeling refreshed as soon as I broke through the surface, shaking salty water from my face. Instead of going any deeper, I swam parallel to the beach, getting into the rhythm of a front crawl. I headed eastward, since there were fewer swimmers in that direction. Closer to town, children, teens, and a few adults splashed, swam, and floated on the waves.

Once I'd gone a good distance, I turned and swam in the other direction until I was in line with my house. I floated on my back for a few minutes, rising and falling with the waves. For the first time since I'd learned that Yvonne was murdered, I relaxed and my racing thoughts slowed down. That was the magic of the ocean and Wildwood Beach. No other place brought me such peace.

Feeling much better, I swam and waded back toward the shore. I'd reached the shallows when I saw Brett coming down the beach toward me, wearing his swim trunks. I waited for him to approach, the incoming tide swirling around my ankles.

"Looks like you had the same idea as I did," Brett said as he reached me.

"It's the best place to be on a day like this."

"I can't argue with that." He took my hands and kissed me. "I need to cool down."

"Want me to come back in with you?" I asked.

He squeezed my hands. "Not if you're cold. I won't be long."

"I'll wait up on the beach then."

As refreshing as my swim had been, it had left me with goose bumps on my arms and legs. I stretched out on my towel and closed my eyes as the sun dried me off and warmed my skin. By the time Brett returned from the ocean and dropped down on his towel next to me, my goose bumps had disappeared.

"Good swim?" I asked.

"Perfect," he said as he wiped water droplets from his forehead.

I sat up so I could give him a kiss. His lips tasted salty from the ocean.

"How are your parents?" I asked once I'd pulled back.

Brett had planned to spend part of the day with them while I was at work.

"Good. I helped my dad with a bookshelf he's building. He's glad to be back to working with his hands again."

Brett's dad had suffered a heart attack during the winter. After receiving bypass surgery, he'd recovered well, though slowly, but he'd retired from his job as a general contractor. Now that he was healthy again, he'd started to grow restless and had decided to work on some small carpentry projects to keep busy.

"He and my mom are thinking of taking in a tennis match or two this week," Brett continued.

"I'd like to do that too. Are you interested?"

"Sure. Are there any matches tomorrow?"

"I think so, but I'd have to check the schedule."

Thinking about tennis reminded me of Easton Miller, and his drowning reminded me of Yvonne's death.

"Have you talked to Ray today?" I asked.

"No. Have you?"

"No, but I found out something about Yvonne's death this morning."

"Of course you did," Brett said with a hint of amusement. He was no stranger to my tendency to get involved in mysteries.

"I wasn't snooping," I said, "but I'm probably not supposed to know this."

"Now I'm intrigued."

Even though nobody was nearby, I kept my voice low. "Yvonne was murdered."

A crease appeared between Brett's eyebrows. "Are you sure?"

"Pretty sure. It sounds like Ray and his deputies have been searching for a murder weapon."

I filled him in on how I'd come to have that information and what Ivan had observed when he found Yvonne's body on the beach.

Brett ran a hand through his wet hair. "So there was a murder and an accidental drowning in the space of about twelve hours?"

"Hmm," I said, thinking.

"You've got a different theory?"

"Not really."

"But?" he prodded, knowing I'd left something unsaid.

"It's just that we assumed Yvonne drowned accidentally, but now we know she didn't. We also assumed that Easton Miller drowned accidentally."

"But maybe he didn't?" Brett finished.

"From what I've heard, no one quite knows how he went overboard."

"Was he alone on his boat at the time?"

"I think his wife was with him," I said. "But if she was, wouldn't she have seen him go overboard?"

"Not if she had her back turned or was below decks."

"True." I gazed out at the ocean as I turned things over in my mind.

"I know that look," Brett said, watching me.

"What look?"

"That one you get when you've got a mystery on your mind and you won't be able to rest until it's solved. Is it Yvonne's murder or Easton's accident?"

"Both," I replied. "I'd really like to know if the two deaths are connected, but without knowing the circumstances of Easton going overboard, I doubt I'll be able to figure anything out."

"And Ray won't want you asking him."

"No, he won't."

Ray wasn't very enthusiastic about my sleuthing habit. He'd warned me to stay out of his investigations in the past, but I wasn't very good at taking that advice. Fortunately, he was a patient man, although I knew I tested that patience now and then. At least my inability to leave mysteries alone hadn't strained Ray's relationship with Brett. I hoped it never would.

"I went to school with a guy who works down at the marina," Brett said. "He might know something about the Miller incident."

That caught my interest. "Do you think he'd talk to me about it?"

"If I introduced you, he probably would."

"Will you introduce me?"

"On one condition," he said with a grin.

"What's that?"

"We stop for ice cream on the way home."

I smiled back at him. "You've got a deal."

* * * *

We decided to turn our excursion into dinner out as well as information gathering and a visit to the ice cream shop. We ate at the Windward Pub, which was located near the marina. The pub's food was as good as always, but the place was packed full with locals, tourists, and people in town for the games. There was such a rumble from all the conversations going on around us that I could barely hear anything Brett said to me as we ate. As much as I enjoyed my shrimp and veggie wrap, I was glad to get back outside, where it was far quieter.

Despite a gentle breeze, the evening wasn't much cooler than the afternoon had been. I was glad I'd dressed for the weather in shorts, a tank top, and flip-flops. Brett and I held hands and walked slowly along the street as we headed for the marina.

"So where will we find Charlie?" I asked Brett. He'd told me the name of the guy he knew at the marina while we were eating dinner.

"Sometimes he's in the office. If he's not there, we might have to look around."

"Hopefully he's working today."

Brett slid his phone from the pocket of his shorts and checked the time. "There's usually someone on duty until seven. If it's not Charlie today, we can try again tomorrow."

I hoped we wouldn't have to wait. One more day wasn't very long, but I knew I'd feel restless until I had a chance to find out what Charlie knew, if anything.

The tiny whitewashed building that sat at the entrance to the marina was locked when we arrived, and no one answered when Brett knocked on the door. My hopes slumped, but Brett shaded his eyes and looked down at the floating dock.

"I think I see him," he said, raising my hopes again.

He set off down the steep ramp, and I followed behind him, holding on to the railing with one hand. Most of the boat slips were occupied, and a few people moved about on the decks of the boats or on the dock. Some of the boats belonged to locals, but there were also plenty of visiting vessels at this time of year.

When we reached the bottom of the ramp, Brett led me off to the right. A stocky man with blond hair was talking to a young couple a few feet away. When the couple climbed aboard a small yacht, Brett raised a hand in greeting and called out to the blond man.

"Charlie!"

When the man looked our way, he smiled with recognition. "Brett. How's it going?" He held out a hand as we approached, and Brett shook it.

"Good, thanks. How about you?"

"Can't complain."

Brett put an arm around my shoulders. "This is my fiancée, Marley. Marley, this is Charlie Quinton."

Charlie grinned as I shook his hand. "I hear the wedding's coming up soon."

"Just a few more weeks," Brett said.

"Are you looking to rent a boat?"

"No, although I wouldn't mind going out fishing one day this summer. We're wondering if you know anything about what happened to Easton Miller the other day."

All traces of Charlie's grin faded away. "That was sad. Did you know the man?"

"I met him earlier in the week," I said. "I was so shocked when I heard about him going overboard."

"Everybody was." Charlie scratched his jaw. "But I'm not sure how much I can tell you. No one knows exactly what happened."

"I heard that he and his wife had gone out for an early morning sail," I said.

Charlie nodded. "That's right. That's something they liked to do—head out early and sit on the deck to watch the sun rise."

"His wife didn't see what happened?" Brett asked.

"Nope. I heard one of the Coast Guard guys say that Mrs. Miller was down in the cabin making coffee when she heard a splash. She ran back out onto the deck, but couldn't spot her husband anywhere. She radioed for help, but his body still hasn't been found. Sounds like she doesn't know how he ended up falling in the water."

"I feel terrible for her," I said.

"It's sad, that's for sure. Hopefully he'll turn up soon. When I heard a body was found yesterday, I thought it had to be him until someone told me it wasn't."

"I thought it was him at first too."

Charlie shook his head. "Crazy. Two unrelated drownings in less than twenty-four hours. That's a first around here."

I didn't correct him about how Yvonne had died. It probably wouldn't be long before everyone knew she was murdered, but I wasn't going to be the one to leak that information.

A man who looked to be in his fifties called out to Charlie from a nearby boat, so we quickly thanked him for the information and headed back up the ramp.

When we were on the sidewalk, Brett took my hand and we headed in the direction of the ice cream shop.

"It doesn't sound like Easton Miller was murdered," he said.

"No," I agreed. "It doesn't. I guess it's just a coincidence that his accident happened so close to Yvonne's death."

"Do you have any theories about who killed her?"

"Not really."

Brett grinned and gave my hand an affectionate squeeze. "I'm sure you will soon."

His gentle teasing brought a smile to my face.

"Maybe," I said, "but not before we've had our ice cream."

Chapter Eight

According to the event schedule for the Golden Oldies Games, there would be tennis matches all week long, including on Monday afternoon and evening. Since Brett and I both had Mondays off, we decided we'd head for the tennis courts later in the day to take in a match or two. I was also planning to head into town in the morning since I knew from the schedule and from talking to Marjorie that her race was starting at nine o'clock.

After a leisurely breakfast with Brett, I set off on foot toward Main Street, where the race walk would start and finish. Brett decided to stay at home for the first part of the day. He was building an arbor for the wedding and wanted to give that project some attention. The plan was to deck the arbor with flowers and have it lead from the yard down to the beach on our wedding day. I could picture what the final product would look like, flowers and all, and couldn't wait to see that vision take shape in reality.

Thinking about the arbor reminded me that I needed to order all of the flowers for the wedding. I decided not to worry about it that morning. Since Brett and I would be returning to town later in the day, I could stop by the flower shop then. For the time being, I was going to focus on Marjorie's race.

I walked along Wildwood Road rather than taking the beach route into town. Before I even reached Main Street, I was glad I'd left my car behind. Traffic was always heavier during the tourist season and, thanks to the road closures for the upcoming races, the streets that were open were clogged with slow-moving cars. Walking into town was probably the faster option.

West of Main Street, Wildwood Road had been closed for the event. As I drew closer, I noticed that several athletes were already gathered near the starting line, many of them stretching or getting last-minute pep talks from their coaches. I spotted Marjorie among them and waved when I caught her eye. She grinned and returned my wave before moving closer to the starting line.

The events at the Golden Oldies Games were divided up not only by sport but also by age group. One of the speakers at the opening ceremonies had mentioned that the oldest athlete registered this year was ninety-six and would be taking part in the horseshoes competition. Even though that wasn't the most physically demanding event, I was still impressed that someone of that age was active enough to be able to participate. I was even more impressed that a ninety-two-year-old would be competing in track and field. Her name was Beryl Madgwick, and she'd been featured in a video at the opening ceremonies. It seemed the Golden Oldies Games gave rise to plenty of inspiring stories.

At age sixty-eight, Marjorie was competing in the third-youngest age group. Several of her competitors had gray hair like she did, but they all looked fit and athletic. Some were smiling, and others looked extremely focused. One or two appeared quite grim as they waited for the race to start.

I hoped Marjorie would do well. I knew she was mostly in it for fun and wasn't expecting to capture one of the coveted top four spots that would result in berths to the national games, but she was still hoping to finish in the top ten.

I found a spot near the curb where I could watch the beginning of the race, and after a few minutes one of the event officials called the racers to the starting line. Seconds later, he fired off the starting pistol and the racers charged off in a big pack. I raised myself up on tiptoes to keep Marjorie in sight as long as possible. As the racers speed-walked around a corner, she was still in the middle of the pack.

With the racers out of sight, some of the spectators dispersed, while others stayed in place. The race route would bring the competitors back down Main Street to the finish line, which was just a stone's throw from where the race had started. I knew I had time to kill before the first racers approached the finish line. The fastest competitors would complete the course in about half an hour. It wasn't even midmorning yet, but the day was already warm, the sun beating down from a cloudless sky, so I wandered off along the sidewalk toward Johnny's Juice Hut, wanting something to quench my growing thirst.

I bought myself an iced green tea and window-shopped for a while before returning my attention to the race. The spectators were looking up the road expectantly, so I found myself a good spot by the curb and sipped at my drink while I waited for the racers to reappear. I didn't have to wait long. Sooner than I expected, the first racer rounded the corner at the end of the street, heading northward.

Cheers rang out from the crowd on either side of the street. Whoever the racer was, she was going to win by a fair margin. She was halfway down the street, and no other racers had appeared behind her. She broke through the ribbon at the finish line to another round of cheers and applause. Seconds later, the next competitors rounded the corner. This time there were four of them packed close together. At almost the last moment, the racer at the rear of the group kicked up her pace and managed to scoot past the others to finish the race in second place.

By that point, more racers were on the home stretch. I spotted Marjorie among them and cheered her on. She kept up a good pace right until she crossed the finish line. She'd secured seventh place, meeting her personal goal and garnering loud cheers from the locals in the crowd.

Still sipping on my cold drink, I wandered down the street and managed to meet up with Marjorie as she drank down a bottle of water.

"Great job, Marjorie!"

"Thanks, Marley," she said with a smile once she'd swallowed a gulp of water. "I'm happy with how I did, and I had a lot of fun."

"That's good to hear."

I noticed Claudia Wu off to the side, her black hair in a ponytail. She wore her racing gear and was going through a series of stretches.

"Is Claudia competing today too?"

"Yep." Marjorie finished off her bottle of water. "Her group is up next. She's the favorite to win. I think I'll stick around and watch."

"I think I might too," I said.

Marjorie took advantage of the protein bars and fresh orange slices that were set out for the athletes, but when the next race was about to begin, she joined me by the curb. When the racers set off, Claudia was near the front of the pack, but as with the last race, all the competitors were close together when they disappeared around the first corner.

While we waited for the last part of the race, Marjorie and I chatted with a couple of other locals who'd come out to watch the event. It wasn't too long before the first racer appeared at the far end of Main Street. No one was too surprised to see that it was Claudia Wu. As with the winner of the previous race, Claudia had a comfortable lead over her competitors. There was more of a race for second and third place and then another gap before the next women reached the finish line.

Spectators and racers alike were congratulating Claudia, and I recognized Rob Mazzoli—the new reporter for the *Wildwood Cove Weekly*—as he moved in for a quick interview. When he was done talking with Claudia, Rob noticed Marjorie and came over our way.

"Congrats on a good race," he said to her. "How do you feel about your performance?"

Marjorie answered that question and a few others while Rob recorded her responses on his phone. After the brief interview, he tucked the device into his pocket.

"I've got to get back to the office," he said. "I need to update the paper's website and social media now that there's a murder investigation underway."

"Murder?" Marjorie stared at him, aghast.

"How do you know that?" I asked at almost the same time.

"The sheriff released a statement an hour ago saying that Yvonne Pritchard's death was suspicious and considered a homicide."

"Oh my word," Marjorie said. "How awful! I can't believe someone killed her. She just interviewed me the other day."

I didn't let on that I'd already known about the murder investigation. Marjorie was still expressing her dismay at the news when Rob left us a minute or so later.

"Why would anyone kill Yvonne?" she asked.

"I don't know," I replied. "But I don't think she was well liked."

"Really? I didn't realize that, but I didn't have much contact with her. She asked me a few questions on Friday night, but we only talked for about two or three minutes. Why didn't people like her?"

"I don't know, exactly. Ed was quite smitten with her, but I saw her arguing with Claudia Wu, and there was another man hanging around the park on Friday night who wasn't happy to see her."

"Poor Ed."

"Yvonne's death hit him hard, even though they only knew each other for a few days."

"I'll have to check in on him and see how he's doing," Marjorie said. "But you say Yvonne argued with Claudia? What about?"

"I'm not sure. I didn't hear much of what they were saying, other than Claudia calling Yvonne a pathetic troll. I don't think Yvonne was as nice as she pretended to be at times. She *seemed* nice enough when she was with Ed, but I heard her saying some not-so-nice things behind his back."

Marjorie frowned. "That's terrible. Ed's got to be one of the nicest guys around."

"I know. She was using him to get free meals, from the sounds of it."

Marjorie was still frowning as her gaze passed over the people milling about until it landed on Claudia. "You don't think Claudia could have killed her, do you?"

"I have no idea, but anything's possible. They obviously didn't like each other, but since I don't know what the problem was between them, I have no way of knowing if Claudia had any real motive to kill Yvonne."

"Maybe we can find out what they argued about. I've talked to Claudia a couple of times over the past few days, so I'm not a total stranger. Leave it to me."

Before I had a chance to say anything, Marjorie dodged around the people standing between us and her target. She hung back for a second or two while a man and woman finished speaking to Claudia. As soon as they walked away, Marjorie moved in.

I casually headed their way, hoping to overhear their conversation.

"...a great race," Marjorie was saying when I drew closer. "Congratulations on securing a spot to nationals."

"Thank you," Claudia said. "I love competing, so I'm looking forward to the next challenge."

Marjorie swiftly steered the conversation in a new direction. "It's terrible what happened to the reporter, Yvonne Pritchard, isn't it? You must have known her, at least to some degree. I'm sure you've been interviewed by all the reporters here."

Although I hung back and pretended I wasn't listening in, I glanced Claudia's way and caught a flash of anger in her eyes.

"It might be terrible that someone killed her, but she was no angel. I hope people don't make her out to be one now that she's dead."

"What do you mean?" Marjorie asked, managing to sound surprised. "I only met her briefly, but she seemed nice enough."

Claudia snorted. "If she ever seemed nice, it was an act, believe me. The woman was despicable."

I edged closer to them, deciding to join the conversation. "I heard her saying rude things about a friend of mine. And I know not everyone was happy to see her here at the games."

If Claudia thought it was impolite of me to insert myself into the conversation, she didn't show it. I suspected she was too focused on her dislike of Yvonne.

"I don't think anyone who really knew her would ever be happy to see her," Claudia said. "Trying to destroy people was her hobby. And you know what? At the opening ceremonies she came up to me and wanted to interview me. The nerve!"

I exchanged a confused glance with Marjorie. "Wasn't that her job?"

"Oh, sure, but we had a history. And not a good one. But if you can believe it, she'd forgotten who I was."

"History?" Marjorie asked.

Fortunately, Claudia seemed to be on a roll with her complaints about Yvonne.

"I wasn't always slim and fit," she said. "Five years ago, I was overweight and living a sedentary lifestyle. I decided I wanted to make a change, so I took up racewalking. I started dropping weight right away, but I had a lot to lose. When I took part in my first competition, I was still quite chubby."

"Don't tell me she ridiculed you for that," Marjorie said.

"Oh, she did. Not to my face, but online. All over social media. She even tweeted photos of me and made fun of my body."

Outrage curled in my stomach. "That's terrible."

"I was devastated at the time. I almost quit the sport because I was so embarrassed. If not for the support of some close friends and family, I would have."

"I'm glad you didn't," Marjorie said. "That was a despicable thing she did."

"And she didn't even remember doing that to you?" I asked.

"She didn't realize I was the same person. She was all sugary sweet, wanting to talk about how I was the favorite to win my event." Claudia's eyes flashed with anger again.

"That must have made you mad," I said.

"Of course it made me mad," she snapped. She narrowed her eyes at me. "Hold on. Are you insinuating that I had something to do with her death?"

"No, no," I said quickly.

She huffed, not believing me, perhaps rightfully so.

"Plenty of people hated that woman," she said. "If you want to point fingers at someone for the murder, you'd better not point them my way."

"Who else hated Yvonne?" Marjorie asked, still completely calm despite the anger sparking off of Claudia.

"That's a long list. But Felicia Venner should be right at the top."

"Who's she?" I asked.

"A track and field athlete. She's here at the games. Felicia and Yvonne had a bitter rivalry that went back decades. In fact," Claudia continued, "I'm surprised they didn't kill each other years ago."

Chapter Nine

"It sounds like the sheriff will have a couple of suspects to look into," Marjorie said once we'd parted ways with Claudia.

We'd moved away from the crowd of people gathered near the starting line so we wouldn't be overheard.

"At least," I said. "Do you know Felicia Venner?"

"No, that's the first time I've heard her name. I wonder what the story is there."

"So do I." And I was already thinking of possible ways to find out.

Marjorie was going to head home for a shower and a change of clothes before taking in some of the other events, so I said good-bye to her and walked along Wildwood Road. On my way home, I couldn't stop thinking about Yvonne's murder and how there could be a long list of people who disliked or even hated her. I recalled the blond man from the park who'd obviously had something against Yvonne. Maybe he belonged on the suspect list too. Without knowing his identity, it would be difficult to find out anything more about him.

Although the murder dominated my thoughts on my trip home, my focus shifted as soon as I turned into the driveway. Bentley was lying in a patch of shade by the house and he jumped up as soon as he saw me and came charging over to greet me. I crouched down and laughed as he wiggled with happiness, his tail wagging like crazy.

The door to the detached workshop stood open, so I headed that way once I'd given Bentley enough attention to satisfy him. I glanced around for Flapjack, but he wasn't in sight.

"Hey," Brett said, coming out of the workshop just before I reached the door. "How did Marjorie do?"

"Great," I replied. "She was aiming for the top ten and came seventh."

"That's impressive."

"So is that," I said with a nod at the nearly finished arbor lying on the grass. "It's going to look amazing."

"Speaking of looking amazing," Brett said with a grin, "I'm sure that's how you'll look when you try on your wedding dress."

My eyes widened. "It's here?"

"It was delivered a few minutes ago. I left the package on the kitchen table."

"Sorry," I said, giving him a quick kiss and then backing away. "I can't wait to see it."

"I figured you'd be eager," he said, still grinning.

I turned and jogged toward the back of the house and up the steps to the porch. Flapjack was lying on the railing, his front paws tucked beneath him. He opened his amber eyes when I arrived, but I only paused for a moment to give him a scratch on the head.

"Sorry, Jack, I've got a package to open."

Once inside, I left the cup with the remains of my iced tea on the kitchen counter and made a beeline for the package on the table. I struggled with the tape for a moment before grabbing a pair of scissors and slitting the package open.

I lifted the lid off the box and parted several layers of tissue paper before uncovering the dress. I held my breath as I carefully lifted the garment out of the box, hoping I wouldn't find any defects or discover that it wasn't as nice as it had looked in the photos online. I lifted the delicate fabric into my arms and let out a sigh of relief. So far it looked even better than it had in the picture.

As soon as I was sure there weren't any tears or other obvious problems with the dress, I set it back in the box and replaced the lid, just in case Brett came inside. I didn't want him getting even a glimpse of the dress before our wedding day.

I grabbed my phone and sent a text message to Lisa.

It's here!

I didn't think she'd need any explanation.

I finished off my tea and rinsed out the cup before tossing it into the recycling bin. My phone chimed, and I snatched it up.

Oh my gosh! Lisa had written back. *Does it fit? Is it gorgeous? I have to see it!*

I haven't tried it on yet, I typed out.

A moment later, I received another message.

Can you bring it over to my place at noon? I'm running errands, but I'll be done by then. And I'll bring food.

I'll be there! I wrote back.

As I set down my phone, I realized I had a huge smile on my face. A flurry of nervousness skittered through my stomach. I hoped my excitement wouldn't get snuffed out when I put the dress on. A tailor could help me adjust it, if needed, but if it was completely the wrong size or didn't suit me, I'd have to return it and start my search all over again.

I considered going upstairs and trying it on before heading over to Lisa's, just to settle my nerves, but in the end, I decided to wait. It would be fun to share the moment of seeing myself in the dress for the first time with my best friend.

My gaze rested on the closed box. Even though I'd decided to wait to try on the dress, it would be hard to think about anything else. I kept myself at least partly distracted by doing some cleaning, but as soon as it got close to noon, I scooped up the box and my tote bag and set off for Lisa's house.

* * * *

Lisa was digging her keys out of her purse when I walked up to her house a short time later. She had a paper bag of take-out food in one hand and pulled out her keys with the other.

"I'm so excited!" she called out when she saw me coming up the walkway. "Did you try it on since we texted?"

"No." I jogged up the steps. "I was tempted to, but I didn't."

Lisa let out a squeal of happiness and hugged me. "Then let's get inside so we can get you into the dress."

Trying on the wedding gown wasn't the first order of business when we stepped into the foyer of Lisa's house. First, we had to greet her kitten, Orion. Lisa had adopted the stray after I'd found him back in the spring. At the time he was tiny and only about ten weeks old. He'd grown a lot since then, but he still made us laugh all the time with his kittenish antics.

As soon as he heard us coming in the door, the black cat came careening down the hallway and pounced on the ends of my shoelaces. Lisa scooped him up into her arms, and I gave him a pat on the head while he purred with happiness.

"Sorry, Orion," Lisa said as she set him down again. "We've got some serious business to take care of." To me she said, "Let's go upstairs. I've got a full-length mirror in my bedroom."

I kicked off my sneakers and followed Lisa up to the second floor. I set the box on her bed and removed the lid.

Lisa gasped as she touched the fabric. "It's so pretty!" She helped me hold up the dress. "It looks even better than it did online!"

"That's what I thought," I said, relieved that she had the same opinion.

"You're going to look incredible."

"I hope so."

Lisa nudged me with her elbow. "You will. You'll see. Come on, put it on."

I traded my shorts and tank top for the dress, taking care not to snag the delicate fabric on anything. The dress had a white satin underskirt and bandeau bodice, overlaid with a sheer, floral embroidered gown with long sleeves.

I had to pinch the back of the bandeau top to keep it from sliding down. I didn't have the curves to fill it out.

"Hold on," Lisa said as I stood in the middle of her bedroom, holding the bodice in place. "I've got some safety pins somewhere." She rummaged around in an enamel box on the top of her dresser. "Here we go."

She stood behind me and pinned a tuck in the satin fabric.

"That should do it," she said a moment later.

I slowly let go of the top, hoping it wouldn't slip. Fortunately, it stayed securely in place.

"I'll do the zipper up for you." Lisa carefully slid the zipper up to the neckline and then moved around to stand in front of me.

I hadn't yet dared to take a look in the mirror.

"Well?" I asked with a rush of nerves.

To my surprise, tears welled up in Lisa's eyes. "Marley!"

"Is it that bad?" I asked, only half-joking.

"Don't be silly." Lisa took hold of my shoulders and turned me so I was facing the mirror. "You look like a princess!"

When I saw my reflection, all I could do was stare at myself, my tongue suddenly unable to work.

"See?" Lisa said.

"Holy buckets," I whispered when I finally found my voice.

Lisa was smiling over my shoulder. "I told you. A princess."

"It's not just the dress." I struggled to overcome the powerful emotions that had hit me like a rogue wave. "I'm getting *married*."

Lisa laughed. "That's why you bought a wedding dress."

Her laughter helped me to feel less overwhelmed.

"I think it truly hit me for the first time, you know?"

She wrapped her arms around me and hugged me. "And you're happy, right?"

I studied my reflection again, my smile almost blinding me. "The happiest I've ever been."

* * * *

I needed to contact the tailor Patricia had recommended. The dress's bandeau bodice had to be taken in, and I was thinking of getting the skirt shortened slightly. I didn't want it dragging too much in the sand. But other than that, the dress was perfect.

My smile stayed on my face all the way through lunch and my walk home. Brett had texted me while I was at Lisa's to say he was making a trip to the hardware store, so I wasn't surprised when I arrived home and he wasn't there. After all the emotions that had run through me while I was at Lisa's house, I wanted nothing more than to throw my arms around Brett and kiss him, but that would have to wait.

In an attempt to keep myself occupied, I booted up my laptop and settled on the couch with it, leaving the French doors open so I could enjoy the slight summer breeze. Bentley settled on his bed across the room from me, and Flapjack padded his way out onto the back porch and stretched out in a patch of shade.

Once I had my Internet browser open, I did a search using Claudia's and Yvonne's names. Claudia's story of what the reporter had done to her a few years ago had shocked me when I'd heard it, and I was still astounded by Yvonne's cruelty. I wanted to see if I could find any of the posts or references to them online. I thought Claudia had told the truth, but I wanted to double-check.

It didn't take much digging to find one of the posts. Someone—a friend of Claudia's, I gathered—had blogged about what Yvonne had done. The reporter had tweeted a photo of a plump Claudia taking part in a race and had added the caption "Race Walk or Elephant Race?" A screenshot of the original tweet was included with the blog post.

Despite already knowing what Yvonne had done, seeing the tweet shocked me anew. How could anyone be so cruel?

I quickly read through the rest of the blog post. Apparently, Yvonne had deleted her tweet in the face of angry backlash from the Golden Oldies athletic community, but not before the author of the blog post had taken the screenshot of it.

I didn't bother searching for any more of Yvonne's cruel posts about Claudia. Seeing one was enough.

Next, I plugged Felicia Venner's name into the search bar. After skimming through the results, I learned that Felicia had competed at the Olympic Games in her twenties and had gone on to have a coaching career. From what I could tell, she was still involved in coaching and had taken up competing in the Golden Oldies Games as soon as she'd turned fifty about five years ago.

When I added Yvonne's name to the search, I found an article the reporter had written about Felicia around that time. By that point, I shouldn't have been surprised by Yvonne's cruelty, but I still couldn't help but wince when I read part of the article.

Failed athlete Felicia Venner is taking a stab at resuscitating her long-dead career in track and field. Now officially over the hill, Venner is scheduled to compete in this year's Golden Oldies Games, a sporting event where all the competitors are oldies, but not necessarily golden, Venner being a prime example.

I didn't bother reading further. The first few lines were more than enough to put me off.

How had Yvonne managed to keep her job?

Maybe she hadn't. Further investigating revealed that Yvonne had worked for a different newspaper when she'd written the article than she had at the time of her death.

I browsed through more of the search results and came across a scathing post Felicia had written on Facebook.

To all my friends who've reached out after seeing the recent article about me, thank you for your support. There's no need to worry about me, though. Yvonne Pritchard has always been a cruel, bitter woman with a shriveled-up heart. Her favorite hobby is trying to tear people down to her miserable level. She's a pathetic hag, and her words mean nothing to me.

Claudia had mentioned that the animosity between Felicia and Yvonne had started decades ago, and I now had a glimpse of just how deep that bitterness ran.

Felicia and Claudia both had reason to dislike Yvonne, and I couldn't help but wonder if one of them hated the reporter enough to kill her.

Chapter Ten

When I heard a car in the driveway a short while later, all thoughts of Yvonne and potential murder suspects fled my mind. I shut down my laptop and left it on the coffee table, getting up in time to meet Brett when he came in the back door.

I barely gave him a chance to greet an excited Bentley before I wrapped my arms around his neck and kissed him. The kiss lasted until Bentley nosed his way between us, wanting some more attention for himself.

"You'd think I was missed or something," Brett joked, petting Bentley on the head.

"You were," I said in all seriousness.

Bentley seemed appeased now, so Brett focused his attention on me, running a hand up and down my arm. "Are you okay?"

"Better than okay," I assured him.

"How's the dress?"

"It needs adjusting here and there, but otherwise it's perfect."

"That explains the smile."

I hadn't realized until that moment that I had a big grin on my face. "That's not the reason."

"No?"

I put my arms around his neck again. "I'm so happy because I'm going to marry you in a few weeks and I'm the luckiest person in the world."

"I don't know about that," he said, holding me close. "I think *I'm* the luckiest person in the world."

"Maybe we're tied," I said, still smiling.

"I can live with that."

We kissed again, but then agreed that we should run some errands. We needed groceries, and normally we'd drive to the store, but having witnessed the state of traffic in town, we opted to go on foot. Between the two of us, we'd be able to carry our purchases home.

On our way to the grocery store, we stopped in at the flower shop, Blooms by the Beach. Since I had plenty to discuss with Sylvia, the owner of the store, I made an appointment to come back later in the week. Then we made our way over to the grocery store on Main Street, where we filled three of our reusable shopping bags with food.

When we left the store, we set off down the street at a leisurely pace. The racewalking event was over, but the streets were still closed off for the running and biking portions of the triathlon. Nothing seemed to be happening on Main Street at the moment, however, and only a few people milled about on the sidewalk.

Brett and I were about to go into the bakery to buy a loaf of bread when I spotted Tommy across the street, hanging around outside Johnny's Juice Hut.

"I'm going to see Tommy for a moment," I told Brett. "I haven't had a chance to talk to him about payment for the wedding photos yet."

While Brett went into the bakery, I dashed across the street.

"Hey, Marley," Tommy greeted when he saw me.

"Are you here to watch the triathlon?" I asked.

"No, I'm meeting Avery."

"The girl you introduced me to the other day?"

"Yep. We're going to get drinks here." He hooked his thumb over his shoulder toward Johnny's Juice Hut.

"I won't keep you long," I said. "Brett and I have talked about payment for the wedding photos, and we wanted to see if you're happy with the amount we came up with."

Tommy shook his head before I had a chance to say the number. "You're not paying me anything."

"But we have to," I protested.

"No, you don't. And I'm not taking any money from you."

"Tommy…"

He shook his head again. "Nope. The wedding cake is Ivan's gift to you, and the photos are my gift. You won't change my mind," he added quickly when I opened my mouth to protest again.

"Are you absolutely sure? We really don't mind paying you."

"Nope. Not happening."

"But—"

"You're the best boss I could ask for, Marley, and you're my friend. The photos are a gift, so forget about the whole money thing."

I couldn't help myself. I threw my arms around him and gave him a hug.

"Thank you, Tommy. Brett and I really do have the best friends."

"Sorry to interrupt," a female voice said.

I released Tommy. Avery had arrived. Today she had her auburn hair in a ponytail. She had a smile on her face, but it struck me as forced.

"You're not interrupting," I assured her. "I need to get going. Thanks again, Tommy. You two have a good time."

Tommy pulled open the door to Johnny's Juice Hut. "See you Wednesday, Marley."

He held the door open for Avery as I headed for the curb. Before crossing the street, I glanced back over my shoulder, feeling a strange prickling sensation on the back of my neck. I thought I caught Avery glaring at me through the window of Johnny's Juice Hut, but when I blinked, she'd turned away. I told myself it was a trick of the light and pushed it from my thoughts.

* * * *

That evening Brett and I attended a tennis match at the courts in Wildwood Park. Normally there were only a couple of benches next to the courts, but bleachers had been set up for the Golden Oldies Games so more spectators could enjoy the event. It was free to watch the matches, and the bleachers were half full by the time Brett and I arrived.

A mixed doubles match started up soon after we found seats and got settled. I didn't recognize any of the players, but as the match came to an end, I spotted a face in the crowd that I'd seen before.

"You see that blond man on the other side of the court?" I whispered to Brett. "The one in the yellow T-shirt?"

Brett's gaze zeroed in on the man I'd seen at the opening ceremonies. "What about him?"

"I saw him glaring at Yvonne on Friday. He was muttering to himself about how he couldn't believe she'd dared to show her face here."

"I'm guessing that earned him a spot on your suspect list."

"Yes, but I don't know his name or who he is." I joined the crowd in applauding for the victorious team as they waved.

"I don't think he's a local," Brett said as the applause died down. "He doesn't look familiar."

"Then I probably need to ask someone involved with the games."

Another match was set to start in a few minutes. Several people got up from the bleachers to leave, stretch their legs, or visit one of the nearby food trucks. Brett and I got up from our seats as well, having decided earlier on that we'd only stay for one match.

As we made our way down the bleachers, I caught sight of another familiar face in the crowd.

"I think I know who I can ask," I said to Brett. "I'll be right back."

I darted around the people milling about at the base of the bleachers and caught up to Pippa as she paused beneath a leafy tree, her gaze glued to her phone as she tapped away at it.

"Pippa."

She raised her head when I said her name and she tucked her phone into her handbag as I approached.

"Are you here to watch some tennis?" she asked.

"My fiancé and I watched the last match. We might catch another one later in the week. When do you play?"

"Tomorrow morning," she said with a faint, joyless smile. "I can't say that my heart is in it anymore, though."

"That's understandable. How's Rowena doing today? Is she still in town?"

"She is. She doesn't want to leave until Easton's been found. She's a bit calmer today, although still terribly upset. I don't think she can truly start to heal until Easton's had a proper burial."

"Is anything more known about what happened to him?"

"No, and I'm not sure there ever will be. Rowena didn't see him go overboard, so how it happened will always be a bit of a mystery. But at least if his body is found, Rowena can have some closure."

"I hope that happens soon."

The blond man in the yellow shirt stopped to purchase a drink from a bicycle vendor not far from us.

I tipped my head his way. "Do you know who that man is?" I asked Pippa.

"Nash Harlow."

"Is he an athlete?" He looked like he might just be old enough to meet the minimum age requirement.

"A coach. He's got several athletes competing here at the games. He coaches younger athletes as well, including a couple who've made it to the Olympics."

"Impressive. Does he coach tennis?"

"Triathlon." Pippa's phone jangled, and she dug it out of her handbag. "I'm sorry, but I need to take this. It's Rowena."

"Of course." I took a step back. "Good luck with your match tomorrow."

I left her to answer her phone call and found Brett waiting for me a few feet away.

"Any luck?" he asked as he took my hand and we walked toward the edge of the park.

"His name's Nash Harlow and he's a triathlon coach. I didn't find out about his connection to Yvonne, though."

"But you know who he is now. That's a start."

"Yes," I said. "It is."

"You should probably talk to Ray."

"About Nash?"

"And everyone else on your suspect list."

"You're probably right."

Brett didn't miss the hint of reluctance in my voice. He gave my hand a squeeze. "It'll be fine. He might not like you getting involved in his murder investigations, but he also wouldn't want you withholding any information that might help him track down the killer."

I knew he was right about that. I needed to share the information I had, even if it meant risking a lecture about keeping my nose out of the case.

"I'll call him when we get home."

Brett drew to a stop as we left the grass for the sidewalk. "How about we go for ice cream first?"

"For the third time in four days?"

"There's no such thing as too much ice cream."

"True, but I'd better remember to go for a run in the morning."

As we resumed walking, someone dashed past us and ran off down the street. It took me a second to recognize the woman.

"That was Pippa."

She'd already disappeared around the next corner.

"The woman you were just talking to?"

I nodded. "Rowena was calling her and now she's running toward the marina. I hope nothing else bad has happened."

We picked up our pace, pausing only briefly to make sure the road was clear before crossing and heading down the street to the marina.

"Something *has* happened," I said when the whitewashed hut came into view.

Two sheriff's department cruisers were parked in front of the building, and a small crowd had gathered near the top of the ramp.

Brett and I jogged the remaining distance. I spotted Charlie standing by the ramp, preventing anyone from going down to the docks below. We worked our way through the crowd toward him.

"What's going on, Charlie?" Brett asked as soon as we'd reached him.

Ray was down on the docks with one of his deputies and a couple of civilian men. At their feet was a lumpy form shrouded by a tarp. I guessed the answer to Brett's question before Charlie responded.

"It's Easton Miller," he said. "His body's been found."

Chapter Eleven

Another deputy arrived and took up Charlie's post at the top of the ramp. Charlie led Brett and me away from the small, curious crowd and over to some shade cast by the building that housed the marina's office. We had more privacy there and a hint of relief from the sun, which was still intense, despite the hour.

"Was he found by the docks?" I asked once we were out of earshot of the rest of the crowd.

A sudden image appeared in my mind of Easton's body bobbing beneath the docks for nearly three days, trapped there as people came and went, none the wiser. Despite the warmth of the evening, a chill trickled along my arms.

"No," Charlie replied, banishing the image from my mind, much to my relief. "A couple of local guys were out fishing and spotted him. He wasn't too far out, though. He probably would have ended up on the beach before long."

Another chill spread over my skin, and I rubbed my arms in an attempt to ward it off. Even though he hadn't been trapped beneath the docks, it was still terrible to think about Easton floating out in the water since he'd gone missing.

"I guess his wife knows," I said.

Most likely that was why Rowena's phone call had sent Pippa running for the marina.

Charlie winced. "Yes, she's still staying on her yacht. She's in a bad way, but she's got a friend with her."

"At least she can get some closure now," Brett said.

We all agreed that was the one hint of good in the unfortunate situation.

Brett and I didn't hang around the marina much longer. I had no desire to watch Easton's body get transported up from the docks, and I knew Ray was too busy to have me interrupt him at the moment. I'd call him in the morning instead, I decided.

Brett and I bypassed the ice cream parlor as we left the marina. We'd both lost our appetites after hearing about Easton, and all we wanted to do was get home.

* * * *

As soon as I finished breakfast the next day, I phoned Ray on his direct line. The call went to voice mail, so I left him a brief message, letting him know why I wanted to speak with him.

Brett took Bentley to work with him, getting an early start, so I set out on a run on my own. Even though Brett and I hadn't ended up indulging in ice cream the night before, I still wanted to get some exercise. Running helped to clear my head, and it was nice to get out for some fresh air before the day grew too warm.

When I returned home, I checked my phone for messages. Ray hadn't returned my call but I had a text message from Patricia, asking if I wanted to join her for tea later that morning. I sent her a quick reply, accepting the invitation, and hurried upstairs to shower and change before heading to her place.

Patricia's house was a beachfront Victorian like my own, although hers was yellow and white rather than blue and white. It was a short walk away from my house, and today I opted to go along the road instead of the beach, since there would be more shade. Although it was only midmorning, the day was already gearing up to be another scorcher.

It only took a couple of minutes to reach Patricia's B&B. As I followed the long driveway toward the house, I heard a woman's voice drifting toward me on the gentle breeze. It took a moment for me to realize that the voice was coming from the upper level of the carriage house where the windows were wide open to take advantage of the sea breeze.

Patricia used the ground floor of the carriage house as a woodworking studio, and the second story had been converted into a suite for B&B guests. I knew the voice wasn't Patricia's, so I figured it belonged to whoever was staying in the suite.

"I understand that the investigation is ongoing," the woman said, sounding short on patience, "but surely you've made *some* progress."

I slowed my steps, realizing the voice belonged to Pippa, Rowena Miller's friend.

"I understand that too, but can you at least tell me when you expect a final ruling on the cause of Easton's death? We... his wife needs closure."

It sounded like she was talking to someone official, and since there was no sheriff's department vehicle in the driveway and I was only hearing one voice, I figured she must be on the phone.

"What about Yvonne Pritchard's death?" she continued a moment later. "I know it's been ruled a homicide, but have you made any other progress with that investigation?"

I didn't want to get caught listening in, so I continued toward the main house, albeit slowly, straining to hear what she'd say next. Unfortunately, all I heard were a few muffled, exasperated words.

I decided to skirt around the house to the back door. As I rounded the corner, I heard a door slam. I glanced over my shoulder. Pippa was jogging down the carriage house's exterior stairway. I picked up my pace, not wanting her to see me. A moment later, an engine roared to life, followed by the sound of a car heading off along the driveway toward the road.

Judging by Pippa's side of the conversation and her obvious exasperation, I thought it was safe to assume that her phone call hadn't provided her with much—if any—information. It made sense that she wanted an update on Easton's case for Rowena's sake, but why was she interested in Yvonne's death? Pure curiosity, perhaps.

Patricia was in the kitchen when I reached the back porch, the French doors standing open to let in the fresh summer air.

"Hi, Marley," she called out when I stepped inside. "Make yourself at home. I'm just slicing up the zucchini bread I baked this morning."

"Sounds delicious," I said, my mouth already watering.

Patricia's baking was never a disappointment.

I paused by a shelf in the family room where a carving was on display. Patricia had a talent for shaping beautiful animals out of wood. I'd seen several pieces of her work before—I'd even purchased a couple—but the elephant displayed on the shelf was one I hadn't seen before.

"Is this new?" I asked when Patricia headed for the dining table that sat between the kitchen and the family room.

"Yes," Patricia said when she saw what I was talking about. "Sienna and I watched a documentary about elephants a few weeks ago and I guess it inspired me."

"It's beautiful."

"Thank you. I'm thinking of making a baby elephant to go along with it."

"That would be adorable."

Patricia fetched the teapot from the kitchen and we sat down to enjoy cups of tea with the scrumptious zucchini bread. We chatted for a few moments about the gorgeous weather and my wedding preparations before I brought up Yvonne's death.

"I guess you've been left with Yvonne's belongings," I said. "Has Ray or one of his deputies told you what to do with them?"

Patricia nodded and took a sip of her tea. "They've been in touch with her next of kin—her adult daughter, Luanne. Apparently Luanne lives in Buenos Aires and isn't able to come to Washington, so she got in touch with her father—Yvonne's ex-husband. He's coming to collect Yvonne's things and is planning to stay in town for a few days, probably so he can try to stay in the loop with the investigation."

"Yvonne's death must have been a terrible blow for Luanne."

"I get the sense that they weren't terribly close, but even so, it must have been a shock."

Patricia was in the midst of refilling my teacup when the doorbell rang.

"That might be the ex-husband now." She set down the teapot. "He thought he'd get here before noon." She pushed back her chair. "Excuse me a minute."

She disappeared down the hall toward the front door. A moment later I heard a man's voice along with Patricia's. They talked for a few moments in the foyer before Patricia showed him to a room on the second floor. She came back down soon after and rejoined me at the table. We were almost finished our tea when we heard footsteps in the hallway.

A man with thinning dark hair appeared in the doorway. He wore a gray suit and looked tired, with bags under his slightly bloodshot eyes.

"Sorry to bother you," he said to Patricia. "Would it be possible to have a glass of ice water?"

"Of course." Patricia got up from the table and fetched a glass from one of the kitchen cupboards. "This is my friend, Marley McKinney. Marley, this is Bryce Harcourt."

"Nice to meet you," I said, "although I wish the circumstances were better. I'm sorry for your loss."

He offered up a hint of a smile. "Thank you."

"Is this your first time in Wildwood Cove?" Patricia asked as she handed him a glass of ice water.

He took a drink before replying. "It is. From what little I've seen from today's drive, it's beautiful."

"Hopefully you'll get to see more before you leave, although I know you're not here to go sightseeing."

"I might have some time on my hands to look around." He downed the last of his water. "Probably not today, though. Sheriff Georgeson asked me to see him in Port Angeles once I got to the peninsula, so that's where I'm headed next."

Patricia took his empty glass from him. "Is there anything else you need before you go?"

"Thanks, but I'm good."

She set the glass on the kitchen counter. "I'll probably be here when you get back, but just in case, I'll give you a key."

She walked with Bryce toward the foyer, and the front door closed a moment later.

When Patricia returned to the back of the house, she paused, her eyes on me. "Is something wrong, Marley?"

I realized I was frowning. "I'm confused."

"About what?"

"Bryce said he arrived on the peninsula today and had never been to Wildwood Cove before."

"That's right. He lives in Portland."

"But it can't be true. I saw him here four days ago."

"Are you sure?" Patricia asked.

"Positive. I saw him at Wildwood Park during the opening ceremonies for the Golden Oldies Games. He was talking to Pippa Hampshire."

Patricia looked as confused as I felt. "That's strange. Why would he lie?"

"That," I said, "is a very good question."

Chapter Twelve

Patricia and I didn't linger over our tea much longer. She needed to get some groceries, and I was thinking about going for a swim in the ocean. I left through the back door and decided to take the beach route home. It wouldn't matter much if I got hot, since I could cool off in the ocean as soon as I got home and changed into my swimsuit.

I'd barely left the Murray property when I met up with Sienna.

"Heading home?" I asked.

"For a bit," she replied. "Ellie's coming over soon. We're going to hang out on the beach, maybe go for a swim." Ellie was a friend of hers from school. "Were you visiting my mom?"

"I was," I replied. "She's just gone out to get some groceries."

"I hope the new guest doesn't show up while she's gone."

"Yvonne's ex-husband? He arrived a little while ago. He's gone to Port Angeles to meet up with the sheriff."

"That's good. I didn't want to be the one to greet him. I wouldn't know what to say. I mean, would he be sad that his ex-wife is dead? Or did he hate her?"

"I'm not sure how he feels about it. But that's not the only thing I'm not sure about."

"What do you mean?"

I told her about the fact that Bryce had claimed he'd just arrived in Wildwood Cove for the first time and how I knew that wasn't true.

"And you're wondering why he lied," Sienna guessed.

"He must have something to hide."

Sienna's eyes sparkled with a light I'd seen before. "Maybe we can find out what that something is. Come on." She hopped over a log, heading for her house.

I hurried after her. "What are you planning to do?" I suspected I already knew the answer.

"You said he went out, right? And my mom's at the grocery store. That means we can search his room without anyone knowing."

"Sienna, that's not a good idea."

She had her keys out and was unlocking the back door. "What if he killed his ex-wife? We can't sit back and do nothing."

I followed her into the house. "Your mom wouldn't like this."

"Mom!" Sienna shouted.

Nothing but silence greeted us.

Apparently satisfied that Patricia hadn't returned unexpectedly, Sienna shut the back door. "She never needs to know. No one needs to know, unless we find something that has to be turned over to the sheriff. Even then, I can say I accidentally found it while I was putting out fresh towels or whatever."

I still had misgivings, mostly because Patricia was a friend of mine and I knew she wouldn't approve in the least. At the same time, I was just as curious as Sienna. If I was completely honest with myself, I was itching for a chance to get a look at Bryce's belongings.

With guilt and curiosity battling it out inside of me, I followed Sienna up to the second floor.

"All the other guests went out after breakfast and said they wouldn't be back till tonight." She turned left at the top of the stairs. "My mom must have given him Yvonne's room." She stopped outside the second door on the right. "This one."

I was having a bad case of second thoughts right at that moment, but Sienna opened the door and disappeared into the room. I followed after her, knowing I was failing at being a responsible adult. Once inside, I left the door open a crack, hoping we'd hear if anyone arrived home while we were snooping.

Sienna made a beeline for the suitcase sitting on the bed. It was unzipped, so she flipped the top open. The suitcase was empty aside from a cell phone charger and a belt.

"He's already unpacked." Sienna wasted no time moving to the chest of drawers.

While she carefully rifled through the contents of each drawer, I focused my attention on the lightweight jacket hanging from the hook on the back of the bedroom door. The first pocket I slid my hand into was empty.

"Nothing," Sienna said with disappointment as she shut the last drawer.

"I guess that's not surprising," I said. "We weren't likely to find the murder weapon lying around."

When I slid my hand into the jacket's second pocket, my fingers touched what felt like plastic.

Sienna sat on the edge of the bed. "Do the cops know what the murder weapon was?"

I pulled the piece of plastic out of the pocket. "I don't know, but since Ivan thinks she was stabbed, it was probably a knife or some other type of sharp object."

"What's that?" Sienna got up and came closer.

"An ID badge." I studied it further. "Bryce works at a hospital in Seattle. He's a pharmacist."

Sienna lost interest and dropped down onto her knees to look under the bed. I returned the ID badge to the jacket pocket before peeking into the small attached bathroom. There wasn't much to see in there.

As I shut the bathroom door, Sienna climbed to her feet.

"Nothing," she said again. The excited light in her eyes had dimmed.

"Don't be too disappointed." I cast a quick look around the room and decided it looked the same as it had when we'd arrived. I led the way out into the hall, and Sienna shut the bedroom door. "I've got other suspects to look into."

She brightened. "Like who?"

On our way back down the stairs, I told her about Claudia Wu, Felicia Venner, and Nash Harlow.

"I saw one of the tweets Yvonne posted about Claudia a few years back. It really was terrible."

"So maybe Claudia wanted revenge," Sienna said as we continued on to the kitchen.

"It's definitely possible. Maybe the fact that Yvonne was all sugary sweet to Claudia the other day was the final straw. She sure seemed angry when I saw them arguing at the park on Friday."

Sienna leaned against the kitchen counter. "What about the other two?"

"Yvonne and Felicia clearly didn't like each other, but I'm not sure how that started. I haven't had time to do any research on Nash yet. That's next on my to-do list."

I expected Sienna to say she wanted to help with that, but her phone buzzed at that moment.

"Ellie's on her way here. I'd better change into my swimsuit."

"Have fun," I said, already heading out the door. I thought it was best if she didn't get too involved in my sleuthing.

"Text me if you find out anything juicy," she called after me.

I waved over my shoulder and headed for the beach, not committing to anything.

* * * *

As soon as I was home, I settled on the couch with a tall glass of sweet tea and my laptop, deciding to leave my swim for another time. I wasn't oblivious to the fact that my concerns about Sienna getting involved in my unofficial investigation mirrored the ones Brett and Ray had whenever I poked around for clues. Ever since Sienna had developed an appetite for solving mysteries, I had a better understanding of Brett's point of view, and Ray's too.

Unlike his uncle, Brett never tried to stop me from investigating. He knew that would mean changing who I was. He did, however, want me to be careful and stay out of danger. I wanted the same for Sienna, so I hoped she wouldn't go snooping on her own.

When I had the Internet browser open, I looked up Nash Harlow. It didn't take much work to find a long list of results relating to the right man. I poked around, skimming various articles, profiles, and websites. Nash's coaching career had started almost two decades ago, and before that he'd competed internationally as a triathlete. That information didn't hold my attention; it was quickly overshadowed by my discovery of a connection between Nash and Yvonne.

Four years ago, Yvonne had written an article about Nash and one of his athletes, but it wasn't about their involvement in a triathlon. The article revealed that Nash—married for more than ten years at that time—was having an affair with one of his twentysomething female athletes.

I sat back and considered what I'd read. I couldn't be sure that there was any truth to what Yvonne had written, but considering the hate-filled glare I'd seen Nash send her way, he'd harbored a grudge against her either way. True or not, I wondered if the allegations had affected Nash's marriage.

I did another quick Internet search, hoping to satisfy my curiosity. I had to do a little more digging to find the information I wanted this time, but it still didn't take too long to uncover it. About a year after Yvonne's article was published, Nash and his wife had formally divorced. The timing suggested that the affair, or at least the allegation, could have triggered the breakdown of their marriage. And if Nash blamed Yvonne for his divorce, he might well have wanted revenge.

Chapter Thirteen

I awoke to another beautiful day on Wednesday morning. The sky was pale pink, and through the open window I could hear birds singing. As soon as I stepped outside, I could tell that the day would be another hot one. It seemed the Olympic Peninsula was caught in the midst of a heat wave. If I'd still been living in Seattle, I would have found the heat a bit oppressive, but here in Wildwood Cove I didn't mind it. Most days the ocean breeze provided some relief, and I always had the option of going for a refreshing swim after work.

On my walk to the pancake house, I noticed a bank of clouds off in the distance, but they were puffy white ones and didn't block out the rising sun. A couple of sailboats were already out on the sparkling water, and a seagull dipped down toward the waves. The scene was so beautiful that it belonged on a postcard.

As usual, Ivan and Tommy were already at work in the kitchen when I arrived at The Flip Side. I said a quick hello to them before going through my usual morning routine. When copies of the local paper were delivered, I paused to have a look at one. As expected, the murder had made the front page, along with a story about the Golden Oldies Games.

I flipped through the paper without reading the articles; I figured I'd do that later. I was about to return the paper to the stand by the front door when another story caught my eye. The article was a short one, so I read it right then. Apparently someone had stolen Felicia Venner's racing gear the day before. When asked by the reporter if the loss would affect her performance, she'd replied, "I won't let it. I've got backup gear. Those were my favorite shoes, but if this was meant to throw me off my game, it won't work. I intend to persevere despite the theft."

I folded up the paper and set it on the stand. Hopefully the theft was a onetime occurrence. The Golden Oldies Games didn't need any more shadows cast over the event.

By then all that was left to do was to flip the Closed sign over at seven o'clock, so I returned to the kitchen to make myself a cup of tea.

"Did you read the paper?" Tommy asked.

"I read about the theft of an athlete's gear, but otherwise I only glanced at the headlines. Why?"

"You know the new reporter for the *Weekly*?"

"You mean Rob?" I poured hot water over my tea bag. "What about him?"

"He found out something, just in time to get it in today's paper."

My ears perked up at that. "Something interesting?"

"Yvonne had drugs in her system when she was killed. Drugs that could have made her drowsy."

My eyebrows shot up. "That's definitely interesting."

"We already knew she was murdered," Ivan grumbled as he placed a tray of breakfast scones in the oven.

I fished my tea bag out of my mug. "We did, but this suggests that the murder was planned."

"Because someone drugged her so she couldn't fight back," Tommy said.

"Exactly."

"Or she took the drugs herself," Ivan said as he punched a button on the oven to set the timer.

"Okay, that's a possibility," I conceded. "Maybe she took something for pain, or maybe she was addicted to drugs." I addressed Tommy. "Any idea what type of drug it was?"

"Nope. Only that it could have made her sleepy."

"Then we can't rule out that she took it herself. But, if the killer drugged her, then he or she had an opportunity to do so. The drug could have been injected or slipped into her food or drink. Too bad we don't know if there were any needle marks found on her body."

The kitchen door swung open. "Needle marks?" Sienna echoed as she came into the room. "There were needle marks found on Yvonne's body?"

"No," I said quickly. "Well, actually, we don't know."

"The sheriff will know," Ivan said with a pointed look in my direction. "Because it's his job to investigate."

"And not mine," I finished for him. "I know."

"You know you can't stop her," Tommy said to Ivan. "It's pointless to try."

Ivan grunted at that and cracked an egg into a bowl.

"There's nothing wrong with talking about it," I said.

Before anyone had a chance to suggest that I wasn't likely to stick to merely discussing the murder, I picked up my cup of tea and headed for the door.

"Come on, Sienna. We'll let the guys work in peace."

As soon as the kitchen door shut behind us, Sienna whispered, "Why were you talking about needle marks?"

I filled her in on what Tommy had told me and Ivan.

"So the killer might have given her the drugs," she said once I'd finished.

We looked at each other and said in unison, "Bryce Harcourt."

"He's a pharmacist," Sienna said.

"So he has access to drugs."

"It must be him! He's the killer!"

"We don't know that for sure yet," I cautioned.

"But he lied about being in town when Yvonne was killed. And she was his ex-wife. Maybe he got sick of paying alimony."

"We don't even know that he *was* paying alimony."

"I bet it was him." Sienna was undeterred. "But how do we prove it?"

"I'll tell Ray that I saw Bryce in town on Friday. He probably already knows Bryce is a pharmacist, but I'll mention it just in case. Since he's Yvonne's ex, I bet Bryce is near the top of the official suspect list. Or he will be once Ray knows he was in Wildwood Cove. Did Bryce show up at the B&B last night?"

"Yep. Around eight o'clock."

"So Ray didn't arrest him."

"But if he was in Port Angeles all that time, there was a lot of questioning."

"*Was* he at the sheriff's office the entire time?"

Sienna shrugged. "I have no idea."

"How did he seem last night?"

"I only saw him for a few seconds. He seemed… normal, I guess. Not that I really know what normal is for him."

So we didn't know if he'd merely been questioned for information about Yvonne or if he'd been grilled as a suspect.

"I'd better phone Ray," I decided.

Leigh arrived at that moment, so I flipped the sign on the door and headed for the office. I had to leave another voice mail for Ray. I kept it short, letting him know I had more information for him. If I didn't hear back from him soon, I'd leave him a longer message, detailing what I knew. While I waited to see if he'd return my call, I tried to keep myself busy with work, but the mystery of Yvonne's death was never far from my thoughts.

* * * *

The pancake house got a bit hectic during the breakfast rush, so I left the office to help Leigh and Sienna with serving customers. All of the tables, inside and out, were occupied, and a short line stretched from the door onto the promenade. The booming business brought a smile to my face, despite the unfortunate incidents of late. The discovery of Easton's body was a hot topic of conversation that morning, but I was relieved to hear many customers also having enthusiastic discussions about the various sporting events going on in town.

The Flip Side was still busy by midmorning, but not overwhelmingly so, and there was no longer a line at the door. Although Leigh was taking a short break, I left Sienna alone so I could make a quick trip to the washroom. On my way back down the hall, I passed the break room and noticed Leigh sitting at the table, her head in her hands. I stopped short and poked my head into the room.

"Leigh? Are you okay?"

She jerked her head up. As soon as she recovered from my sudden appearance, she released a heavy sigh.

"I'm okay," she said. "Just..."

I stepped into the room. "What?"

A strand of bleached blond hair had escaped from her messy bun. She tucked it behind her ear. "You don't want to hear about my problems."

"Of course I do. If you want to share them."

Leigh stared at the tabletop for a moment. "I'm worried about Greg," she said, referring to her husband.

"Is he sick?" I asked with concern.

"No. At least, I hope not. I don't know what's wrong. That's what's worrying me."

I sat down across from her. "What makes you think something's wrong?"

"He's been acting strange. Preoccupied."

"Did you ask him about it?"

"I did, but he swears it's nothing," she answered.

"You don't believe him?"

Leigh shook her head. "The last time he acted like this he'd lost his job and didn't want to tell me. It took three days before he finally broke the news to me."

"Do you think that's what happened this time too?"

"I wondered, but the other day I peeked into the hardware store and saw that he was working, just as he was supposed to be." Worry clouded her hazel eyes. "What if something's really wrong? What if it's something terrible?"

I reached across the table and squeezed her hand. "There's no point in jumping to conclusions. You could be worrying for no reason."

"*Something's* going on," she said.

"Maybe you should try talking to him again."

"Maybe." She got to her feet slowly, as if her worries were weighing heavily on her shoulders. "I'm sorry about this, Marley."

"Don't be. Let me know if there's anything I can do, okay?"

She thanked me and gave me a weak smile before returning to the dining room. I followed her there to see how things were going. When I was satisfied that Leigh and Sienna had everything under control, I decided to head to the office to deal with some invoices. I'd only made it a few steps when Ray walked into the pancake house.

"Morning, Marley," he said, removing his hat as I approached him. "I got your messages. Since I was in town, I thought I'd stop by for a chat. Can you spare a few minutes?"

"Of course."

I glanced around. The pancake house was still nearly full, so the dining area wouldn't offer much privacy.

"How about we talk in the office?" I suggested.

Ray nodded his assent.

"Can I get you some coffee? Maybe something to eat? Ivan just took a tray of breakfast scones out of the oven."

A hint of a smile touched Ray's face. "I won't turn down either one. Thank you."

I told him I'd meet him in the office and stopped by the kitchen to pick up a cup of coffee for Ray and a scone for each of us. I added a splash of cream to the cup of coffee, knowing that's how Ray liked it. I'd come to know him and his wife, Gwen, quite well since I'd moved to Wildwood Cove, thanks to numerous gatherings with Brett's family. I didn't know their daughter, Jourdan, quite as well yet, since she was away at college most of the year, but I was hoping to see her a few times while she was in town during the summer.

Once I'd carried the food and coffee into the office, Ray and I settled into the two chairs in front of the desk.

"You must have your hands full this week," I said as Ray took the first sip of his coffee. "Two deaths, a theft, and all the extra traffic from the tourists and athletes."

"It's been hectic, that's for sure." He tore a small piece off his scone. "I gather from your messages that you've been busy too."

He kept his tone even, so I couldn't tell if he was annoyed or not.

"Business has been booming here at The Flip Side, but I don't think that's what you're referring to." I didn't need to wait for confirmation. "I really haven't done all that much snooping. I've just learned some things from talking to people and observing what's been happening around me."

"If you talk to the wrong people about the wrong things, it can be more dangerous than you might think."

"I know," I assured him. "And I have no intention of getting mixed up with another murderer." Before he could say he'd heard that before, I hurried on. "But I've heard and seen some things that I thought you should know about."

He nodded at me to continue as he took another sip of coffee.

I began by telling him about the night of the opening ceremonies when I'd seen Claudia arguing with Yvonne. "Claudia had reason to hate Yvonne," I said, going on to detail why that was the case. "And she's not the only one."

I filled him in on Nash's history with the reporter and mentioned what I'd heard about Felicia Venner.

"Oh, and there's the ex-husband," I added. "I know you've talked to him already, but do you know he's a pharmacist?"

"I do know that," Ray said after swallowing the last bite of his scone.

I tore a piece off my own and savored the delicious flavors of apple, cinnamon, and maple. "So he had access to drugs. And I've heard that Yvonne had drugs in her system when she was killed. Drugs that could have made her drowsy and easier to kill."

Ray raised an eyebrow.

"I didn't get that from snooping," I rushed to assure him. "Not that last part, anyway. It was in the paper."

Ray didn't comment on that. Instead, he wrote something down in the notebook he'd produced while I was relaying all my information.

"Has there been an autopsy on Easton Miller yet?" I asked as he snapped his notebook shut.

"It's underway as we speak."

"So you won't know if he had drugs in his system for a while yet?"

"I have no reason to suspect that the two deaths are related," he said, catching on to my line of thinking. "Of course there won't be any official ruling until the postmortem is complete, but the most likely scenario is that Dr. Miller simply fell overboard and drowned. It's unfortunate and tragic, but these things happen every year."

He picked up his hat from where he'd set it on the desk.

"There's something else," I said before he could get up to go. "I met Bryce Harcourt at the Driftwood B&B right before he paid you a visit in Port Angeles. He said he'd just arrived in Wildwood Cove and that he'd never been here before, but that's not true."

Ray's eyebrows drew together. "What makes you say that?"

"I saw him at Wildwood Park on Friday night."

I clearly had Ray's interest now.

"Are you sure about that?"

"I'm sure. He was talking to Pippa Hampshire."

Ray opened his notebook again and jotted something down. "I'll look into it," he promised before standing up and placing his hat on his head. "Thank you for the information. But, Marley…"

"I know," I said as I got to my feet. "Leave the investigating to the professionals. But I wanted to make sure you had all this information."

"And I appreciate that."

He sounded a bit weary. I wondered if it was because of the hectic week or because he was tired of giving me the same warnings over and over.

"Thank you for the scone and coffee."

I walked him to the door before returning to the office. I knew what he'd said was true—there were boating accidents and drownings every year. From everything I'd heard, it certainly sounded as though Easton's death had been a sad but simple accident. Even so, I couldn't quite shake the feeling that two deaths were somehow related.

Chapter Fourteen

Later on in the day, when the lunch rush was winding down, Levi arrived at the pancake house and got settled in at a small table. I wondered if he was planning on meeting Pippa, but when Leigh asked if he was ready to order, he didn't indicate that he was waiting for anyone.

Once Leigh had taken his order and provided him with a glass of Coca-Cola, I approached his table.

"No Pippa today?" I said once we'd exchanged greetings.

"One of her friends has a tennis match, so Pippa's cheering her on. I'll head back over there in a bit, but I needed something to eat and the food here is fantastic."

"I'm glad you like it," I said with a smile. "How did Pippa's match go this morning?"

"Great." A proud grin stretched across his face. "She won, so she's moving on to the next round. She plays again tomorrow."

"That's great. She must be pleased."

Levi's grin faded. "She is, but she's not able to enjoy it as much as usual."

"That's understandable. How's Rowena doing?"

"Not so good." Levi paused long enough to take a sip of his Coke. "She and Easton go way back. They even knew each other when they were kids."

"I remember someone saying that they went to school together."

"Yep. And they grew up in the same neighborhood. They didn't start dating until their senior year of high school, but they've been together ever since."

"Wow." My heart ached for Rowena. "So he's always been in Rowena's life."

"And now she has to learn to live without him. It won't be easy for her."

"Have you known the Millers for a long time?" I asked.

"Nah. I've been dating Pippa for a year, and I've known Rowena and Easton for less time than that. But long enough to know they were really in love." He shook his head. "I don't know how Rowena's going to cope."

"I'm glad she's got Pippa, at least. I'm sure that's a great comfort to her."

"It is. They're best friends."

I was about to leave him in peace when he spoke up again.

"Any word about who killed Yvonne?" he asked. "You must hear a lot of news and gossip in a place like this."

"I don't know much about the official investigation," I said.

That was true enough. I didn't want to share that I had my own suspicions.

"The sheriff's probably got a list of suspects a mile long," Levi said. "That woman was a real piece of work."

"You didn't like her?" I wasn't all that surprised.

"Did anyone?"

Leigh arrived with Levi's order of bacon cheddar waffles, so I excused myself and left him to eat. As I worked, my mind drifted back to the topic of Easton's death.

Maybe Ray was right and the drowning was purely accidental. Rowena was the only person on the yacht with him at the time he went overboard. And if what Levi said was true, the Millers had been a devoted couple, very much in love.

But what if it *wasn't* true? Sometimes couples put on a good front for the rest of the world, keeping up the appearance of a perfect relationship, but behind the scenes the story could be quite different. I had no way of knowing if that was the case, however.

Maybe once the autopsy and toxicology reports were in, Ray's theory would become the official ruling. But until that happened, I knew I'd continue to wonder if there'd been two murders in Wildwood Cove that week.

* * * *

After I'd closed and cleaned The Flip Side that afternoon, I returned to the office to retrieve the box holding my wedding dress. I'd brought it to work with me that morning so I could swing by Sally North's tailor shop on the way home. Before leaving the pancake house, I lifted the lid off the box, unable to resist taking another peek at the gown. Every time I looked at it, excitement fluttered in my stomach.

Sometimes I couldn't believe how well things were going in my life. After the deaths of my stepfather and stepsiblings, and before I'd moved to Wildwood Cove, I had in many ways hidden away from the world. I'd buried myself in a job that I didn't hate but didn't love, and my one relationship that had gone beyond a few dates didn't end well.

Looking back, I knew I hadn't made the best choices when it came to my relationship with my previous boyfriend, Ryan. Now I wondered if I'd done that on purpose, although subconsciously so. As much as part of me had wanted to find love, I'd ignored red flags that should have told me early on that Ryan wasn't the guy for me. Maybe because the fact that he wasn't right for me meant I'd never truly give my heart to him. And if I never fell completely in love, then I wouldn't have to risk losing someone else who held a piece of my heart.

Moving to Wildwood Cove had changed my life, had changed *me*. It was partly the place; I'd always loved Wildwood Beach, and the ocean had a way of soothing me while also making me feel alive. But even more than the place, it was the people here who'd brought me out of hiding so I could live life to the fullest again. I had such great friends here in Wildwood Cove, and Brett... He was largely responsible for healing my heart.

And now we were getting married. I wouldn't have said that it was a dream come true because what we had together was better than anything I'd ever dreamed, anything I could have wished for.

Letting the fabric of my wedding dress slide through my fingers, I carefully packed it away again. I tucked the box under my arm and set off on foot into the heart of Wildwood Cove.

Sally North's shop was situated on Pacific Street, nestled between a small restaurant and a thrift shop. A bell jingled when I opened the door and stepped inside. There was a small reception area with a desk, a couch, and a coffee table. An open door directly across from where I stood led into another room. A shadow moved beyond the doorway, and Avery appeared a second later.

"Hi," I said with a small dose of surprise. "I didn't realize you worked here."

"I don't, really," Avery said. "It's my aunt's shop. I stopped by to say hi, and now I'm watching the place for a few minutes while she runs a quick errand." She looked at the box I was holding. "Do you need something altered?"

"Yes. I was hoping to find out if your aunt can make a couple of changes to my dress."

"I'm sure she can. She can do pretty much anything with a needle and thread."

"Is it all right if I wait?" I asked.

"Sure. She won't be long."

I took a seat on the couch, resting the box on my knees.

Avery leaned against the desk, her gaze fixed on me. "How long have you known Tommy?"

Somehow I wasn't surprised she'd brought Tommy into the conversation.

"He started working at the pancake house two springs ago, so over a year now."

She continued to watch me with her gray eyes. I wouldn't have called her gaze hostile, but it certainly wasn't friendly. I recalled the prickling sensation I'd experienced outside of Johnny's Juice Hut and felt certain she'd been the cause of it. I suspected I knew why she was acting cool toward me.

"How about you?" I asked, pretending I hadn't noticed her attitude.

"We met last week, but we clicked right away."

I didn't think I'd imagined the hint of defensiveness in her tone.

"He's already taken some awesome photos of the athletes," she continued.

"I saw one on the front page of the paper," I said. "He's a very talented photographer. I'm lucky he'll be taking the pictures at my wedding."

Avery perked up. "Wedding?"

"I'm getting married in August." I tapped the box on my lap. "It's my wedding dress I need altered."

"Oh, cool." She sounded relieved, and the iciness in her eyes melted away.

I knew then I'd been right in suspecting she was worried we might have designs on the same guy.

Silence fell between us. It was on the verge of becoming awkward when the front door opened with a jingle of the bell above it. A middle-aged woman with curly dark hair entered the shop.

"Thanks for hanging around, Avery," she said before turning to me. "Hello. I'm Sally North. Are you here to see me?"

"She needs her wedding dress altered," Avery said before I had a chance to respond. "I'll see you tomorrow, Aunt Sally."

"Bye, hon," Sally said as Avery disappeared out the front door. She smiled at me. "Sorry about the wait."

"No problem," I assured her. "I've only been here a few minutes."

I introduced myself and told her about my dress.

"There are a couple of things I'm hoping can be altered," I explained.

"Bring the dress in the back and I'll have a look."

Sally led the way into a larger room with several dress forms standing along one wall. A folding screen blocked off one corner of the room, and two chairs sat in another corner.

I set my box on a long worktable and removed the lid.

"That's gorgeous," Sally remarked as I withdrew the gown.

I told her about needing the bandeau top taken in. "And I was hoping the skirt could be shortened a bit. The wedding will be on the beach, and I don't want the hem to drag in the sand too much."

"Both should be easy fixes. Do you have time to try it on for me now? I've got about an hour before my next appointment."

"Sure. That would be great."

I ducked behind the folding screen and changed into the dress before stepping back out into the open. I held up the top so it wouldn't slide down. Sally quickly remedied that situation with tucks and pins. Then she had me stand on a stool so she could work on the hem.

"Have you taken in any of the sporting events this week?" she asked as she worked.

"A couple. I watched a friend's race and went to a tennis match the other night."

"I guess you've probably heard the news about the tennis player who died."

"I did," I confirmed. "It was terrible news. I had a chance to meet him and his wife at my pancake house last week."

Sally shook her head sadly as she moved around behind me. "I still can't believe it. I went to school with him and his wife, Rowena, in Seattle. Rowena and I stayed in touch over the years, and I was hoping to catch up with her during the games. I never imagined something like this would happen."

"I think it was a shock to everyone," I said.

"Easton was a good man." She paused as she worked away at pinning the hem at the back of the dress. "You know," she continued after a moment, "I always thought Rowena had a charmed life. Her family was well-off, she was popular at school, she was a talented athlete, and she went on to have a wonderful marriage. But more recently, life hasn't been so kind to her."

"I heard that she and Easton lost their son a couple of years ago."

Sally reappeared in front of me, assessing the way the skirt of my dress was hanging with a critical eye. "That's right. He was a talented tennis player too, just like his parents. But his car went off the road one night and into a river."

My chest tightened. "That's awful." I knew too well how difficult that would have been for his family.

"I think it would have broken Rowena completely if she hadn't had Easton in her life," Sally said. "I don't know what she'll do now. I'm planning to stop by her yacht in the morning to see how she's holding up."

"I know her friend Pippa Hampshire is keeping an eye on her."

"I don't know Pippa, but I'm glad Rowena's got someone to lean on." Sally surveyed the dress one last time and then nodded with approval. "That should do it. I can have the alterations finished for you by the end of next week."

With Sally's assistance, I carefully stepped off the stool, making sure not to get my feet caught up in the fabric.

"That's fantastic. Thank you so much."

"Careful of the pins," she warned as I slipped behind the folding screen.

I heeded her advice and managed to get out of the dress without any pins poking me. When I had my clothes on again, I handed the dress over to Sally.

"You don't think Easton's death could be related to the reporter's death, do you?" I asked, managing not to sound like it was something I'd already considered.

"Oh, gosh, no. I don't see how it could be. I heard the reporter was murdered."

"She was."

"Then they're definitely not related. I was told Rowena was the only one on board the yacht with Easton when he went overboard. And anyone who suspects her of killing her own husband would be barking up the wrong tree. Heck, they'd be in the wrong forest. Those two were devoted to each other. Rowena would never kill him and she had no reason to, anyway."

"No money troubles or infidelity?"

"Absolutely not. They both come from well-off families and Easton had a successful dental practice. Besides, like I said, they were devoted to each other. Easton's death was an accident, pure and simple. It had to be."

I pretended to accept her word for it, but the truth was that I still wasn't quite convinced.

Chapter Fifteen

As I walked away from Sally's shop, my stomach gave a rumble of hunger. Instead of heading straight home, I made a detour to the Beach and Bean so I could grab a frozen lemonade and a maple pecan muffin. My plan was to get the items to go and leave the bustling coffee shop, but as I stood in line at the counter to place my order, I reconsidered.

Rowena Miller was sitting by herself at a small table tucked away at the back of the coffee shop. The place was crowded and every table was occupied, but Rowena seemed oblivious to all the chatter going on around her. She sat with her hands clasped around her cup, staring blankly at the tabletop.

I wondered if I should leave her alone, but by the time I had my drink and muffin in hand, I decided to speak to her briefly and then leave her in peace. I could almost feel her grief as I approached. It was like an invisible but palpable cloud around her.

She didn't notice me even once I stood right next to her table.

"Rowena?"

She raised her head slowly. Her eyes were blank at first, but she recognized me a second later.

"The owner of the pancake house, right?"

"That's right. Marley McKinney." I hesitated a second before continuing. "I'm so sorry about your husband. I don't want to bother you, but I just wanted to say that."

"Thank you." Her eyes grew misty but cleared a second later. "And you're not bothering me." She glanced at my drink and the small paper bag that held my muffin. "Will you join me? I'm probably not great company, but I could use the distraction."

"Of course." I set my snack down on the table. "Can I get you anything first?" I asked with a glance at her nearly empty cup. "Another drink? Something to eat?"

"No, but thank you. I don't have much of an appetite these days."

"That's understandable." I sat in the seat across from her and took a sip of my lemonade.

Rowena attempted a smile, but it died away before it fully took shape. "Your pancake house is certainly popular. That's not a surprise, though. The food there is delicious."

"Thank you. This is usually a busy time of year at The Flip Side, but it's been extra busy lately with the athletes and coaches in town for the games."

"Yes, the games." She tipped her cup to check the contents, but made no move to drink what was left. "I'm afraid I haven't been supporting my fellow athletes like I'd planned."

"I'm sure everyone understands."

She smiled sadly. "Yes. I've had so many messages on my phone, and others passed on by Pippa. Everyone's been very kind." Her hand shook as she finally raised her cup to finish her drink.

"Will you be returning to Seattle soon?" I asked before taking a sip of my frozen lemonade.

"Not until next week. I'll be leaving the yacht here; I have cousins who will deal with it for me. Pippa is going to drive me back home, once the games are over. She offered to drive me earlier, but I don't want her missing out on any of the games, and I don't want to leave until Easton's... until he's been released."

"Do you know when that will happen?"

"Probably in the next day or two." She dug around in her handbag and produced a tissue.

I asked my next question before I had a chance to think better of it. "And his death is still considered accidental?"

Rowena's gaze snapped up to mine. "It *was* an accident."

"He didn't have any drugs in his system when he went overboard?"

"Of course not!"

"Sorry," I said quickly, not wanting to upset her further. "I only ask because Yvonne Pritchard took or was given a drug before she died, one that could have made her drowsy and possibly easier to kill."

Rowena's shoulders relaxed, and she dabbed at her nose with the tissue. "My husband had nothing to do with that woman. Why would you think his death was related to hers?"

"Only because they happened so close together and both were found in or near the water."

"Well, that's where the similarities end. That woman hurt people right, left, and center, but my Easton didn't have an enemy in the world. Yvonne was murdered. My husband died in a terrible accident."

Tears welled in her eyes, and I regretted pushing the conversation as far as I had.

"I'm sorry for upsetting you," I said.

"It's more the whole situation that has me upset. I hope I wasn't too brusque with you."

"Of course not." I slipped the remains of my muffin into the paper bag and stood up. "I'd better be off, but I really am sorry for your loss."

"Thank you," she whispered, more subdued again.

As I left the coffee shop, I took a long drink of my frozen lemonade. I regretted it a second later when I ended up with a brain freeze. When the pain subsided and I could think clearly again, I decided I could cross Rowena's name off my suspect list.

My suspicion that Easton's death could be related to Yvonne's seemed unfounded. Rowena was the only one with the opportunity to kill her husband, and I now knew she hadn't harmed him. Her grief was intense and genuine. Now that I'd witnessed it firsthand, I didn't doubt that for a second. She'd loved him deeply and she now missed him terribly.

While it was something of a relief to know that the murderer hadn't already struck twice, I didn't feel any closer to figuring out who the killer was. I decided I'd focus on the puzzle later. At the moment, I had some errands to run.

* * * *

I walked toward the marina and sat on a bench while I finished off my muffin and frozen lemonade. I was relieved to see that nothing was out of the ordinary today. Boaters were coming and going down at the docks while people passed by me on the sidewalk, licking ice cream cones or munching on fish and chips. No more bodies had been pulled from the water, and I hoped it would stay that way.

As nice as it was to sit there watching the world while the sun warmed my skin, I didn't let myself stay there too long. Once I'd finished my snack, I headed for Timeless Treasures, the antiques shop on Main Street. The owner, Mr. Gorski, was helping me track down a special item I wanted to buy as a birthday gift for Brett. The last time I'd checked in with Mr. Gorski, he hadn't yet found the right item at the right price.

This time, however, my luck was better. I had to wait a few minutes while Mr. Gorski helped another customer, but then he called me over from across the shop where I was admiring a porcelain mantel clock.

"I've got good news for you today, Marley," he said as I headed his way. "I got in touch with a dealer I know down in Oregon, and he's got just what you want in stock. Take a look." He turned the monitor of his computer around so I could see the screen.

Excitement bubbled up in my chest. "It's gorgeous!"

The picture on the screen showed a salvaged ship's wheel with a brass hub. It appeared to be in good condition, and the wood had a beautiful reddish tone.

"It's a forty-two-inch mahogany wheel, just like you wanted," Mr. Gorski informed me.

"It's perfect." I tried to keep my growing excitement in check, needing to know more before I made any final decisions. "What about the price?"

"Slightly over your budget, but not by much."

He quoted me the price. It was a bit more than I'd planned to spend, but I thought it was worth it.

"And it can be delivered by early August?" I checked.

"Within the next couple of weeks," he assured me.

"Then I'll take it," I said with a surge of happiness. "Thank you, Mr. Gorski."

"My pleasure."

After wrapping up my business at Timeless Treasures, I headed for the hardware store, feeling like I was walking on a cloud. A few weeks back, Brett had revealed that he'd always wanted an authentic ship's wheel to display on the wall. We'd been working together to renovate and update our Victorian for several months, and I loved the idea of adding a nautical element to the family room. Hopefully Brett would like the wheel I'd purchased.

By the time I reached the hardware store, the effect of my frozen lemonade had worn off and I'd gone from pleasantly warm to hot. The air-conditioning inside the store was a welcome relief. I headed straight for the aisle where I knew I'd find light bulbs. The light in my office at The Flip Side had burnt out the week before. It wasn't a big deal since the days were long and bright at this time of year, but I wanted to get a replacement while I was thinking about it.

As I turned down the right aisle, I caught sight of Leigh's husband, Greg, up ahead. I was about to raise a hand to wave at him when he darted out of view. I continued on to the end of the aisle to see if I could spot him again, but he was gone.

That was strange.

Maybe he'd been in a hurry to get to another part of the store, but I couldn't shake the feeling that Greg had been trying to avoid me.

Chapter Sixteen

My thoughts hopped around like agitated rabbits for the rest of the day. Despite my best efforts, I couldn't settle my mind, and I found myself unable to sit still for more than a few minutes at a time. Brett and I ate barbecued shrimp and veggie skewers for dinner as storm clouds rolled in to darken the previously bright blue sky. By the time we'd cleaned up after our meal, the first low rumbles of thunder could be heard in the distance.

When every last dish was put away, Brett settled on the swing on the back porch, checking his email on his phone. Bentley flopped out near Brett's feet and I stood by the porch railing, watching Flapjack as he prowled along a log at the top of the beach. After a few minutes, I wandered after him and scooped him into my arms. I gave him a cuddle as I carried him back up to the porch, and he rewarded me with a purr that almost matched the distant thunder. I set him on the railing, and he hunkered down, his tail twitching as he kept an eye out for birds.

I left him there and eyed the space on the swing next to Brett, wondering if I should give relaxing another try. Brett took my hand, tugging me closer, so I sat down next to him, setting the swing in motion.

"You've been restless all evening," he said, running his thumb over my knuckles. "What's going on?"

"Too much on my mind, I guess."

"Because of the murder? The wedding?"

"Both, but mostly the murder. The wedding plans are going well so far, so I'm not too worried. Just anxious for the day to get here."

"Me too."

I leaned against him and he put his arm around me. His presence and the gentle movement of the swing eased some of the tension from my muscles and slowed my thoughts by a notch or two.

"Have you heard anything new about the murder investigation?" Brett asked.

"No. Have you?"

"No. All I know is that Ray's working long hours to deal with that case and everything else."

"He mentioned that when I saw him."

"At least there haven't been any serious accidents on the roads this week despite all the extra traffic."

"Hopefully it'll stay that way. We don't need any more tragedies."

"That's for sure." Brett ran a hand over my hair before resting his arm across my shoulders again. "How's your investigation going?"

"Not too well," I said as I watched the stormy clouds over the ocean. "Except now I think I'm convinced there's only been one murder."

I told him about my conversation with Rowena at the Beach and Bean.

"Her grief is genuine. I'm sure of that. I really don't think she killed her husband."

"But you still have a long list of potential killers in Yvonne's case?" Brett guessed.

"Unfortunately. I haven't managed to eliminate anyone else."

"Did you share everything you know with Ray?"

"I did. Hopefully it'll be of some help. I keep going over everything in my mind, but I don't get anywhere. I'm missing something. Possibly a whole lot of things."

"You'll find all the pieces and fit them together." He sounded so sure.

"I wish I could be as confident as you are."

He gave me a gentle squeeze. "I have enough confidence in you for the both of us."

I snuggled closer to him as a fork of lightning lit up the gray sky far across the water.

"I don't want to worry about mysteries and puzzles tonight," I said. "All I want to do is enjoy this."

"This?"

"You and me. Us."

Brett kissed the top of my head. "That sounds good to me."

* * * *

By morning, the storm was nothing but a memory. The sun was shining again, and the only clouds in the sky were a few puffy white ones out over the water. The Flip Side was as busy as ever, and it wasn't until midmorning that the line out the door disappeared and the rush died down. I took advantage of the lull—if it could be called that—to change the light bulb in the office and answer a few emails. I'd considered telling Leigh about my trip to the hardware store and her husband's odd behavior, but in the end I decided not to, at least not yet. It would only add to her worries. Whatever was going on with Greg, hopefully it would resolve soon so Leigh could relax. If Brett had been acting strangely and wouldn't tell me why, I'd be beside myself with worry, so I had a good deal of compassion for Leigh.

When I returned to the dining area a short while later, I waved to Marjorie, who'd arrived in my absence and was sitting at a small table near the back of the restaurant. She was on her own today, but Sienna was over there chatting with her. I cleared and wiped down a table after a group of four diners left, and when I'd finished, Sienna was still talking with Marjorie. As I glanced their way, Sienna said a couple more words and then headed for the kitchen.

When she came back through the swinging door a moment later, she hurried to my side.

"You should talk to Marjorie," she whispered.

"For a reason other than to say hello?" I guessed.

"Yep." Sienna's eyes were bright with excitement. "She's been *investigating.*"

I wasn't sure if I should be excited like Sienna or apprehensive. Either way, I couldn't deny that I was curious.

I was about to ask Sienna what exactly Marjorie's investigation had entailed, but she'd already grabbed two orders from the pass-through window and was off to deliver them to waiting customers. No matter, I could find out right from the source.

I stopped to chat with a group of regulars and filled a couple of coffee mugs, but then I made my way over to Marjorie's table.

"I hear you're turning into an amateur sleuth," I said by way of greeting.

Marjorie grinned at me. "We could form a club."

"Ray would love that," I said.

She laughed. "Can you sit down a minute?"

"Sure." I pulled out the chair across from her and sat down.

"I'm not sure you'd call what I did sleuthing. All I really did was ask a few questions."

"That's usually what I do too," I said. "You can learn a lot simply by asking the right questions of the right people."

"Exactly!" Her eyes bright, Marjorie leaned closer and lowered her voice. "I've been wondering about Felicia Venner ever since Claudia Wu mentioned her name."

"Do you know how their rivalry started?"

"Back in the day, they were both rising stars in track and field, training with the same coach. The people I talked to said they both got jealous of the time the coach spent with the other one."

"How did their animosity play out?" I asked. "It obviously didn't stay completely private if so many people know about it."

"It does seem to be common knowledge," Marjorie agreed. "And, no, they didn't keep it private. Apparently they argued and sniped at each other all the time, and then one day they got into an all-out catfight at the track during a national championship."

"Yikes."

"That's not the worst of it."

This time I was the one to lean farther over the table. "What else happened?"

"A week or two after the fight, Felicia accused Yvonne of hiring someone to shove her down a flight of concrete steps."

I winced. "Ouch. Was she hurt?"

"Oh, yeah. She had to have surgery on her knee and missed an entire season of competing. She ended up switching coaches. She did compete again after recovering, but she didn't have the success she wanted, or the success that Yvonne had."

"That must have made it sting all the more."

"I'm betting it did."

I sat back and thought over everything Marjorie had told me. "Did anything ever come of Felicia's accusations?"

"It doesn't sound like it. She couldn't prove anything, and Yvonne swore she had nothing to do with it."

"Felicia didn't see who pushed her?"

"Just a brief glimpse. It was a man in dark clothing with a hood pulled up over his head. But whoever he was, Felicia still seems to think to this day that he was doing Yvonne's dirty work."

"Interesting."

"I thought you'd think so."

"What did the people you talked to think about Felicia as a potential suspect in Yvonne's murder?"

"I didn't come out and ask anyone that directly. I was worried I might ruffle too many feathers."

"That's always a risk." I'd certainly done my share of feather ruffling in the past.

"But," Marjorie continued, "I got the sense that a couple of people think it could have been Felicia."

"I'd have to agree with them," I said. "If her grudge has festered for all these years, coming face-to-face with Yvonne here at the games might have caused Felicia to snap."

Marjorie leaned back as Sienna swept over to the table and set down a plate of banana nut pancakes in front of her. One of Ivan's latest creations, the pancakes had the perfect blend of bananas, cinnamon, and nutmeg, with chopped pecans to add some crunch.

"Have you told Marley everything?" she asked Marjorie.

"Every last detail."

"Thank you for sharing," I said as I stood up.

A group of six diners had just entered the pancake house and two more were coming in the door behind them. It seemed the lunch rush was about to start.

"I'd better get back to work, but I appreciate everything you told me."

"My pleasure," Marjorie said.

"Is there anything else I can get you?" Sienna was asking as I left to go greet the new customers.

For the next hour or so I didn't have a chance to pause between taking orders, serving meals, and cleaning tables. It was after one o'clock when business finally slowed down a bit.

"So, what do you think?" Sienna asked as she followed me into the kitchen.

I set down a load of dirty dishes and wiped my hands on my apron. "About what Marjorie said?"

"It was great intel," Sienna said, her eyes shining with excitement. "Felicia Venner definitely belongs on the suspect list."

I caught Ivan watching us with suspicious eyes, so I took Sienna's arm and led her out of the kitchen.

"I agree," I said once we were out of Ivan's earshot. I kept my voice low so customers wouldn't hear us either. "I plan to do some more digging."

"We should go straight to the source."

"We?"

Sienna pressed on like she hadn't heard me. "I know the perfect cover for questioning Felicia. I can pretend I'm doing a summer internship for the *Wildwood Cove Weekly*. I'll say I'm interviewing some of the athletes for the paper."

"I don't think that's a good idea."

"What do you mean? It's a great idea!"

Two diners were ready to pay for their meals, so I stepped away from Sienna to attend to them. When I returned minutes later, she was no less enthusiastic about her idea.

"It's a great way to get information from Felicia and to gauge her reactions when I ask questions."

"And if she's the killer?" I said. "You could be putting a target on your back."

"I bet you were planning to ask her questions."

"But I'm an adult."

Sienna rolled her eyes at that. "She'll be way less suspicious of me asking questions than if you grill her."

"That might be true, but we can't count on it."

Sienna picked up the coffeepot. "It's a good plan, and I think we should put it into action later today."

Before I could object again, she hurried off across the room to offer coffee refills.

When we crossed paths again a while later, she whispered, "You can come with me if that would make you feel better."

"Oh, I'm definitely coming with you. There's no way I'm letting you question a potential killer on your own."

She smiled triumphantly. "I knew you'd come around eventually."

She dashed off before I could say anything else. I still had my misgivings, but I knew she wasn't going to take my advice and give up on her plan. When it came to investigating, she could be as stubborn as I could be. I'd just have to make sure she was as safe as possible while she dug for clues.

In the meantime, we still had work to do. I noticed a man with spiky brown hair take a seat at one of the small outdoor tables, so I headed outside to take his order. It wasn't until I arrived at the table that I realized the newcomer was the photographer I'd seen at the park on the night of the opening ceremonies. I remembered overhearing him introduce himself to a group of athletes as Jay Henkel. He was facing the ocean and talking on his phone, which was probably why he didn't notice me approach. I was about to step into his line of sight when I froze.

"Have you heard?" he said cheerfully into his phone. "The wicked witch is dead!"

Chapter Seventeen

My stomach churned. I still stood frozen, hardly able to believe what I'd heard.

"She washed up on the beach." Jay's latest words were delivered with no less glee than his previous statement.

If I'd had any doubt that he was talking about Yvonne before, it had vanished in an instant.

Not wanting to hear any more, I stepped forward so he'd see me. When his startled gaze darted my way, I held up the coffeepot and forced a smile.

He nodded once and then said into the phone, "Hold on a second."

"Do you need another few minutes?" I asked, impressed that my voice sounded cheery rather than disgusted.

"Nah. I'll have the Belgian waffles with strawberry syrup and a fruit salad." He returned his phone to his ear. "I'm back."

I retreated into The Flip Side, not wanting to hear another word of his conversation. Even though Yvonne hadn't been the nicest woman, it still struck me as terribly callous to talk about her death in that way. Callous and chilling.

If he was that cold and heartless, was he capable of committing murder?

* * * *

I couldn't shake the chill that had settled deep inside me after hearing Jay talking about Yvonne. It stayed with me the rest of the workday, lingering like an unwanted companion. I thought about telling Sienna and the others what I'd overheard, but in the end I held back. I didn't want to get Sienna fired up about another suspect. It worried me enough that she was so eager to question Felicia Venner. Part of me hoped she'd lose enthusiasm for her plan by the end of the workday, but I wasn't the least bit surprised when that didn't happen.

"Do you know what Felicia looks like?" she asked me after I'd closed the pancake house and Leigh had left for home.

"No," I replied. "I guess that'll make it hard to find her."

"I bet we can find a picture of her online." Sienna already had her phone out.

I wiped down one of the tables while she searched the Internet. It didn't take her long to find what she was looking for.

"Got it!"

She held up her phone so I could see the photo of a woman with shoulder-length fair hair. She appeared to be in her late fifties, which made sense. That put her close in age to Yvonne.

"It seems to be a recent photo," Sienna said, turning the phone so she could look at the screen again. "It says this is from last year's Golden Oldies Games in Everett."

"Okay, so we know what she looks like." I finished cleaning another table. "Tracking her down might still be a problem, but I guess we should start at the track and field venue."

All the track and field events were taking place at the local middle school.

Sienna tapped at her phone again. "I'll see if I can find out if she's competing today."

I continued cleaning as she checked the schedule for the games.

"It looks like she's got the day free, but other age groups are competing in track and field this afternoon."

"So she might be there to watch," I said.

"Let's hope so."

Sienna tucked her phone away in her pocket and helped me with the rest of the cleaning. Within half an hour we were out the door. Ivan had seemed suspicious that Sienna had stuck around, but we said good-bye to him and Tommy so quickly that he didn't have a chance to question what we were up to. As I locked the door behind us, a twinge of guilt made *me* question it.

"Why don't you leave the interview to me," I suggested. "I'd really rather you didn't get involved."

"Marley, we already went through this," she said calmly. "She'll be way less suspicious of a teenager asking her questions."

I sighed as I kept pace with her on the sidewalk. Her determination was eerily familiar. I'd have as much luck keeping her out of the investigation as I would keeping myself out of it.

It didn't take long to reach the school grounds, but by the time we arrived I was wishing I'd stopped off at home to change into cooler clothes. I'd forgotten to pack a pair of shorts in my tote bag that morning and now I was ready to wilt. A teenage girl stood at the gate to the sports field, handing out competition schedules. I accepted the one she offered to me, not so much because I was interested in the events taking place that afternoon, but more because the sheet of paper gave me something to fan myself with.

"Maybe we should split up," Sienna said as we stood near the edge of the field, taking in the sight of all the athletes, officials, and spectators. The bleachers weren't completely filled, but there was still quite a good crowd.

"I think it would be better for us to stick together," I countered. "I don't want you talking to Felicia without me close by."

"I promise I won't ask her any questions until you're there with me, but it could take us hours to search this place if we don't split up."

I knew she was right about that. "All right," I relented. "But I'm holding you to that promise."

Sienna traced an X over her heart and flashed a grin at me before disappearing into the crowd. I set off in the opposite direction, keeping my eyes peeled for Felicia.

I thought I spotted her on several occasions over the next few minutes, but each time I got closer I realized I'd honed in on the wrong fair-haired woman. I'd made it about a third of the way around the perimeter of the field when my phone buzzed in my hand.

Found her! A text message from Sienna read. *By the long jump.*

That was at the opposite end of the field. With longing, I eyed a nearby vendor who was selling canned drinks from a cooler filled with ice. The line to purchase beverages from him was five deep, so I passed him by with regret, continuing around the perimeter of the field.

By the time I spotted Sienna waving at me, my event schedule had gone limp. I stuffed it into the back pocket of my jeans.

Sienna grabbed my arm when I reached her.

"See? That's her." She pointed toward three women standing in a tiny patch of shade cast by the equipment hut in one corner of the field.

Sure enough, one of the women matched the photo of Felicia that Sienna had found online.

As we kept an eye on the group, the other two women walked off, leaving Felicia on her own, watching as the next competitor got ready to take a run at the long jump.

"This is my chance!"

Sienna darted off before I'd absorbed her words.

I hurried after her, but then slowed down as she walked right up to Felicia and started chatting with her. I sidled closer until I could hear what they were saying, all the while pretending that I was focused on the competition unfolding in front of me. In reality, I barely noticed what the athletes were doing.

Felicia had obviously bought Sienna's story about working for the local paper. She happily answered questions about her experience at the games and how she'd become involved in track and field. The amiability between them continued until Sienna nudged the conversation in the direction she wanted it to go.

"I've heard you used to have a fierce rivalry with your fellow competitor, Yvonne Pritchard. Was that a thing of the past, or was it still going on when you arrived in Wildwood Cove?"

I gave up my pretense of watching the competition so I could focus on Felicia. The friendly smile had vanished from her face, and her gray eyes had turned flinty.

"I don't want to talk about Yvonne Pritchard." She nearly spat out the reporter's name.

Sienna didn't appear fazed at all. "Now that Yvonne's been murdered, do you regret that you didn't get along with her?"

"I regret nothing." Felicia had lowered her voice, but each word practically sizzled and popped with the heat of her anger.

I edged closer.

"And like I said," Felicia continued, "I don't want to talk about that snake of a woman."

"I'm sorry," Sienna said with an innocent and apologetic smile. "My editor wanted me to ask these questions. She told me it would make for a juicy story."

Felicia's eyes flashed. "Then I suggest you look for a new summer job. Otherwise you'll end up no better than Yvonne."

Sienna typed something into her phone. "So you thought she was pretty bad?"

The fury on Felicia's face set off alarm bells in my head. She looked like she wanted to slap Sienna. I quickly moved to the teenager's side.

"Thanks for taking the time to answer some questions," I said.

Felicia focused her steely gaze on me. "Who are you?"

"My mentor," Sienna said before I had a chance to respond.

That only seemed to incense Felicia even more. "So *you* put her up to asking those questions?" She jabbed a finger at me. "You should be ashamed of yourself! Teaching this young lady to make disgusting insinuations!"

"I was just asking questions," Sienna said, still managing to sound innocent. "It's not like I was accusing you of killing anyone."

"And you'd better not!" Felicia leaned closer and lowered her voice again, although it lost none of its heat. "Both of you, listen to me. If you print even the slightest suggestion that I had something to do with Yvonne's murder, you'll be facing a lawsuit."

"We're not accusing you of anything," I said quickly, hoping to placate her.

"Good," she said, although she didn't sound any happier. "Because I didn't care one whit about Yvonne. That was all in the past, and as far as I'm concerned that's where it belongs."

With one last, furious glare at us, she stormed off.

"Whoa," Sienna said once she'd gone. "Touchy subject."

I gave a vague nod of agreement, most of my attention elsewhere.

As Felicia had stalked off, I'd noticed Jay Henkel standing nearby, listening in. He was walking away now, but his shoulders were shaking with laughter.

Chapter Eighteen

"Marley?"

Sienna called my name as I took off after Jay.

"Excuse me!" I said as I jogged up to the photographer's side.

He glanced my way without recognition, but then he did a double take and drew to a stop. "Hey, the pancake lady."

"Um… sure." I didn't let that throw me off. "Do you know Felicia Venner?"

Jay blew a speck of dirt off the camera hanging around his neck. "Why are you asking?"

"You laughed when you overheard her back there. I was wondering why you thought what she said was so funny."

Sienna appeared at my elbow, but Jay didn't acknowledge her presence.

"I laughed because she was lying through her teeth."

"You mean about her rivalry with Yvonne Pritchard being a thing of the past?" Sienna asked.

Jay finally glanced her way, if only for a split second, before focusing his attention on the latest woman getting ready to compete in the long jump. "Yep. Talk about a load of crap."

I noticed he still hadn't directly admitted to knowing Felicia, but he obviously knew something about her. "How do you know she was lying?"

His attention snapped back to me and Sienna, and he appraised us with cool eyes. "What's your interest?"

"I've got a summer internship with the local newspaper," Sienna piped up. "Marley's my mentor. I want to write an article about Yvonne Pritchard."

Jay let out a humorless bark of laughter. "And what? You'll make her out to be a saint?"

"Not if she wasn't," Sienna said.

The way Jay stared at me then sent an unpleasant chill slithering up my spine. "So, let me get this straight. You work at the pancake house *and* the local newspaper?"

"Not exactly," I said, hoping I wasn't about to get tripped up by our fibs.

Sienna jumped in to save me. "She *owns* the pancake house. She *volunteers* at the paper."

"I guess that's small towns for you." Jay didn't sound impressed, but the cold suspicion in his eyes faded. He turned on the LCD screen of his camera and flicked back through a series of photos. "Does this look to you like Felicia's feud with Yvonne was water under the bridge?"

He turned the camera so Sienna and I could see the screen. The photo had clearly caught the two women mid-argument, their faces contorted with anger. Felicia was pointing a finger at Yvonne, as if she'd been jabbing it at the reporter as she'd done to me moments earlier.

"When was that taken?" I asked.

"Last Friday. Not exactly ancient history." Jay hit a button and several other frames of the women's argument flashed across the screen. "They argued for several minutes before Felicia took off."

Jay hit the button one more time. The last photo to appear didn't feature Felicia and Yvonne. Instead it showed Levi and Pippa, their arms around each other as they kissed.

"Why do you have a picture of them?" I asked.

Jay turned the camera so he could see the photo. As soon as he did, he switched off the screen. "That's another one who didn't like Yvonne," he said, failing to answer my question.

"Pippa Hampshire?" Sienna asked with surprise.

"Her boy toy," Jay corrected. "I overheard the two lovebirds talking the other day, and he sure didn't have anything nice to say about Yvonne."

"Why? What did Levi have against her?" I asked.

Jay shrugged. "Who knows?"

His gaze drifted over my shoulder, and what little interest he might have had in our conversation seemed to go with it.

"Excuse me, ladies, but I've got work to do. Good luck with your article, kid," he added without any sincerity.

"I don't like him," Sienna said as we watched him walk off.

"Neither do I."

Jay had left me chilled and uneasy after I'd overheard his phone call at the pancake house, and now I trusted him even less. He'd obviously taken the photos he'd shown us without the subjects' knowledge and they weren't the type of photos a sports photographer would be expected to take. Did he make a habit of sneaking photos of people in their private or unflattering moments? If so, why?

* * * *

Sienna and I didn't spend much more time talking about Jay. Within moments of the photographer walking away, we spotted a familiar face over by the track. A group of athletes had gathered near the start line in preparation for a semifinal round of the 100-meter sprint. Standing near some coaches and members of the media, Tommy snapped pictures of the competitors. As Sienna and I drew closer, the athletes took their marks and the starting gun fired seconds later.

"Whoa," Sienna said as the athletes took off. "They're as old as my grandparents and they run way faster than I can."

"It's impressive," I agreed.

Within moments, the race was over. Tommy had jogged down the track to capture photos of the victorious runner, so we kept walking until we caught up to him. When Tommy lowered his camera and backed away from the athletes, Sienna called his name.

He grinned when he saw us. "Here to watch the races?"

"To investigate," Sienna said.

"Who are you investigating?"

"A woman named Felicia Venner," I said. "She's the one who had her gear stolen. She and Yvonne had a rivalry going back decades."

Sienna picked up the story. "She told us she didn't care about that anymore, but then some photographer guy showed us a picture he'd taken of the two women arguing. They looked like they still hated each other's guts."

"And I think the photographer belongs on our suspect list too," I said.

"We photographers aren't above suspicion?" Tommy joked.

"Only you," Sienna replied. "The other guy kind of gave me the creeps."

"And you didn't hear what he said earlier today." Despite my previous plan not to mention Jay's phone conversation, I shared what I'd overheard with Sienna and Tommy.

Sienna shuddered. "Wow. That's cold."

"It chilled me to the bone when I heard it," I admitted.

Tommy was usually so laid-back that it was a surprise to see a hint of concern in his eyes. "Should you really have questioned him if he's a cold-blooded killer?"

"We don't know he's a killer," Sienna said.

"And we were questioning him about Felicia," I added. "Not as a suspect."

"Even though he is one now." Sienna paused for a second. "But what's his motive?"

I swatted at a bug that flew near my face. "I don't know, but he clearly didn't like Yvonne for some reason."

"Maybe I can find out why," Tommy said.

"By talking to Jay?" I didn't like the sound of that plan. I wanted all of us to steer clear of the Seattle photographer in the future.

"Nah. I've got a better idea. Rob used to work in Seattle. Maybe he's heard of Jay."

"Rob the reporter?" Sienna asked.

"Yep."

"It's worth asking," I said.

Tommy pulled his phone out of his pocket. "What's his last name?"

"Henkel."

Tommy made a note of that on his phone. "I'll check with Rob the next time I see him."

"Thanks, Tommy."

"Let us know if you find out anything," Sienna requested.

He gave us a mock salute. "I will."

Sienna and I left Tommy to take pictures of the high jump competition that was just getting underway. As we passed through the gate and onto the sidewalk, Sienna scrunched up her nose.

"Now I'm confused," she said.

"Me too," I admitted. "We've got too many suspects."

"Exactly! We're leaving with more questions than we had when we got here."

"That's true, unfortunately. Our suspect list keeps getting longer. There's got to be a way to cross off some names."

"I still think our best suspect is the ex-husband," Sienna said.

"I'd almost forgotten about him," I admitted.

"It's hard for me to forget about him when I see him around my house."

"So he's still in town?"

"Yep. I tried asking him some casual questions this morning. Like, how long he's sticking around and what he's doing while he's here, but he kind of avoided the questions and my mom told me to leave him alone."

"Did she know why you were asking questions?" I was worried Patricia might think I was encouraging her daughter to investigate crimes.

Was I encouraging her?

"I think she figured I was interested because the murder victim was his ex."

"She knows you've got him pegged as the potential killer?" I asked with mild alarm.

"No, I'm pretty sure she doesn't. I think she put it down to a sort of morbid curiosity."

We waited for a couple of cars to pass before crossing the street.

"If only I could get hold of his phone for a while," Sienna continued. "Maybe we could find out why he was in town last week."

My alarm resurfaced, far stronger this time.

"Promise me you won't even try to get a look at his phone," I said. "If he were to catch you…"

"All right, I won't touch his phone."

"Or any of his personal belongings. Any *more* of his personal belongings," I amended, remembering that we'd already looked through his things at the B&B.

"We could be passing up a chance to get some really good clues."

"Sienna…"

"Okay, okay. You win." She sounded a bit disappointed, but not annoyed. "So what can we do to figure this thing out?"

"That's a good question," I said. "One I'm going to have to think about."

Chapter Nineteen

By the time I arrived home, Brett was already there. Bentley and Flapjack were napping in the shade while Brett picked cherry tomatoes from the plants growing in one of the raised garden beds. After greeting the animals, I gave Brett a hand and soon we had a bowl full of the juicy little tomatoes. We headed for the back porch and snacked on our harvest while I told him about my afternoon.

"It feels like I'm losing my knack for solving mysteries," I confessed as we sat on the porch swing. "I have so many suspects and no clue where to go from here." Before Brett had a chance to say anything, I added, "And I know the police are working on it, but it really bugs me not to be able to figure anything out."

"Would it help to tell me what you know so far?" Brett asked.

"Maybe." I scrubbed my hands down my face, suddenly tired of thinking.

"Or we could go for a run. That usually helps to clear your head."

"That's probably what I need," I said. In fact, now that he'd made the suggestion, I realized I was craving some exercise. I glanced up at the bright sun. "It's still pretty hot, though."

"We could go for a short run, then a dip in the ocean."

"And then nachos for dinner?"

"You speak my language," Brett said with a grin.

Bentley had been lying near our feet, but now he jumped up and gave an excited bark, his tail wagging as he watched us.

"I think he knows there's going to be cheese," I said.

Brett gave Bentley a pat on the head. "It's like a sixth sense. We haven't even opened the fridge."

Bentley gave another bark and ran into the house through the open French doors.

"Who's going to tell him we're not eating until later?" Brett asked as he got up from the swing.

"I'll leave that to you. You know what happens when he looks at me with sad puppy dog eyes."

"He's got you wrapped around his paw."

"It's not my fault he's so cute."

"I'll break the news to him." Brett took my hand and pulled me to my feet.

My stomach gave a loud rumble of hunger.

Brett laughed. "Sounds like we should get moving so we can have those nachos."

"The sooner the better."

* * * *

We set an easy pace for ourselves because of the heat. After following Wildwood Road into the center of town, we veered off into a quiet residential neighborhood with shady, tree-lined streets. Several other locals were out and about enjoying the beautiful evening, some with canine companions and some without. Many of the people we passed were heading toward the beach. We saw several familiar faces, but we only exchanged quick greetings as we continued on our way.

The air smelled of the ocean and freshly cut grass. Many of the houses had window boxes or hanging baskets bursting with colorful flowers. The pleasant sights and smells helped to soothe me, as did the steady rhythm of running.

Once we decided we'd strayed far enough from home, we headed back toward Wildwood Road. Before we got there, I slowed to a walk and Brett did the same beside me. We were on Leigh's street and I'd spotted her out in her front yard, talking with a neighbor while Greg mowed the lawn. Their youngest daughter, Kayla, sat on the front steps, combing her doll's hair.

Before we reached Leigh's house, her neighbor went back to weeding her garden and Leigh turned our way. I waved, catching her attention. When Greg noticed us too, he shut off the lawn mower.

"Beautiful evening, isn't it?" Leigh called out as we approached.

"Gorgeous," I said as Brett and I stopped on the sidewalk.

"I can't say I'd choose to go running in this weather, though," she said, eyeing our running gear. "Aren't you two on the verge of getting heatstroke?"

"Not quite," Brett said. "But we do plan to jump in the ocean when we get home."

"That sounds like a good idea," Greg commented.

Leigh and Greg's oldest daughter, Amanda, appeared at the top of the steps. "Mom, Grandma's on the phone and she wants to talk to you!" She held up a cell phone and waved it in the air.

"Sorry," Leigh said to us. "I'd better take that."

Brett and I said good-bye to her as she jogged up the front steps and into the house.

"How are you doing these days?" Brett asked Greg.

"All right, thanks. How about you guys?"

"Pretty good," I answered. Before I could think better of it, I added, "I saw you at the hardware store the other day, but you disappeared before I had a chance to say hi."

Greg's gaze shifted away from mine. "Oh? That's too bad."

"I got the feeling you didn't want to talk to me."

Greg kept his eyes fixed on the lawn mower as he cleared his throat. "I was probably just busy. Why would I not want to talk to you?"

"I don't know. Something to do with Leigh, maybe?"

I could feel Brett watching me. I knew he was wondering why I was grilling Leigh's husband.

Greg finally looked up from the lawn mower, a crease across his forehead revealing how worried he was. "Did she tell you something was wrong?"

"She's worried that you're hiding something from her," I said. "Whatever it is, I know it's not my business, but if you can put Leigh's mind at ease…"

Greg glanced over his shoulder at the house. His wife hadn't reappeared. He let out a deep breath, his shoulders sagging. "I was trying to do something special for our fifteenth anniversary, but I've messed everything up. I know Leigh thinks I've been acting cagey, and I thought she might have asked you to figure out why."

"She didn't," I said. "She just confided in me that she was worried about you."

"How did you mess up?" Brett asked.

"The night I proposed to Leigh we were in Seattle to see *The Phantom of the Opera* at the Paramount. We had such a great time that we still talk about that night. Our anniversary is coming up in a couple of weeks, and I found out that *Phantom* is playing again at the same theater. I knew Leigh would love it if I got us tickets. I was going to book us a room at the same hotel and take her out to dinner before going to the theater."

"So what went wrong?" I asked.

"The tickets are all sold out. I called the box office a couple of times, hoping more tickets would come available, but they haven't. It was a perfect plan, and now I feel like nothing else will measure up."

"But if Leigh didn't know about your original plan, she can't be disappointed," Brett pointed out.

"I know. I just really wanted to do this for her, you know?" He glanced at the house again, but Kayla was the only one in sight. "I guess I need to get over it and make reservations at a nice restaurant closer to home."

"You might need to give Leigh an idea why you've been so secretive," I said. "Even if you don't tell her everything."

Greg rubbed the stubble on his chin. "You're probably right about that. I never meant to worry her."

"And don't give up on your plan yet," I said, the wheels turning in my head.

Greg's forehead creased again, this time with confusion. "I really don't think I'll be able to get tickets to the show."

"I might be able to help," I said. "I can't make any promises, but give me a couple of days and I'll see..."

I trailed off as Leigh emerged from the house and came down the steps to join us. All three of her daughters followed after her.

"The girls want to go for ice cream," she told Greg.

He glanced at the small patch of lawn left untrimmed. "Give me five minutes to finish this and we'll all go."

"You want to join us?" Leigh asked me and Brett.

"We'd better pass this time," Brett said.

"We're going to have dinner in a bit," I added.

The girls were getting antsy for their ice cream, so we exchanged a few more words and then left Greg to finish cutting the lawn. We walked instead of jogging, both of us too hot to want to go any faster.

"What was that all about?" Brett asked when we were out of Leigh's earshot. "Do you really think you can help Greg?"

"I'm not sure yet," I said. "But after we've had our swim, I'll call my mom and find out."

* * * *

Our short swim in the ocean was exactly what we needed after getting uncomfortably hot. The water was blissfully cool, and I had goose bumps on my arms by the time we left the water and walked up the beach to our house. While Brett made guacamole and grated cheese to go on top of our nachos, I curled up on the porch swing and phoned my mom. She and her husband, Grant, lived in Seattle, where I'd grown up, and one of her closest friends had worked at the Paramount Theater for years. She'd taken early retirement a year or so ago, but I was hoping she still had some connections there.

After chatting for several minutes about life in general, I explained to my mom why I'd called.

"I'll talk to Tracy," she promised once I'd filled her in. "I know she'll want to help out, but whether she actually can…"

"I know it's not a sure thing," I said. "But I thought it was worth a try."

"It definitely is. Leigh's husband obviously wants to make this a special anniversary for her. A laudable goal, if you ask me."

"I agree."

We chatted about the upcoming wedding for a while but when I caught the scent of dinner in the air, I brought the call to an end. I'd barely hung up when Brett carried a platter of nachos out to the table on the porch. He returned to the kitchen, reappearing a moment later with a tray holding salsa, guacamole, and two tall glasses of ice water.

My stomach grumbled loudly as I snagged a nacho laden with cheese and black olives. "These smell delicious." I added a generous dollop of guacamole and took a bite. "Mmm. And they taste even better."

"Any luck with the tickets?" Brett asked as he grabbed a couple nachos of his own.

"Mom's going to talk to her friend Tracy. Hopefully she'll be able to help us out." I took a long drink of water. "At least one mystery is solved now. Ever since Greg dodged me at the hardware store, I couldn't stop wondering why."

"He should have realized that acting suspicious would only make your sleuthing senses tingle."

I smiled, knowing he was teasing. "At least there's nothing bad going on between them. I think it's romantic that Greg wants to make their anniversary so special for Leigh."

Brett piled guacamole and salsa onto his nachos. "But he might be setting the bar too high for the rest of us."

"What do you mean?"

"Now I'll have to make sure I come up with anniversary plans that measure up."

"As long as we get to spend our anniversaries together, whatever we do to celebrate will be perfect."

"Can I quote you on that next summer?" Brett asked with a grin.

"You won't need to," I assured him. "I'll still feel the same way next year and every year after that."

Brett leaned over and kissed me. "You'd think we were in love or something."

"How could I not love a guy who makes such delicious nachos?"

"It's only one of my many talents."

This time I kissed him. "Don't I know it."

Chapter Twenty

The rising sun almost blinded me when I looked out over the water the next morning. The waves sparkled so brightly in the dazzling light that I had to turn my eyes away. I walked along the beach on my way to work, enjoying the incredible beauty of the summer morning. Since it was so early, hardly anyone else was in sight. A young couple walked hand in hand toward the eastern end of the cove, a German shepherd trotting along beside them, and closer to town a man was jogging through the soft sand, getting a good workout.

As I drew closer to the man, I thought I recognized him. A few steps later I was sure I did. I almost called out a hello, hoping to catch Levi's attention and draw him into a conversation. After what Jay had said about Levi's feelings toward Yvonne, I wanted to figure out if his animosity toward the reporter was strong enough to provide a motive to kill her.

I thought I was about to get my chance to get his attention when he slowed to a stop. He kicked off his running shoes, stripped off his T-shirt, and broke into a jog again, this time heading over a sandbar to the water. When he was almost waist-deep in the water, he dove into an oncoming wave, resurfacing seconds later.

I slowed my pace, wondering if he'd gone into the ocean for a quick swim and would emerge from the water almost right away. Luck didn't seem to be with me, though. He struck off, swimming parallel to the shoreline, his strokes as sure and as strong as a competitive swimmer's.

Not wanting anyone to catch me staring at him, I continued on my way. When I reached the paved promenade that would lead me to The Flip Side, I paused and glanced back at the water. Levi was still swimming. His shirt and shoes weren't too far away from where I stood now, though. Maybe I could still have a word with him.

Picking up my pace, I let myself into the pancake house and dropped off my tote bag in the office. I said a quick hello to Ivan and Tommy, and then maneuvered one of the small tables meant for outdoor dining through the front door. Each day after closing I moved the tables indoors for safe storage. Maybe I shouldn't have bothered, but it gave me peace of mind. I'd had trouble with vandalism in the past, and although the person responsible was now dead, I felt better keeping everything locked up.

When I had all the outdoor tables in place, I strolled to the end of the promenade and shaded my eyes, searching for Levi. This time I had more luck. He was heading out of the water and up the beach. I walked casually, not wanting to appear too eager, and met up with him close to the spot where he'd left his shirt.

"Morning," I called out cheerfully.

Levi ran a hand across his face, scattering a few droplets of water. "Morning," he returned when he'd had a chance to recognize me. "You're a fellow early bird, I see."

"I'm definitely a morning person. And the pancake house opens at seven, so I always get an early start."

Levi grabbed his T-shirt from the sand and shook it out before using it as a towel, wiping down his face and upper body.

It wasn't difficult to see why Pippa found him attractive. With his well-toned physique and good looks, he wouldn't have been out of place on the cover of a surfing magazine. I wondered if Jay's description of him as Pippa's boy toy was accurate, or if the couple had a deeper connection. That wasn't what I really wanted to know about, however.

"How's Rowena doing?" I asked.

"About as well as can be expected, I guess." Levi pulled his damp T-shirt over his head. "Pippa's taking her to watch some of the track and field in the afternoon. Hopefully it'll be a bit of a distraction."

"I'm glad Rowena's got Pippa as a friend."

"Yeah. The two of them are close. And Pippa... she's got a good heart. She'd do anything for a friend, especially Rowena."

I didn't fail to notice the way his blue eyes softened when he mentioned Pippa's name. To me that was like announcing he was in love with her without having to say the words.

"Have you heard any news about the murder investigation since we last talked?" I asked. "I know there haven't been any arrests yet."

"Nothing so far." Levi ran a hand through his wet hair. "Sometimes those investigations take months, even years."

"True," I conceded. "But with the games almost over, a lot of witnesses and maybe even the killer could be getting ready to leave town."

"You think it was someone who's only in town for the games?" He shrugged before I had a chance to respond. "I guess that makes sense. Yvonne probably didn't know anyone in Wildwood Cove until she got here."

"I guess the murderer could be someone from the peninsula," I said. "But there seems to be a lot of people connected to the games who disliked or even hated her."

Levi's gaze tracked a seagull as it circled over the water.

It seemed he wasn't going to reveal what I wanted to know without more prompting. "You didn't like her."

His gaze snapped back to me. "Who told you that?"

"You gave me that impression the other day."

Levi snatched up his shoes from the sand. "There wasn't much to like."

"That doesn't really surprise me," I said. "One of The Flip Side's regular customers was really taken by her, but I overheard her saying some nasty things behind his back."

"That sounds about right. She was a real piece of work."

"How did you know her?"

"I didn't. Not until I arrived in town."

"But your paths crossed in the days before her death?" I guessed.

"Unfortunately." A note of bitterness had entered his voice. "She wanted to interview Pippa."

"Didn't Pippa want to be interviewed?"

"About her participation in the games, yeah."

"Yvonne was a sports reporter. Isn't that what she wanted to talk about?"

"No. All she wanted to focus on was Pippa's relationship with me. People look at us as a couple and all they see is the age difference. And okay, I guess I get that, at least a little bit. But really, it's not anyone's business."

I couldn't argue with that.

"And Pippa's an amazing woman. An amazing athlete. So, yeah, it ticked me off that Yvonne only wanted to write about our relationship. It was rude and totally unfair to Pippa. It upsets her when people grill us about our relationship. Makes her feel judged. I don't care what people think about us, but it gets to Pippa, you know?"

"I can imagine," I said.

"Anyway, I'd better go. Pippa will be awake now. I might see you later, though. Your place serves the best food in town."

I smiled at that. "I'm glad to hear it."

"Catch you later."

He set off across the sand, heading in the direction of the B&B.

So it was true that Levi didn't like Yvonne, but had the reporter upset Pippa enough that Levi would have wanted revenge? It seemed like a flimsy motive for murder, but it wasn't something I could discount entirely.

Even though the sun was already warm on my shoulders, a slight chill prickled over my skin. *Someone* had killed Yvonne Pritchard, and if Ray and his deputies didn't catch the murderer soon, I feared the investigation would stall. And with an unsolved murder hanging over Wildwood Cove, it wouldn't be easy to carry on as normal.

* * * *

A little over an hour after The Flip Side opened for the day, Lisa and Chloe showed up. We'd arranged to meet up at the pancake house that day, so I wasn't surprised by their arrival. The law office where Lisa worked had shut down for a couple of weeks of summer vacation, and Chloe was on summer break from her job teaching second grade in Port Angeles. We'd decided to take advantage of their free time to chat about their bridesmaid dresses.

"Did you choose your dresses?" I asked, noting the shopping bags they carried.

"We bought them in Port Angeles yesterday," Chloe replied, practically bubbling with excitement.

"Don't worry," Lisa added. "We've got the receipts so we can take them back if you don't like them."

"I'm sure I'll love them." I led them down the hall to the office. "You both have better fashion sense than I do."

"I'm not so sure about that," Lisa said.

I glanced down at my graphic tee and worn jeans. "I am."

When we reached the office, Chloe stopped and put her hands on her hips. "I have a complaint, Marley."

I wasn't sure if I should be apprehensive or not. She didn't look mad.

"Lisa's seen your wedding dress and I haven't!"

"Oops," I said. "Sorry. It's at the tailor's."

"Show her the photo we took at my place," Lisa urged.

Before taking off the dress, I'd snapped a quick picture of my reflection in the mirror. I found the photo on my phone and showed it to Chloe.

"Oh my gosh!" She took the device from me so she could get a closer look. "Marley!" Tears welled in her eyes.

"Don't cry!" I grabbed a tissue from the box on my desk and handed it to her. "We're not even at the wedding yet."

"But it's beautiful. *You're* beautiful."

"Right?" Lisa chimed in. When Chloe sniffled, Lisa nudged her arm. "You're going to get me going too."

"No tears," I said. "You're supposed to be showing me *your* dresses."

Chloe returned my phone to me and dabbed at her eyes with the tissue. "Okay," she said with determination. "No more tears."

She and Lisa removed their purchases from the shopping bags. The style of the dresses was the same, but they were different colors. Lisa's was made from emerald green satin while Chloe's was deep blue.

"What do you think?" Lisa asked as they held up the garments.

"They're perfect." I had to take a second to rein in my emotions so I didn't break my own rule about tearing up. "They're like the colors of the ocean."

Lisa and Chloe beamed at each other.

"That's exactly what we thought," Chloe said. "We knew you'd like that, especially since you're having a beach wedding."

"They really are perfect." I let the fabric of Lisa's dress slide through my fingers. "Are you both happy with them?"

They assured me that they were.

"Then it's settled," I said with a smile. "Those are officially your bridesmaid dresses."

Lisa and Chloe let out squeals of happiness, and the next second I was squished in the middle of a group hug. I didn't mind one bit.

"Now for the next order of business," I said once they'd released me. "Who's hungry?"

Chapter Twenty-One

It took over an hour for Lisa, Chloe, and me to get through the stacks of banana nut pancakes and sides of fruit salad that we ate in the office. We did more chatting and laughing than eating, and when they left the pancake house, I continued to bubble with happiness. I'd had some good friends in Seattle when I lived there—I still kept in touch with a couple of them—but my friendships with Lisa and Chloe were two of the best I'd ever had, and I counted myself lucky to have them in my life. In a month, I'd be marrying into Chloe's family, and that made me even luckier. I knew not everyone loved their in-laws, but I wouldn't have that problem.

I returned to the dining area in time to take over for Sienna so she could hurry off to a dental appointment. The lunch rush kept me and Leigh plenty busy, and I didn't realize that Levi and Pippa had arrived at The Flip Side until they were already eating the meals Leigh had served them. They sat at one of the small tables out in front of the pancake house, which explained how I'd missed their arrival. Leigh was looking after those tables. Nevertheless, as I was making my way around the restaurant, offering coffee refills, I decided to head outside and say hello.

"He must have wanted *something*," Pippa was saying to Levi as I refilled coffee mugs at the neighboring table. She sounded annoyed, not quite her usual composed self.

"He just wanted to ask a few questions about Yvonne." Levi spoke quietly, but I was still able to pick up his words.

"But you barely knew the woman."

"No, but I spoke to her before she died."

I couldn't hesitate any longer than I already had. I either had to approach their table or go back inside the pancake house. Otherwise I'd look conspicuous and they'd probably figure out I was eavesdropping.

Making up my mind, I turned toward their table.

"Afternoon." I held up the coffeepot and gave them a cheery smile. "More coffee?"

"Please." Pippa nudged her mug my way. She attempted a polite smile, but her features were taut.

"Will you be attending the banquet next week?" I asked, making conversation while I topped off both their mugs. The banquet was for the athletes, coaches, and volunteers, a way to wrap up the Golden Oldies Games.

"We will," Pippa responded. "And Rowena will be going with us."

"Oh, that's good," I said.

"They'll be honoring Easton at the banquet," Levi explained. "And Yvonne."

Pippa frowned, but said nothing.

"That's nice," I said.

With both their mugs full, I couldn't think of another reason to hang around. I excused myself and returned inside.

From what I'd overheard, I gathered Levi had been questioned as part of the murder investigation. The information Jay had given me about Levi's issue with the reporter must have reached Ray and his deputies as well. Levi had indicated to Pippa that the questions were nothing serious, but was that the truth?

Leigh was in the middle of taking a long order for a party of six when one of the tables outside became vacant, so I slipped out to fetch the dirty dishes. Pippa and Levi were just getting ready to leave their table. Pippa gathered up her purse as Levi dropped some bills on the table.

"I don't want you to worry," he said to Pippa as he stuffed his wallet into his pocket. "I'll make sure everything's fine."

She still appeared tense. "I think I've proven to you that I'm not fragile."

Levi put an arm around her and led her off down the promenade. I watched them go, not knowing what to make of Levi. He seemed like a decent guy, but that was nothing more than an impression. I didn't really know much about him when it came down to it. I felt like I shouldn't discount him entirely as a potential killer, although others certainly had stronger motives to harm Yvonne than he did.

As I carried the dirty dishes into the kitchen, I tried to stamp out a flicker of frustration. I needed to eliminate some suspects from my list. I felt like

I was spinning my wheels, kicking up a bunch of sand but getting nowhere. I was tempted to give up on the whole mystery and narrow my focus to my upcoming wedding, but when I exited the kitchen I saw Ed sitting across the pancake house with Gary. Ed didn't look quite as devastated as the last time he'd eaten at The Flip Side, but he still wasn't his usual jovial self.

Leigh had just finished taking their orders, but when Ed caught my eye, I knew I couldn't avoid him.

"I guess you know by now that Yvonne didn't die by accident," he said as soon as I approached their table.

"I do," I confirmed. "I'm so sorry."

"Are you still looking into her death?"

"I am," I said, wondering how much I should reveal. I decided to be open with him. "But I've got a long list of suspects that seems to keep getting longer."

Ed's face fell. At first I thought it was because I'd let him down by not solving the case yet, but then Gary spoke up.

"So it's true then?"

"What's true?" I asked.

"That a lot of people wanted Yvonne dead," Ed said sadly. "That's what we're hearing around town."

"I don't know if a lot of people wanted her *dead*, but... Yvonne did have a habit of rubbing people the wrong way."

Ed nodded, his face somber. "I've heard a lot of stories over the last few days. At first I didn't want to believe any of them, but now I think I didn't know the true Yvonne."

"Unfortunately, I think that might be the case," I said gently.

"But she still didn't deserve to be murdered," Gary said.

"That's right." Ed sat up straighter. "She didn't. She still deserves justice."

"She does," I agreed. "But I don't know if I'm the one to help her get it."

"You can't give up, Marley." Ed was fired up by his newfound determination. "You can figure it out. I know you can."

"I appreciate your faith in me," I said. "But I'm really not sure how much I'll be able to do."

"But you won't give up, will you?" Ed pleaded. "Whatever bad things Yvonne might have done in her life, the killer's done worse."

That was probably true, but even if it wasn't, I didn't want to disappoint Ed. Although I lacked Ed's belief in my investigative abilities, I assured him that I'd keep trying. If I didn't want to let Ed down, I had no other option.

* * * *

My appointment at the flower shop was scheduled for that afternoon. As soon as I was finished up at The Flip Side for the day, I walked over to Blooms by the Beach, where Sylvia—the shop's owner—led me over to a small table with two chairs. She offered me tea or coffee, but I declined, and we got down to business. She had a binder full of photos of flower arrangements, bouquets, and centerpieces.

"We can always come up with something custom as well," she assured me as I opened the binder to the first page. "This is a great source of ideas, though."

"Everything's so beautiful," I said after I flipped through a few pages. "I don't know how I'm going to choose."

"It can be a bit overwhelming if you don't come in with a firm idea of what you want. Why don't we start by talking about your favorite flowers and whatever ideas you might have? Then I can show you some samples that might fit."

That suggestion brought me a rush of relief. The vast selection had me more overwhelmed than I'd realized.

"I know I don't want any lilies," I said. "They're gorgeous, but I've got pets and I know they're poisonous."

"We can definitely avoid those." Sylvia wrote something in the spiral notebook she'd brought to the table.

I told her about the arbor that Brett was building. "I was hoping we could weave some colorful flowers into it and maybe some greenery."

"That would look stunning." Sylvia flipped through the binder. "I can show you photos of similar things we've done in the past."

We spent several minutes poring over the photos. When Sylvia flipped to a picture of an archway decorated with sunflowers and greenery, I immediately pointed to it.

"I love that. The sunflowers are so bright. Happy."

"And perfect for an August wedding," Sylvia added. "That's a great choice."

Once we'd decided on the type of greenery to put on the arbor with the sunflowers, we moved on.

"What else will you need?" Sylvia asked.

"Two centerpieces for the food tables, my bouquet, and bouquets for the two bridesmaids. I'd like a lot of color, especially for my bouquet. Maybe we can use sunflowers again, but mixed in with something else?"

"Absolutely." Sylvia flipped through the binder again. "How about something like this?"

The photo she pointed out showed a beautiful bouquet of sunflowers and deep pink gerbera daisies with plenty of bright greenery. Just looking at the photo made me happy. I didn't doubt that the real thing would be even more gorgeous.

"That's it," I said without hesitation. "That's exactly what I was hoping for."

We spent another half hour going over all the details before everything was finalized. I had a moment of worry as we finished up, wondering if I'd made the right decisions, but then I brushed that concern aside. There probably wasn't a wrong decision. The flowers I'd chosen would look beautiful. It didn't matter if they weren't what someone else would have chosen for their wedding. I knew Brett would be happy. All he'd requested was no daffodils, since he was allergic to them.

When Sylvia and I talked about payment, I almost winced at the cost, even though it was—barely—within the budget Brett and I had set for the flowers. We had the money to pay for the flowers, and the rest of the wedding, but I didn't want to know what a more elaborate event would have cost.

As I tucked my credit card back in my wallet, a man in his late fifties or early sixties entered the shop.

Sylvia's assistant, Bridget, greeted him and asked, "How may I help you?"

"I'm looking for a bouquet of flowers for my wife." He smiled with pride. "She just won her triathlon competition."

"That's wonderful!" Bridget exclaimed, coming out from behind the counter.

Sylvia and I added our congratulations. As Bridget showed the man around the shop, pointing out some ready-made bouquets and explaining the other options available, Sylvia and I hashed out the last details about delivery of the flowers for the wedding. By the time we were wrapping up, the man had picked out a bouquet of lilies for his wife and Bridget was ringing up his purchase.

"Is your wife coached by Nash Harlow?" I asked, unable to keep my curiosity in check.

"No. Thank goodness," the man answered.

Interest sparked in Bridget's eyes. "Is there something wrong with Nash… whatever his name is?" she asked.

Apparently I wasn't the only curious one in the shop.

The man frowned. "I've heard he has trouble keeping his hands to himself when he's around women."

"Oh, dear," Bridget said as she punched buttons on the cash register.

"I heard there was a bit of a scandal a few years ago when he had an affair with one of his athletes," I said.

The man nodded. "It ended his marriage. She might not have thought so, but it was probably the best thing for his wife. I doubt that was the first time Nash had cheated on her."

I wondered if Yvonne's article had played a role in Nash's wife finding out about his affair, or if it had come to light another way. If the article was responsible, that strengthened Nash's motive for murder, in my mind.

The man finished paying for his flowers and left the shop. I followed him out the door a minute later, after thanking Sylvia for her help. Once out on the sidewalk, I pushed thoughts of the triathlon coach aside and checked my phone for messages. I'd received a text from Sienna about half an hour earlier.

Can we meet? it read. *I've got news!*

I tapped out a quick response and picked up my pace, my curiosity driving me toward home.

Chapter Twenty-Two

When I arrived home, Sienna was heading up to my house from the beach. She stood on top of a log and waved as I came along the driveway. When I drew closer, she hopped down and met me by the steps to the back porch.

"How did it go at the flower shop?" she asked. I'd mentioned my appointment to her that morning.

"Great," I replied. "I think the flowers are going to look amazing."

"I'm sure they will."

I unlocked the back door and as soon as I opened it, Bentley burst out, his tail wagging.

"You survived the dentist," I observed as Sienna dropped to her knees to shower Bentley with attention.

"Yep. No cavities!"

"That's always a relief."

"Tell me about it. I can't stand having my teeth drilled." She shuddered.

Flapjack sauntered out onto the porch, and I picked him up to give him a cuddle.

"So what's your news?" I asked, unable to wait in suspense any longer.

Sienna gave Bentley one last pat on the head and sat down on the porch swing. I joined her there, Flapjack settling on my lap.

"When I got home from the dentist, Sheriff Georgeson was just leaving."

"Do you know why he was there?" I asked, intrigued.

"To talk to Levi."

"Really? From what I overheard at The Flip Side, it sounded like he'd already been questioned this morning."

"Questioned twice in one day?" Sienna said. "He must be a top suspect. He wasn't even on my radar until Jay told us about him not liking Yvonne."

"Same." I stroked Flapjack's sleek fur. "Any idea what Ray asked Levi?"

"I wasn't there when it happened, so I only know what I could get out of my mom. All she said was that they were talking about some article Yvonne was writing, one the sheriff found on her laptop. Then Ray was talking to Pippa and she said Levi was with her all Friday night and Saturday morning."

"So Pippa gave him an alibi. Did Ray believe her?"

Sienna shrugged. "My mom couldn't tell. She didn't want anyone to know she could hear what was going on so she kept out of sight. She's not normally an eavesdropper, but she said she was worried we might have a killer under our roof. I told her if she did some more eavesdropping, we might be able to solve the case. She didn't think much of that."

"You didn't mention your interest in the case, did you?" I knew Patricia wouldn't approve of her daughter digging around for clues.

"Of course not. She thinks I'm curious about what's going on around the house, but that's all. She doesn't know how nosy I really am." She said that last part with a mischievous smile.

"Let's keep it that way. And remember what you promised."

"I remember. No snooping. Asking my mom questions doesn't count, though."

"No, that should be safe enough."

As long as Patricia didn't find out that she wasn't the only one her daughter had questioned.

"So…" Sienna set the swing in motion. "Do you think Levi's alibi is for real? Or would Pippa lie for him?"

"I'm not sure. Any chance you know about their comings and goings last Friday and Saturday?"

"Nope. They're staying in the suite above my mom's studio, not in the house, so a lot of the time I don't know when they're around."

Which meant we had no way of confirming Levi's alibi.

"I wonder if any of our other suspects have alibis," I mused.

"How would we find out? Should we ask more questions?"

"Not yet," I said quickly, not wanting her to get any ideas. "I need to think about what to do next."

Sienna hopped up from the swing. "And I'll keep my eyes and ears open."

"Sienna…"

"Don't worry, Marley. I won't ask any questions without you around." She gave Flapjack and Bentley each a scratch on the head. "I have to go, but I'll see you in the morning."

"See you," I returned as she jogged down the steps.

I headed inside after Sienna had gone, the animals following me. Brett's family was coming over for a barbecue and I needed to get ready. Everyone was bringing something to eat, so I didn't have too much to do, but I wanted to make sure the house was tidy.

Fortunately, that didn't take long. All I had to do was put a few things away and sweep up the sand that we'd tracked into the house over the last couple of days. As I worked, I tried to slip puzzle pieces together in my head, hoping to make an important connection or two, but I didn't get anywhere. That seemed to be the story of my sleuthing life lately.

Too many pieces were still missing. One of the biggest question marks hovered over Bryce Harcourt's name. Ray hadn't arrested him, so maybe the fact that he'd lied about being in Wildwood Cove last week wasn't enough to get handcuffs snapped around his wrists. Still, not being in jail yet didn't mean he *wasn't* guilty. Maybe Ray and his colleagues needed to gather more information before they could charge him with Yvonne's murder.

I wondered if there was a way I could find out if that was the case. Ray would be the best source of that type of information, but he tended to remain tight-lipped about his investigations, which was understandable.

I considered what Sienna had said about the article found on Yvonne's computer. Since Ray had asked Levi about it, maybe Levi was mentioned in the article. Perhaps Yvonne had decided to write about Levi and Pippa's relationship. If anyone else had been the journalist, I would have wondered why they'd bother to write about that subject. Since Yvonne was behind it, the whole point might have been to attempt to embarrass or upset the couple. That seemed to be Yvonne's style.

If the article was about Pippa's romantic relationship with her personal trainer and Levi knew Yvonne was writing it, maybe he'd decided to take drastic measures to make sure it never got published. Not knowing how Levi had reacted and responded to Ray's questions on the subject made it hard for me to assess the viability of that theory.

As I put away the broom, my thoughts returned to Nash Harlow. I poured myself a glass of sweet tea and grabbed my phone, taking both out onto the porch. I settled on the swing, tucking one leg up beneath me, and searched online for more information about Nash. After a few minutes of sorting through articles and other information I didn't find helpful, I came across a YouTube video featuring the coach.

I let the video play. It showed a sit-down interview of Nash from about three years ago. I didn't recognize the woman conducting the interview.

She was asking Nash questions about two of his top young athletes who were, at the time, getting ready to compete in a triathlon at the world level.

After the first couple of minutes, I almost shut the video off, thinking it wasn't going to be of any help to me. Then the interview took a more interesting turn.

"How has recent media coverage of your affair with one of your athletes affected your relationship with the other triathletes you coach?" the reporter asked. "Has it caused any strain or distraction?"

Nash's face clouded over. "What does that have to do with anything?" Despite his stormy tone of voice, the reporter seemed unfazed.

"Has it had an impact on the training of Rick and Michelle?" she asked, referring to the athletes who were getting ready for the world championship.

Nash's face flushed with anger. "It hasn't had any effect on my athletes at all, but it ruined my marriage. Some trash reporter wrote about my private life in an attempt to destroy me. Why do I deserve that? Why?" He leaned forward, his eyes practically bugging out at the reporter.

She didn't wince or back off an inch. "So you blame the media for the breakdown of your marriage, not your own actions?"

Nash stood up so fast that his chair toppled over. "This interview is over!"

He ripped the microphone from his lapel and threw it to the floor, storming off camera right before the video ended.

I sat back, the swing moving gently as I sipped my iced tea and considered what I'd seen. Nash hadn't taken any responsibility for his actions and had blamed the media for the failure of his marriage. Most likely he'd specifically blamed Yvonne. I doubted anything had changed since then, considering his feelings toward the murdered reporter.

He certainly had enough anger to be the killer, but did he have an opportunity to commit the crime?

Figuring that out would have to wait. I could hear Brett's truck approaching along the driveway at the front of the house and I knew his family wouldn't be far behind him. With Bentley racing ahead of me, I made my way down the porch steps to greet Brett.

An hour later, everyone had arrived for the barbecue and the table on the back porch was laden with food. Brett and his dad were sharing barbecue duty, grilling hamburgers and shrimp skewers that Brett had marinated before leaving for work that morning. While waiting for the meat and shrimp to cook, we all snacked on potato chips, veggies, and dip.

"How's the wedding prep going?" Brett's mom, Elaine, asked me.

"Moving along well, I think," I said. "I got the flowers all ordered this afternoon. They should look great."

"And Lisa and I have our bridesmaid dresses," Chloe chimed in as she took a cherry tomato from the veggie platter.

"They're gorgeous," I said before munching on a chip.

"But Marley's dress is even more beautiful." Chloe nudged me with her elbow. "Show my mom the photo."

"I want to see it too!" Jourdan, Chloe and Brett's nineteen-year-old cousin, grabbed a carrot stick and joined us at the end of the table.

I glanced Brett's way. Chloe correctly interpreted my hesitation.

"He won't see. Just give them a quick look."

"All right." I grabbed my phone.

When I returned to the porch, Brett and Chloe's aunt Gwen was also waiting to see the photo. I brought it up on the screen and passed my phone over to Elaine.

She gasped and put a hand to her mouth. "Oh, Marley." Tears filled her eyes, and she seemed unable to say anything more.

She passed the phone to Jourdan, who shared it with Gwen.

I put an arm around Elaine. "You're not supposed to be crying yet. There's still a month until the wedding."

"I'll try to hold off," she said, blinking her eyes to ward off the tears. "But you look so perfect in the dress, and seeing that picture somehow makes it all feel so real."

"That's what it was like for me when I put the dress on for the first time."

Gwen and Jourdan both exclaimed over the photo before handing the phone back to me.

"What's going on over there?" Brett called from where he was standing near the barbecue grill.

"None of your business," Chloe replied with a cheeky smile.

I stopped next to Brett on my way inside to grab a salad from the fridge.

"I was showing them my wedding dress," I said before kissing him on the cheek.

He put a hand to my arm to stop me from walking away. "I can't wait," he whispered in my ear.

"To see the dress?"

"For all of it."

I kissed him again. "Same here."

Soon all the food was ready, so we sat down at the table and dug into a delicious meal while enjoying each other's company. There was one empty seat at the table, meant for Ray. It wasn't unusual for him to miss all or part of our gatherings because of work. Gwen had explained that he was putting in extra hours lately because of the murder investigation and all the other issues that typically arose during tourist season when the local population swelled. He was hoping to make an appearance at some point, and he finally showed up when the rest of us were polishing off our food.

Brett quickly set him up with a burger, and Ray added a handful of chips to his plate as he sat at the table. He was still in uniform and he told us he was likely to return to work to put in a few more hours before calling it a night.

I didn't bring up his investigation while he was eating, letting him enjoy his burger in peace. Later on, while Brett was down by the firepit getting a small blaze going, I joined Ray by the railing. He took a sip of soda from his glass and looked out at the view.

"No arrests yet?" I asked.

He sent a sidelong glance my way. "Not yet."

"Remember how I mentioned Nash Harlow before?"

"The triathlon coach." It was a statement rather than a question.

"I know you don't want me getting involved, but I came across a video that I think you should see, if you haven't already."

"A video of Harlow?"

"An interview of him from a few years ago. One second."

I dashed into the house and grabbed my phone for the second time that evening. Everyone else was down by the firepit when I returned and played the video for Ray.

When it reached the part where Nash's temper flared, I thought I saw Ray's eyes sharpen with interest. It was hard to tell, though. He was good at keeping his expression neutral.

"Can you email me the link?" he requested when the video ended.

I knew then that he was definitely interested.

"Sure." I did that right away.

"And, Marley…"

"I know," I said quickly. "You want me to leave the case alone. But there's one more thing." I rushed to continue before he could protest. "Bryce Harcourt. Has he explained why he lied about being in Wildwood Cove last week? Because I know Patricia Murray is worried about having a murderer staying at her B&B. His room's right down the hall from Sienna's!"

Ray set his glass on the railing. "The Murrays aren't in any danger from Harcourt."

"Are you sure?"

He glanced up at the sky with a shake of his head, but he didn't seem angry. "You really can't help yourself, can you?"

"Not really," I admitted. "But Patricia truly is worried. And there's Levi. He's a suspect too, right?"

"Levi Carter hasn't been ruled out yet, but Bryce Harcourt isn't the killer. He lied about being in town when his ex-wife was killed because he thought he'd be a suspect, but we've ruled him out. He's in a relationship with a woman who competed in the games earlier this week. He was here to see her and they were together when Yvonne was killed."

"And you're sure?"

He didn't hide his exasperation. "Yes, Marley, I'm sure."

"Okay. Thank you." I knew he'd shared a lot more than he typically would have, and I appreciated that. "Is it all right if I pass that on to Patricia?"

"I suppose that won't hurt."

I thanked him again, and we joined the others down by the firepit. Ray left a few minutes later to head back to his office in Port Angeles, but everyone else got settled in folding chairs or on the rustic wooden benches set around the firepit. The beach was fairly busy, with lots of people out enjoying the beautiful evening, but it grew quieter as time passed. At one point I spotted Pippa and Levi walking hand in hand toward town. I sat snuggled up to Brett's side, his arm around me as we chatted and laughed with his family.

When the sun sank out of sight, we brought out the marshmallows and toasted them over the flames. After burning my first one into a charred lump that fell off my stick and into the fire, Brett toasted marshmallows for both of us. I was in the midst of savoring the gooey deliciousness of one he'd handed me when my gaze strayed beyond the dancing flames to the darkening beach.

As I swallowed down the marshmallow, my heart rate picked up.

A shadowy figure stood off in the distance, watching us.

Chapter Twenty-Three

"Who's that?" I spoke so quietly that Brett was the only one to hear me.
"Who's who?" he asked.

I nodded toward the shadowy figure. "Over there."

By the time the words were out of my mouth, I was already on my feet.

With so many people nearby, I didn't feel unsafe approaching whoever was on the beach, but a hint of wariness accompanied me. Why watch us from the darkness? If it was a friend or neighbor, they could have walked right up and said hello.

The person took a step backward as I drew closer, as if they were about to retreat. Then they seemed to realize they were caught and stayed put.

"Avery?" I said with surprise when I was close enough to recognize her.

Brett came up behind me, resting a hand on my lower back.

Avery flashed a smile at me. "Sorry if it seemed like I was lurking. I thought I recognized you, but I wasn't sure. And I wondered if…"

Although she trailed off, I figured I knew what she'd left out. "You thought maybe Tommy was here with us?"

She shrugged and her smile was sheepish this time. "Yeah."

"He's not." My voice had more of a blunt edge than I'd meant it to.

"Okay…"

Awkwardness wedged itself between us.

"Brett, this is Avery." I made the introduction more to fill the silence than out of politeness. "She's volunteering at the games. Avery, this is my fiancé, Brett."

"Nice to meet you," Brett said.

"You too." Avery took a step backward. "I'd better get going."

Without another word, she headed off along the beach toward town.

Tension eased out of my muscles, and I sensed Brett relaxing next to me. I hadn't realized until that point how on edge we'd both been.

"That was…" Brett started to say.

"Strange?" I suggested. "It was."

"She's a friend of Tommy's?" Brett asked as we headed back toward the glow of the fire.

"Something like that. They just met recently. I don't know if they're friends or if they're dating, but if they *aren't* dating, I'm pretty sure Avery wants them to be."

We didn't say anything more about it as we rejoined Brett's family, but it took several minutes of sitting by the fire for me to lose the chill that had settled over me.

* * * *

I eventually managed to push Avery to the back of my mind until I saw Tommy at The Flip Side the next morning. The uneasy feeling she'd instilled in me left me concerned for Tommy. Was she *too* interested in him?

Maybe I was making a mountain out of a molehill. I hoped that was the case. I was curious to know how Tommy felt about her, but I didn't want him to think I was prying.

"I talked to Rob last night," Tommy said after I'd greeted him and Ivan.

"The reporter?" Ivan asked.

"Yep." Tommy sliced up a banana as he talked. "Marley and I were hoping he'd know something about Jay Henkel."

Ivan raised his eyebrows in a silent question.

"He's a sports photographer in town for the games," I explained.

"And one of Marley's suspects," Tommy added.

Ivan narrowed his eyes at me.

I thought he was about to voice his disapproval of my penchant for investigating, so I quickly said, "He didn't like Yvonne, and he has a habit of taking photos of people without them knowing."

"Isn't that what sports photographers do? Take photos?"

"Sure," I said, "but these aren't sports photos." I told him about the pictures of Felicia and Yvonne arguing and the one of Pippa and Levi kissing.

"What does he do with the photos?" Ivan asked as he mixed up some breakfast scone batter.

The delicious scents of apple and cinnamon wafted my way.

"I'm not sure," I said.

Tommy unpeeled another banana and sliced it up as well. "I've got an idea, thanks to Rob."

"So he does know Jay?"

"Not personally, but he's heard of him. Rob used to work at the *Seattle Insider*."

"Where Yvonne worked?"

"Yep. And Jay worked there for a while too. Until Yvonne got him fired. Now he's freelance."

The oven timer dinged. Tommy set down his knife and wiped his hands before opening the oven and removing a tray of maple pecan sticky rolls. The enticing aroma almost distracted me from our conversation, but not quite.

"How did Yvonne get Jay fired? That sounds like a motive for revenge and maybe even murder."

"That's what I thought." Tommy removed a second tray of sticky rolls from the oven. "Rob doesn't know all the details, but the rumor was that Jay was using photos to blackmail or influence people."

"What people?"

Tommy shrugged. "Rob thought maybe people at the *Insider*. To help his career, maybe?"

"Interesting."

"Has he been blackmailing people in Wildwood Cove?" Ivan asked.

"That's a very good question," I said.

"But even if he was, would that have anything to do with the murder?" Tommy returned to slicing bananas for strawberry banana crêpes, a summer favorite at The Flip Side. "We don't know that he was blackmailing Yvonne, and isn't it usually the blackmailer who gets iced, not the one being threatened?"

"Usually," I agreed. "But I don't think we should ignore Jay's history. And if he held a grudge against Yvonne for getting him fired…"

"Does he have an alibi?" Ivan asked.

I stifled a smile. Ivan seemed almost as interested as Tommy and I did now.

"I have no idea," I said. "I'm not doing that well with figuring out alibis. I know Yvonne's ex-husband is in the clear and Pippa gave Levi an alibi, but I'm not sure I trust that one completely."

"She could have lied for him," Tommy said.

"Exactly. Heck, the ex-husband's girlfriend could have lied for him too—that's supposedly who he was with at the time—but Ray seems to believe his alibi, so I guess it's solid."

I wandered over to where the sticky rolls were cooling. I closed my eyes with bliss as I breathed in the delicious smell.

"Those are for the concession." Ivan's stern voice sent my eyes flying open.

"I know," I said, forcing myself to turn my back on the sticky rolls. "I'm just enjoying the smell."

"I'll have them ready to go in a few minutes," Tommy said. "The volunteer should be here to pick them up around seven."

I'd promised to donate a batch of the sticky rolls to an all-day event called the Summer Fun Games. It was meant to give people of all ages a chance to participate in races and other activities, riding on the wave of interest from the Golden Oldies Games. Other restaurants around town were also donating food, all of which would be sold to raise money for a local charity that helped get underprivileged kids involved in organized sports. Local businesses had also donated gift certificates and other prizes for the winners of the various events.

I moved farther away from the sticky rolls. It wouldn't be easy not to steal one for myself while they sat on the counter.

Ivan seemed to read my mind. "I've got another batch on the go. You can have one later."

As Tommy placed the sticky rolls in a large bakery box, my phone rang in my back pocket. When I pulled out the device, I saw that it was my mom calling.

"Morning, Mom," I said into the phone as I wandered out of the kitchen.

"Morning, sweetie. How was the barbecue last night?"

"Great, although I wish you and Grant could have been there."

"So do I, but we'll be coming over to visit soon."

"I'm looking forward to it," I said sincerely. I hadn't seen my mom in weeks.

"The reason I'm calling so early is that I heard back from Tracy last night."

"And?" I asked, with a spark of hope.

That hope flared with her next words.

"I've got good news."

* * * *

My mom's phone call left me with a smile on my face, although I had to rein it in when Leigh arrived for work so she wouldn't question me about my cheeriness. As much as I wanted to share the good news with

Greg right away, I didn't have his cell phone number, so that would have to wait. Shortly after arriving at The Flip Side, Leigh had announced that her whole family would be attending the Summer Fun Games later on, so hopefully I'd get a chance to talk to Greg then. Brett and I were also planning to spend some time at the event in the afternoon or evening.

The workday was as busy as usual and the hours zoomed by. After closing the pancake house, I tried to get tidied up as quickly as possible so I could leave a bit earlier than I normally would. When I arrived home, Brett was already there, having wrapped up work early himself. I changed into denim shorts and a tank top, and then Brett and I set off for the park.

It was a good thing we'd decided to walk, because there wasn't a single parking space in sight when we got close to Wildwood Park. It looked as though half the town had shown up to take part in the Summer Fun Games. Hopefully that would translate to lots of money raised for the charity through event entry fees and the sale of refreshments.

Before checking out the races, Brett and I swung by a concession stand that was selling baked goods. As we'd expected, one of the volunteers had come by the pancake house that morning to pick up the batch of sticky rolls Ivan and Tommy had made first thing. I wasn't surprised when the volunteer manning the table told us that the rolls had sold out within the first hour that the stand was open.

Hand in hand, Brett and I strolled around the park, watching the various events going on around us. As we passed through some pleasant shade cast by a leafy tree, a man standing nearby announced that the adults' three-legged race would begin soon.

"Last chance to join in!" the man called out. "Two dollars per team to enter! All for a great cause!"

"What do you say?" Brett asked me.

"I'm game if you are."

We handed over our entry fee to the volunteer and joined the other racers at the start line. Once each team was fastened together, the volunteer raised his voice again.

"On your marks, get set... Go!"

Brett and I charged away from the start line. I was afraid I'd fall flat on my face, but Brett and I worked well together and raced toward the finish line. For a second I thought we'd win, but another team edged ahead of us right before we crossed the finish line.

"Second place." I leaned down to untie my leg from Brett's. "Not bad."

"Congratulations to our winners!" the volunteer said. "You've each won a five-dollar gift certificate to the Beach and Bean."

When the volunteer handed the gift certificates to the winners, my jaw almost dropped.

"What's wrong?" Brett asked, noticing my surprise, even though I managed to keep my mouth from gaping.

I nodded at the winning team. "That's Claudia Wu and Bryce Harcourt."

"Claudia Wu, as in one of your suspects?"

"And Bryce is Yvonne's ex-husband. I met him at the B and B the other day. Ray mentioned that he was here with his girlfriend, but I had no idea he meant Claudia."

Now that I knew one of my other suspects had provided Bryce with his alibi, I had to wonder if Ray was right to believe he no longer warranted any suspicion.

Chapter Twenty-Four

Claudia and Bryce raised their clasped hands in victory as the volunteer handed them their prizes. After thanking the man, Bryce gave Claudia a quick kiss on the lips.

"We probably shouldn't stare." Brett gave my hand a gentle tug.

I forced my gaze away from the couple, but it wasn't easy.

"Do you know what this means?" I whispered.

"Not really," Brett admitted.

"Bryce's alibi was provided by someone who hated Yvonne."

"So you can scratch two suspects off your list? Or do you think Claudia would have been willing to cover for Bryce?"

"Or they were both involved in Yvonne's murder. I don't know which." I watched the couple walk off, holding hands. "I'm going to talk to them."

I followed after Claudia and Bryce as they headed for one of the concession stands. Brett caught up to me in a couple of strides.

"Do you think that's a good idea?"

"I'll be careful about what I say."

I hung back as Bryce and Claudia paid for two cups of lemonade. Once they had the drinks in hand, I approached them with a smile.

"Congratulations on winning the race," I said.

Claudia was the one to respond. "Thank you. You guys gave us a run for our money."

"I didn't realize the two of you knew each other." I kept the comment casual.

"You know Bryce?" Claudia sounded surprised.

"A friend of mine runs the B and B where he's staying," I explained. "We met the day he arrived in Wildwood Cove."

I thought I detected a flash of apprehension in Bryce's eyes. "That's right. I thought you looked familiar." He took a step backward. "Claudia and I are going to check out some of the other events," he said quickly, giving her hand a tug.

"Enjoy the rest of the afternoon," Claudia said.

I thanked her, but Bryce was already walking off, pulling Claudia along with him.

"He couldn't get away from us fast enough," Brett commented quietly.

"He's nervous, but why? Ray believes his alibi. Maybe he's still got something to hide. Maybe Claudia lied for him and he's afraid Ray might figure that out."

"Do you think they could both be involved in Yvonne's death?" Brett asked.

"It's possible."

"We should probably steer clear of them from now on."

"You're right," I said. "Maybe we should enter another race." I caught sight of familiar faces across the park. "There's Leigh and Greg. Let's head over that way."

As we wended our way around several families with young kids, I told Brett about the phone call I'd received from my mom. "Tracy managed to get free tickets for Leigh and Greg, but I haven't had a chance to tell him that yet."

"Do you want me to distract Leigh so you can talk to him?"

"That would be perfect."

I waved, catching Leigh's attention as we approached. She and Greg were watching as their three daughters got ready to compete in a children's egg-and-spoon race.

"Have you entered any of the events yet?" Leigh asked us.

"We came in second in the three-legged race," Brett replied. "How about you two?"

"Greg and I haven't entered anything yet," Leigh said, "but the girls are on their third races."

As Brett asked Leigh about the races the girls had run, I caught Greg's eye and stepped out of Leigh's earshot. With a glance at his wife, Greg followed suit.

"I've got good news for you," I said quietly. When I told him about the tickets, a grin spread across his face.

"That's incredible, Marley. Thank you so much."

"You're welcome," I said. "The tickets will be waiting for you at the box office on the night of the show."

"That's perfect. Leigh will be thrilled. How can I ever repay you?"

"You don't have to," I assured him. "I'm glad I could help."

Leigh glanced around for her husband, so Greg swiftly returned to her side while I moved closer to Brett and took his hand. We were just in time to watch the egg-and-spoon race get underway. Amanda and Brianna—Leigh and Greg's oldest two daughters—placed third and fourth in the race, but Kayla dropped her egg halfway through and ended up in tears. Brett and I wandered off as Leigh and Greg hurried over to the finish line.

"Isn't that Ed over there at the horseshoes?" Brett asked.

When I looked in the direction he'd indicated, I smiled. "It is. And it looks like he's having fun."

Ed tossed a horseshoe and grinned as the people around him clapped him on his back and congratulated him for a good throw.

"It's nice to see him happy again," I said.

After watching the horseshoe competition for a few minutes, I decided to try my hand at the women's shotput event. I didn't do very well, only managing to throw the heavy ball a few feet. Brett seemed amused by my failed effort.

"It's not funny," I said, poking him in the stomach as I returned to his side. "Let's see how well you do."

He was up to the challenge, but he had to wait for the women's event to wrap up before he got a chance to compete. I knew he'd do far better than I did, but I wasn't expecting him to win the competition.

"Two free ice cream cones from Scoops," he said with a grin as he waved the gift certificate he'd won.

"A good prize," I acknowledged.

"I'm hoping you'll share it with me."

"That's an offer I won't turn down, but can we get some dinner first? I'm starving, and I don't think ice cream will be enough to fill me up."

"It looks like they're selling burgers over there." Brett pointed to a grill set up next to a table at the western end of the park. "Maybe they've got veggie burgers too."

"Let's check it out."

We worked our way across the park, and got in line at the burger stand, which had a sign indicating that there were both meat and veggie burgers available. We'd only been in line for a minute or so when I sensed someone come up behind us.

"Hey, guys."

Brett and I both turned at the sound of Tommy's voice.

My smile wasn't quite as bright as it might have been, because Avery was standing right next to Tommy. I detected a hint of wariness from Brett too, although I doubted it was obvious to anyone else.

"Are you enjoying the games?" I asked.

"We haven't been here long, but so far so good," Tommy said.

Avery tucked her arm around Tommy's. "We might enter one of the races after we eat. Tommy's treating me to dinner."

I knew Tommy well enough to notice the hint of discomfort behind his grin. I suspected he wasn't as into Avery as she wanted him to be.

"We had a go at the three-legged race," Brett said.

"We came in second," I added. "But Brett won a prize in the shotput."

Brett smiled. "Free ice cream."

"Cool." Tommy's grin seemed more natural this time. "I wouldn't mind winning that prize."

"Too bad there's no archery competition," Avery said.

The line shifted so we all shuffled forward a few feet.

"Right," I said. "You're volunteering at the archery event. Is that still going on?"

"Until Wednesday."

The line moved forward again, and it was time for Brett and I to put in our orders. With several patties already on the grill, we didn't have to wait long to get our food.

After we'd added condiments to our burgers, we searched for a place to eat. The park's picnic tables were all occupied, but Brett and I found a free patch of shade and sat down on the grass. Tommy and Avery wandered off in another direction after getting their food. I couldn't help but feel relieved. I enjoyed Tommy's company, but I couldn't get myself to warm to Avery.

"I could use some lemonade now," Brett said as he polished off the last of his burger.

"Me too." The food and the hot sun had left me desperate for a cold drink.

Brett got to his feet and offered a hand to help me up. We got in line at the lemonade stand, but as we waited, I noticed Rowena standing on the sidewalk at the edge of the park, watching a lawn bowling competition involving both teenagers and adults.

I put a hand to Brett's arm. "I'm going to talk to Rowena for a moment. I'll be back soon."

As I approached Rowena, I noted that she still looked sad, but not quite as melancholy as the last time I'd seen her.

"Hi, Rowena," I greeted when I reached her side. "How are you doing?"

"Hi, Marley," she returned. "Not bad, considering. Pippa thought it would do me good to get out in the fresh air and I think she was right. Spending my days cooped up on the yacht leaves me with too much time to think."

I could understand that. "I'm glad you were able to come out and take in this event. Is Pippa here too?"

"She's competing in the lawn bowling."

When I followed Rowena's line of sight, I spotted Pippa among the players.

"This evening we're going to watch some of the tennis," Rowena continued. "I'm looking forward to that."

"My fiancé and I saw some earlier in the week. The match we watched was a good one."

"There are lots of great players competing in the Golden Oldies Games."

"I've definitely been impressed by what I've seen so far," I said.

The lawn bowling competition came to an end, and we applauded along with the rest of the spectators. Pippa hadn't won, but she seemed happy anyway. She came over to join us with a smile on her face. Once we'd exchanged hellos, Pippa checked to make sure Rowena was doing all right.

"I'm fine," Rowena assured her. "You were right—it's been good for me to get out."

"I'm glad to hear it," Pippa said before turning her attention to me. "Have you heard anything about Yvonne Pritchard's murder case?"

"Nothing recently," I said.

Rowena shook her head sadly. "It's terrible what happened to her."

"Did you know Yvonne?" I asked.

"I knew her name," Rowena said. "But I'd never seen her in person until I arrived in Wildwood Cove. I hope her murder gets solved quickly. She must have family in need of closure."

"She has an adult daughter, I know that much," I said. "And her ex-husband is in town."

"An ex-husband," Pippa mused. "I wonder if the police are looking at him as a suspect."

"Let's talk about something more pleasant," Rowena requested, her eyes growing sadder.

"Of course," Pippa said quickly. "That was insensitive of me."

"No, don't worry about it. But shouldn't we be heading over to the tennis courts?"

Pippa consulted the slender silver watch on her wrist. "You're right. Adrian's match is scheduled to start in twenty minutes. We'd better go find seats."

"It was nice to see you again, Marley," Rowena said to me.

"You too. Enjoy the tennis match."

Both women smiled at me before setting off in the direction of the tennis courts.

I was about to rejoin Brett over by the lemonade stand when a woman gasped and a handful of people scattered in all different directions. I swung around in time to see Jay give Levi a hard shove that sent him stumbling backward. More people scurried out of the way.

Levi quickly regained his balance and swore at Jay. Then, before I could even blink, Levi punched Jay in the jaw.

Chapter Twenty-Five

Parents grabbed the hands of their children and rushed them away from the fight. Jay recovered from the blow to his jaw and lunged toward Levi. Two men grabbed Jay from behind, hauling him away from Levi. At the same time, Brett got in front of Levi, blocking his path to Jay.

"There are kids here." Brett put a firm hand on Levi's shoulder. "This isn't the place."

My heart lurched with fear at the prospect of Levi turning on Brett in the haze of his anger. To my intense relief, Levi stepped back and held up his hands in surrender. He was breathing hard, his eyes narrowed, but as the other men pulled Jay farther away, some of the tension eased out of his taut muscles.

Pippa rushed over. "What on earth was that all about?" she demanded of Levi. "Are you hurt?"

"I'm fine." Levi shot a stormy glance at Jay, who was shaking off the men who'd subdued him. "That jerk needed to be taught a lesson."

"You shouldn't waste your time on him," Pippa scolded. "You could get charged with assault!"

As if a switch had flicked, Levi's focus shifted from Jay to Pippa and the remaining tension in his body drained away.

He put a hand to her face. "I'm sorry, babe. I shouldn't have let him get to me."

"What did he do?" Pippa voiced the question I wanted to ask.

Unfortunately, we didn't get a good answer.

"Never mind," Levi said, rubbing the back of his neck. "Let's get out of here."

Pippa took his hand and they started walking toward Rowena, who was waiting for them a short distance away.

"Was it the photos?" I asked before they could take more than a couple of steps.

Levi spun around to face me. "You saw the photos?"

"What photos?" Pippa asked, clearly confused.

"I saw *some* of Jay's photos," I clarified. "Enough to know he doesn't have much respect for people's privacy."

Levi's jaw tensed. "He doesn't have much respect for anything."

"What photos?" Pippa asked again.

"I'll explain later." Levi took her arm and steered her away from me.

Rowena joined them, and the three of them disappeared into the crowd. Now that things had settled down, everyone was getting back to what they'd been doing before the fight broke out.

Brett rested a hand against my back. "What was that all about?"

"I'm not exactly sure," I said. "Did you see who started the fight?"

"No, they were already in the thick of it when I heard the commotion and turned around."

"At least it didn't get any worse." I took his hand and gave it a squeeze. "And I'm glad you didn't get hit. You scared me when you ran into the mix."

He kissed me on the forehead. "I wanted to make sure no one else got hurt."

That was just like him, watching out for everyone else. I gave him a hug.

"We lost our spot in line," he said as he wrapped his arms around me.

"Doesn't matter," I said, unconcerned. "We can try again."

I wanted to kiss him, but I was acutely aware of all the people around us, so I contented myself with holding his hand as we got back in line to buy some lemonade. There were even more people ahead of us this time, but eventually we got our drinks.

As we enjoyed our lemonade, we wandered around the park again, watching the various games and races. When we spotted Sienna and her friend Bailey competing in the teen egg-and-spoon race, we stopped to cheer them on. They came in fourth, but they were in high spirits. It was good to see Bailey smiling. Back in the winter she'd gone through a rough patch and had seemed sad or angry most of the time. Now she was like a different person.

Brett and I chatted with the teens for a few minutes before moving on to watch a sack race that was about to start.

"Want to join in?" Brett asked once we realized that the next race was for adults.

"I think I'll just focus on my lemonade," I said. "You?"

"I'm good here." He closed his hand around mine.

"Is that…?" I stepped to the side to get a better view of one of the women climbing into a burlap sack at the start line. "It is! It's Beryl Madgwick."

"Who?" Brett scanned the line of racers without recognition.

"She's one of the oldest competitors at this year's Golden Oldies Games," I explained. "She was featured in one of the videos at the opening ceremonies. She's down there at the far end."

Brett's eyebrows rose when he got a look at her. "How old is she?"

"Ninety-two. Can you believe it? She competed in the track and field events, and now she's going to be in the sack race."

We weren't the only ones whose attention had been caught by the senior's participation in the race. Jay was back—thankfully focused on photography rather than fighting—and Tommy was there too. They both snapped photos of Beryl as she got ready to hop her way to the finish line. When the race began, Jay and Tommy hustled along the sidelines to capture photos of Beryl in action.

I clapped and cheered as the racers crossed the finish line. Beryl had finished in the middle of the pack, but considering that all the other competitors were at least twenty-five years younger than her, I thought she'd done impressively well. Clearly, I wasn't the only one. Tommy and Jay moved in for more photos of her, and I recognized Rob from the *Wildwood Cove Weekly* as he navigated his way through the crowd to speak with Beryl.

"She puts us thirtysomethings to shame," Brett said.

"Right? She's incredible."

We were moving off to check out some of the other games when I realized that Felicia was standing a few feet away from us. She didn't see me. She was too focused on glaring at Beryl, who was still chatting with Rob.

"If looks could kill…" I said under my breath.

"What's that?" Brett stopped and turned back to me.

I tipped my head in Felicia's direction.

"What's up with that?" he asked when he saw Felicia giving Beryl the evil eye.

"I'm not sure."

I took Brett's hand and we wove our way through the crowd, leaving Felicia and Beryl behind us.

"I don't know about these games," Brett said quietly as we walked.

"The ones right here?"

"The Golden Oldies Games," he clarified. "Although some of it seems to have spilled over to these ones."

"Some of the craziness, you mean?"

"That's one word for it. The games might be all fun and good sportsmanship on the surface, but beneath that…"

"You're right. I think most of the athletes and others involved in the games are probably good people, but there's definitely a lot of animosity between some of them. Yvonne seems to be the source of a lot of the anger, but not all of it."

"Like the two guys who were fighting."

"Like them," I agreed. "I know Jay had a picture of Levi and Pippa kissing, but I wonder if there were others."

"You mean more private ones?"

"That's what I'm thinking. I'm not sure the picture I saw would be enough to make Levi so mad. Then again, he does seem pretty protective of Pippa."

I let out a sigh as we paused to drop our empty drink containers in a recycling bin.

Brett gave my hand a squeeze. "Getting tired?"

"A little. Mostly I'm tired of my mind being such a jumble."

"Maybe you're trying to do too much these days, focusing on too many things."

"You're probably right, but I don't know how to shut my mind off," I said.

"How about a walk on the beach? Maybe that will help you to relax."

"But we can stop for ice cream first?"

"Of course."

"Then let's get out of here."

Brett was in full agreement with me until someone called his name. We stopped in our tracks.

"It's Mr. Clinton," Brett said quietly.

"Your grumpiest client?" I asked with apprehension.

"The one and the same."

"Brett Collins, I need a word with you!" The elderly man was storming toward us.

I stepped away from Brett. "I'll meet you over there." I nodded toward a tree growing by the side of the road.

I swiftly abandoned Brett to face Mr. Clinton on his own. I only felt a hint of guilt for doing that. He dealt with Mr. Clinton's grouchiness on a regular basis and tended to take it in stride.

The park was more crowded than ever now, and I had to edge my way around two families who were laughing and chatting together. I found a small patch of free space between the tree and the curb and stopped there, checking my phone for messages while I waited for Brett.

I smiled when I saw that Lisa had sent me photos of Orion. I sent her a recent photo of Flapjack in return. I'd snapped the picture the other day when the tabby was chasing a butterfly out in the yard. Maybe I was biased, but I thought it was adorable.

I didn't have any other messages, so I returned my phone to my pocket, hoping Brett would be free to leave soon. I barely had my phone tucked away when someone shoved me hard from behind.

Before I could stop myself, I flew off the curb and into the street.

As I crashed to the pavement, a bicycle zoomed right toward my face.

Chapter Twenty-Six

All I had time to do was close my eyes.

The impact came, but not where I expected. I thought the bike would smash into my face, but instead it hit me hard in the arm. My eyes shot open as the cyclist went flying and the bike clattered down on top of me.

I was only half aware of voices shouting and exclaiming around me. I was too stunned to truly notice anything aside from the pain pulsing in various parts of my body.

"Marley!"

The sound of Brett's voice snapped me out of my haze.

Somebody lifted the bike off of me as Brett crouched by my side.

He put a hand to my face. "Are you hurt?"

"Only a little." I pushed myself into a sitting position, my whole left side protesting. "I think."

"Maybe you should stay put." Brett shifted his hand to my shoulder. "I'll call an ambulance."

"No," I said quickly. "I don't need an ambulance. Does the cyclist?"

"No, I'm okay."

I looked up to see a man in cycling gear heading our way. He had a long scrape down one arm, but he seemed to be moving normally.

"Just a few bumps and scrapes," he said. He took his bike from the man who'd lifted it off of me and thanked him before turning back to me. "What about you? I'm really sorry. You came out of nowhere and I didn't have a chance to stop. I tried to swerve..."

I shook my head, but stopped when my neck and shoulder ached. "It wasn't your fault."

"Are you sure you're okay?" Brett asked. The deep crease between his eyebrows told me how concerned he was.

"Okay enough to get up off the road before something else hits me."

I held out a hand and Brett took it, carefully helping me to my feet.

"I don't need an ambulance," I reiterated when I was standing, albeit not entirely steadily. I knew he'd been about to suggest that again.

A middle-aged woman brought a folding lawn chair over toward the curb. "Why don't you sit down for a minute, dear? You look like you need to."

"Thank you," I said gratefully as I eased myself into the chair.

Pippa appeared out of the crowd. "I heard there was an accident." Her gaze landed on the cyclist. "I'm a doctor. Does anyone need medical attention?"

"I'm fine." The cyclist nodded at me. "She got the worst of it."

"I'm not badly hurt," I said as Pippa approached.

"Let her take a look at you," Brett advised, still looking worried.

"What happened?" Pippa asked as she assessed my appearance with a practiced eye.

"I fell onto the road and got hit by the bicycle."

"Did your left arm take most of the impact?"

At first I thought she'd figured that out from the way I was resting my arm on my lap, but when I looked down I realized that there were other obvious signs as well. My skin was scraped and already turning purple with bruises.

"My arm and my side," I said. "My arm hurts the most, including my wrist."

"May I have a look?"

I let her take my arm in her hands, and I answered a few questions as she assessed my injuries.

"I don't think anything's broken," Pippa said a couple of minutes later. "But if you want an X-ray to be sure…"

I shook my head before she could finish. "I don't think I broke anything either. I've sprained this wrist before, and it doesn't feel any worse than it did then."

"Let me give your side a quick check."

After she did that, she seemed satisfied that I wasn't badly hurt.

I thanked her for her help before saying, "I thought you and Rowena had left the park."

"We did," she said. "But our friend's tennis match was delayed so we thought we'd come back and grab a bite to eat. Are you going to be all right for getting home?"

"Yes. My fiancé's here with me."

Brett rested his hands on my shoulders from behind the chair. "I can go get my truck so you don't have to walk home."

"That's okay. I can walk."

I thanked Pippa again, and she left to find Rowena.

The small crowd that had gathered after the bicycle hit me had mostly dispersed, everyone's attention back on the activities happening in the park. As much as I was glad not to be gawked at, I knew the downside was that I might have missed the chance to speak with potential witnesses.

"I don't suppose you saw what happened before I fell onto the road, did you?" I asked the cyclist.

"Before? I barely even saw you fall. One second the road was clear and the next you were there."

"I know. It happened so fast."

"Are you sure you're all right?" he asked.

"Absolutely. Sorry about what happened."

"So am I. Take care."

He hopped back on his bike and cycled off.

I stood up without too much difficulty and thanked the woman who'd let me use her chair.

Brett tucked a curly lock of my hair behind my ear. "Ready to go home?"

"I am, but…"

"Brett? Marley?"

We both turned at the sound of the familiar voice

Deputy Kyle Rutowski strode toward us. He was in uniform, although without his hat.

"I heard there was an accident." He noticed my bruised and battered arm. "I was about to ask if you knew what happened, but I take it you do."

"Marley was hit by a cyclist," Brett explained.

"The cyclist didn't stick around?"

"He did," I rushed to assure him. "But he wasn't hurt and I'm okay so he just left a moment ago."

"Do you need to go the hospital? Your arm doesn't look so good."

"A doctor checked me out," I said. "I really just want to go home."

"Fair enough. I'm glad you weren't hurt any worse."

"Thank you. But there is one thing. I should have asked right away if anyone saw what happened, but by the time I thought of it, most of the potential witnesses had already moved on."

"Why do you need witnesses?" Brett asked. "I thought you said it wasn't the cyclist's fault."

"It wasn't his fault, but it was *someone's* fault that I ended up on the road. I was pushed off the curb."

Concern clouded Brett's face. "Intentionally?"

"I think so. I felt two hands on my back, and it was a really hard shove. I suppose it *could* have been an accident, but I don't think so."

"Do you have any idea who it was?" Rutowski asked.

"No clue," I replied. "I didn't even catch a glimpse of them."

"Are you okay to hang around for a minute?"

"Sure," I said, although all I wanted was to head home with Brett.

Rutowski turned to address the people milling about on the grass nearby. "Can I have your attention, please? If anyone was here in the moments before the accident happened, I'd appreciate a word with you."

About half a dozen people came forward, including the woman who'd offered me her chair. Unfortunately, it quickly became clear that no one had seen who'd pushed me. Most people had been focused on other things and had only noticed me after or just as the bike had struck me.

"It doesn't sound promising," I said quietly to Brett as we listened in on Rutowski's conversations.

Brett settled an arm across my shoulders but didn't respond. I glanced up at him and was surprised to see him frowning. It wasn't often that he wore such a dark expression. I was about to say something to him when Rutowski wrapped up his questioning of the witnesses.

"No luck?" I guessed as he returned to me and Brett.

"Nobody saw anything until you were already on the ground," Rutowski said.

That was disappointing but not surprising.

"Is there any reason why someone would want to hurt you?" Rutowski asked.

"Well…"

He raised one eyebrow. "Let me guess—you've been looking into the murder of the sports reporter."

The whole sheriff's department probably knew about my habit of getting involved in investigations.

"I've asked a few questions," I admitted. "But there's a long list of suspects and I really don't think I'm close to figuring out who did it."

"The killer might not know that." It was the first time Brett had spoken for several minutes.

"That's true." Kyle was close to my age, but the stern look he gave me then somehow made me feel much younger than him. "You know from experience that messing with a murderer can be dangerous."

"I do."

Rutowski sighed. Maybe he knew it was hopeless to warn me off. Although at the moment I had no desire to investigate anything. All I wanted to do was go home and lie down. I wasn't even interested in ice cream anymore.

Rutowski flipped open his notebook. "You'd better give me a list of who you've questioned. One of them could be the killer."

With my whole body—and especially my left arm—aching, it wasn't easy to think clearly, but I made my way through all the people I could think of until Rutowski had what I thought was a complete list.

As Kyle shut his notebook, I leaned into Brett's side, suddenly more weary than I'd been in a long time. Brett rubbed my back as my eyes threatened to drift closed.

"Why don't you head home?" Rutowski suggested. "You look like you could use some rest."

Brett and I thanked him and set off along the sidewalk at an easy pace.

"It won't take me long to jog home and get my truck," Brett said, eyeing me with concern.

"I can walk," I assured him.

We both fell silent, and by the time we left the park far behind us, we still hadn't spoken again. I glanced at Brett. His uncharacteristic frown hadn't disappeared.

I gave his hand a squeeze. "Hey. You don't need to worry. I'm okay."

His blue eyes met mine, but his frown didn't ease up. "I can't help but worry, Marley. Somebody tried to kill you."

"I don't know that they were actually trying to kill me."

"What if the bike had hit you in the head? What if it had been a car?"

That thought had passed through my mind as well, but it was too frightening to dwell on.

"Maybe it was just a stupid prank pulled by a random stranger." Even as I suggested it, that scenario didn't feel very plausible.

Brett didn't say anything, but I could tell he felt the same.

My weariness intensified. "I'll lie low for a while. To be honest, I don't feel up to much else right now. I'll focus on work and our wedding. Hopefully Ray will have the case wrapped up before long."

Brett shook his head, but I was relieved to see that a slight grin had replaced his frown. "I don't think you know how to lie low, not when there's a mystery waiting to be solved."

"I'm pretty sure I'll succeed, at least for tonight," I said as we turned into our driveway.

Brett glanced my way with a mixture of worry and affection in his eyes. "I'll believe it when I see it."

Chapter Twenty-Seven

A dose of over-the-counter painkillers helped me sleep that night, but in the morning I woke up sore and reluctant to get out of bed. After I'd snoozed the alarm a couple of times, Brett rolled over and kissed me.

"How are you feeling?" he asked in a sleepy voice.

"Not too bad."

He shifted closer and wrapped an arm around my waist. "Really?" He sounded like he didn't believe me.

"Okay, I'm sore," I admitted. "But not so much that you need to worry."

"I'm going to worry anyway."

I brushed his hair off his forehead. "I intend to be in one piece for our wedding."

"And forever after that, I hope." He kissed me again. "Why don't you stay home from work today? I'm sure Leigh and Sienna can handle things."

I was tempted to agree to that idea until I remembered what day it was.

"I can't. You and I both need to be at The Flip Side this morning."

"Right. The cake testing." Brett grinned. "Then what are we waiting for?"

"Cake is a good motivator," I said.

"Especially when we know Ivan's making it."

"That's for sure." Still, I made no move to get up.

Flapjack hopped up onto the bed and padded his way over to us. He let out a loud meow and clawed at the covers.

I ran a hand over his fur. "Besides, Flapjack's not going to let us laze around all day."

Brett's grin faded. "But if you need to rest, I'm sure we can reschedule with Ivan. And I can look after the animals."

I threw back the sheet, the only cover I'd used during the warm night. "It's all right. I'm getting up."

That was easier said than done. My sore muscles had stiffened up while I slept, and my bruised arm let me know whenever it brushed against anything.

"I might scare off the customers," I said after I was dressed and examining the mass of black and purple bruises that ran along my arm. "Or scare off their appetites, at least."

"You should be taking it easy anyway," Brett said. "Why don't you leave the serving to Leigh and Sienna today?"

"I might have to," I conceded. "My wrist is going to be a bit of a problem."

Brett pulled a T-shirt on over his head. "You still think it's just sprained?"

"Yes, but it aches. I don't think I can carry any heavy loads of dishes."

Brett gently took my hand in his and examined my wrist. "How about I wrap it for you? But you should still leave the lifting to Leigh and Sienna."

I agreed to that, and Brett wrapped my wrist with a tensor bandage. I also agreed when he suggested that we drive to The Flip Side. I'd miss my early morning time on the beach, but I probably wouldn't have enjoyed it as much as usual anyway.

My slow start to the day meant that we arrived at the pancake house later than was usual for me, but there was still half an hour to spare before opening.

As soon as Ivan and Tommy saw my bruised arm and bandaged wrist, I had to tell them what had transpired the evening before.

"I wish I'd seen who shoved you," Tommy said with regret. "But I was way across the park. I didn't know anything had happened."

"Even the people who were right there didn't see who did it," I said.

The stormy expression on Ivan's face was almost frightening. It matched the thunderous boom of his voice. "You could have been killed if a car had hit you!"

"Believe me, I know."

I reached out and took Brett's hand, giving it a squeeze. He'd tensed up over the past few minutes, and I knew his worries about me had returned to the surface.

Despite not wanting to think about anything the night before, I hadn't been able to stop myself from wondering who'd shoved me. As nice as it would have been to believe it was an accident and that I had nothing further to worry about, I couldn't get myself to accept that explanation.

So many of the people I suspected of possibly killing Yvonne were present at the park that evening. Any one of them could have become angered or threatened by questions I'd asked them. And if Yvonne's killer had pushed me into the road, he or she clearly wasn't averse to causing further harm. But no matter how hard I tried to remember more about the moments before I went flying off the curb, I didn't recall any of my suspects being nearby. That didn't mean they hadn't been there—I'd been more focused on my phone than anything else—but I had no hope of fingering the culprit.

Going over and over the incident in my mind was getting me nowhere, and talking about it wasn't proving any more useful. All it was doing was feeding my worry that someone could be out to get me, and I knew it was doing the same for Brett.

"Let's talk about something else," I suggested. "Like cake."

"Good idea," Brett said.

He pulled a stool up to the kitchen's large island and nudged it toward me. I sat down as he brought another stool over for himself.

The thunderclouds hadn't left Ivan's eyes and his frown was even deeper than normal, but he set plates in front of me and Brett before fetching a large serving platter that held five small, rectangular cakes.

"Vanilla, lemon, chocolate, carrot, coconut," he said, pointing to the five cakes in turn.

He handed us forks and then cut two pieces off the first cake, transferring them to our plates. I took a bite and chewed slowly, taking the time to savor the sample.

The vanilla cake was light and fluffy, with just the right amount of flavor. Not that I was surprised. Ivan's creations were never anything short of delicious.

"Yum," I said once I'd swallowed. I immediately took a second forkful.

"That's really good," Brett said before he, too, indulged in some more.

As we polished off the small samples, Ivan transferred pieces of the next cake onto our plates. This one was a white cake as well, but flavored with lemon. It had a great texture and flavor, just like the first one, although I preferred the vanilla to the lemon. That, however, didn't stop me from eating the whole piece.

The next cake we tried was the chocolate one. I closed my eyes and sighed with happiness when I took the first taste.

"Ivan, that's amazing." I made short work of the rest of the piece.

"This is the front runner in my book," Brett said once he'd swallowed down his last bite.

"Two more," Ivan said. Although he spoke in his usual gruff voice, I knew him well enough to tell that he was pleased by our reactions.

We tasted the carrot cake and then the coconut one. Neither one was the least bit disappointing.

"Well?" Ivan demanded once we'd sampled each cake.

"I need to sample them again to make up my mind," Brett said with a grin.

My expression matched his. "Me too."

"You both have a favorite." It sounded like Ivan was accusing us.

"The chocolate one," I admitted.

"Definitely," Brett agreed.

"But they're all good," I continued. "Especially the vanilla and the carrot. And I know my mom will love the vanilla one."

"So will Chloe," Brett said. "And my parents love carrot cake."

"So does Grant." I pulled the platter of cakes toward us and cut Brett and me another slice of the carrot cake. "So it's going to take a lot of research to decide if we should really go with the chocolate."

"You can have all three," Ivan said.

"Really?" I asked.

He gave a curt nod. "Three tiers. Chocolate on the bottom, then the vanilla, then the carrot cake on top."

I exchanged a look with Brett and knew we were on the same page.

"Ivan, that would be perfect. Are you sure you want to do all three?"

His eyebrows drew together, making his expression almost menacing. "Of course. You're getting three tiers."

"Thank you, Ivan," I said with a smile.

"Yes, thank you." Brett stood up and held out his hand.

Ivan shook it and then got back to his work without another word. Brett and I stayed in the kitchen and helped ourselves to more cake. Tommy sidled over for a few samples of his own.

I eventually stopped eating, but only because my stomach was getting uncomfortably full. Brett took a few more bites and then called it quits as well.

When Leigh and Sienna arrived, I had to explain once again how I'd ended up so bruised. Since I was still sore, I took a rain check for the hug Leigh wanted to give me for helping out Greg—he'd told her everything the night before—but seeing her so happy was really all the thanks I needed. She and Sienna tested each one of the cakes and approved our choices. They both assured me that they could handle everything up at the front of the house, so once The Flip Side was open, I headed for the office.

"Do you want me to stick around?" Brett asked as I opened the window to let in the gentle summer breeze.

"I always enjoy your company, but you'd be bored."

He wrapped his arms around me and rested his chin on the top my head. "I could grab my laptop from home and come back here to do some work."

"I thought you were planning to finish up the arbor today."

"I can change my plans."

I gave him a squeeze before letting go. "No need. I'm going to catch up on some work on the computer. I'll be fine."

"You don't have to stay here all day, you know," he said.

"I know." Although I felt better being close at hand just in case anything came up while The Flip Side was open.

"Call me if you want me to come pick you up."

I assured him that I would and walked him to the back door. I was returning to the office when Ray came down the hallway toward me.

"Morning," I said as I gestured for him to precede me into the office. "I'm guessing you're here about what happened last night."

Ray removed his hat. "Rutowski told me about the incident. I'm glad you weren't seriously hurt."

"Thanks. So am I."

"Have you remembered anything since last night? Anything about the person who pushed you?"

"I've *tried* to remember, but I don't think there's anything *to* remember. I didn't see who it was."

"That's probably what they were counting on. This most likely happened because the killer feels threatened by the questions you've been asking."

"I've come to the same conclusion," I admitted.

Ray ran a hand through his dark hair. "Listen, Marley, I know you can't shut off your curiosity, and I know you have good intentions…"

"But I should leave the investigating to the professionals," I finished for him. I held up my bandaged wrist. "This is a constant reminder to do just that."

Ray didn't seem too convinced, probably because of my track record. As much as I wanted to keep my head down and mind my own business right at the moment, I knew full well that could change. No doubt Ray knew it too, but he took his leave and I spent the rest of the day focused only on The Flip Side.

Chapter Twenty-Eight

Monday was my first of two days off, and when I got up in the morning I was still determined to mind my own business. After breakfast, Brett showed me the finished arbor and we maneuvered it across the yard so we could decide where we wanted it for the wedding. Even without the flowers and greenery that would decorate it for the event, the arbor looked gorgeous. It would be a great place for wedding photographs.

After we'd agreed on the perfect placement for the arbor, I settled on the porch swing with Flapjack and read a few chapters of a book I'd bought a couple of weeks earlier. Brett was busy in his workshop and Bentley was keeping him company, so Flapjack and I relaxed, enjoying the peace and quiet.

I was thinking about getting myself a cold drink when I noticed someone heading up the beach toward the house. I put a foot down on the deck, stopping the swing's gentle movement. Flapjack was sound asleep on my lap, but he didn't seem to mind when I woke him up by shifting him aside. He simply curled up on the swing and closed his eyes again.

"Ed?" I called out as I got to my feet.

Ed left the beach and approached the porch steps.

"Hi, Marley. Is this a bad time?"

"Of course not. Come on up."

He joined me on the porch, but he seemed ill at ease. I urged him to take a seat and he lowered himself into one of the chairs on the porch. I took the one across from him.

"Is anything wrong?" He'd never come by the house before, and I thought he looked preoccupied.

"I came by to apologize."

"What for?" I asked with surprise.

He nodded at my bandaged wrist. "I heard about what happened. People are saying someone pushed you onto the road because they were worried you were getting too close to the truth."

"I don't know if that's true or not," I said, even though I suspected it might be.

"But it could be. And if that's why it happened, then it's my fault."

"That's not true, Ed."

He shook his head. "I'm the one who asked you to investigate. I never should have done that and I'm sorry."

"Please don't worry about it, Ed. We both know my reputation. I would have ended up looking into things even if you hadn't asked me to. I'm drawn to mysteries like a moth to a flame."

"Still, I'm not sure it's worth it."

"It's not worth trying to find the killer?"

"Sheriff Georgeson should keep trying, but I don't think Yvonne's worth risking your safety."

Despite what he'd told me the last time I'd spoken with him, his statement still surprised me. "Because she wasn't who you thought she was?"

Ed nodded. "And it's worse than I realized. After hearing what everyone was saying about her, I decided to do some digging. Actually, my niece helped me. I'm no good at all that Internet stuff. She found me several of Yvonne's articles to read."

"And they weren't very nice," I guessed.

"That's an understatement. How did those things even get published?"

"She worked for the *Seattle Insider*. It's about half a step above a tabloid."

"That explains it." His hands tightened on the arms of his chair. "How did I not clue in that she was like that? I guess I was blinded by a pretty face."

"She put on an act when it suited her," I said. "Don't beat yourself up about it."

Ed heaved himself to his feet. "Please don't put yourself at risk anymore, Marley. I hate to think of anything worse happening to you."

"I'll look after myself." Maybe it wasn't quite the assurance he was looking for, but it seemed to be enough.

After he left, I returned to the swing and set it in motion. As it moved gently back and forth, I considered what I knew about Yvonne's murder. It seemed likely that whoever killed the reporter was from out of town. With the Golden Oldies Games set to close later in the week, everyone would head back to wherever they were from. No doubt that would make Ray's investigation more difficult, but I hoped it wouldn't stall it completely.

Flapjack stood up and stretched before nuzzling his head against my injured arm. He pressed against one of my bruises, so I quickly pulled my arm away and gave him a scratch on the head. The spurt of pain reminded me that I'd planned to spend the day doing nothing but resting and relaxing. Solving murders didn't qualify as either, so I picked up my book and immersed myself in its story.

* * * *

By Wednesday morning I was feeling much better. My bruises had turned ugly shades of brown and green, but they were far less painful. My wrist still ached, but I was managing without the bandage now. I'd surprised Brett—and myself—by leaving the mystery of Yvonne's murder alone during my time off. Thoughts of suspects and motives had never strayed too far from my mind, but I'd managed to stay focused on other things.

When I stepped inside The Flip Side at six o'clock, enticing smells wafted toward me. I followed my nose to the kitchen, where Tommy was in the midst of filling two boxes, one with maple pecan sticky rolls and the other with apple cinnamon scones drizzled with a delicious maple glaze.

"For the volunteers," Ivan said when he caught me eyeing the baked goods.

I held my hands up in surrender. "I wasn't going to steal any."

He eyed me suspiciously, but then went back to his work.

Tommy closed up the boxes and stacked them. "All ready to go."

The closing banquet for the Golden Oldies Games was taking place on Thursday and would be followed by an outdoor party in the evening. Volunteers were spending the next two days setting up and preparing for the events. I'd offered to take some food by to keep everyone fueled.

"I'll run them over to the school in a couple of hours," I said after thanking Tommy.

The volunteers wouldn't start setting up for the banquet in the school gymnasium until eight o'clock, so there was no point in heading over there right away. I kept myself busy getting The Flip Side ready to open, and later with some work in the office. Once eight o'clock rolled around, I left Leigh and Sienna to take care of the customers and set off. I'd brought my car that morning, knowing I'd be transporting food across town.

It only took a few minutes to get to the elementary school and find a parking space. The school's front door was unlocked, so I headed down the hallway toward the back of the building where the gymnasium was located. The double doors to the gym stood open. Inside, several people were rushing around. Numerous tables had been set up and draped with white cloths. Three volunteers were busy unloading folding chairs from a large dolly and setting them up around the tables. Several teenagers were hanging decorations on the walls while a couple of women stood huddled over a clipboard, holding a quiet discussion.

I hesitated inside the door for a moment, not seeing anyone I recognized. A moment later, I spotted Avery hurrying over to help out with the chairs. After our odd and awkward encounter on Friday night, I didn't really want to approach her. Fortunately, Sally North came through the door behind me. I'd heard she was one of the event volunteers.

She smiled when she recognized me. "Hi, Marley. How are you doing today?"

"Great, thanks." I held up the bakery boxes, hoping she wouldn't notice my bruises and ask me about them. "I brought the promised scones and sticky rolls."

Sally's smile brightened. "Fantastic! Are the rolls those delicious maple pecan ones you serve at The Flip Side?"

"The same."

"I know from personal experience that they're heavenly, so all the volunteers are going to appreciate them. Thank you so much."

"You're welcome," I said as I handed over the boxes.

"I'll put them in the cafeteria. That's where we've got the coffee and tea for the volunteers set up. Will you be at the party tomorrow night?"

"I hope to be." The post-banquet party would take place at Wildwood Park. The dinner was only for athletes and coaches, but the party was for anyone who wanted to attend. There would be food trucks, live music, and fireworks to wrap things up after dusk.

"Then maybe I'll see you there." Sally almost turned away, but then stopped. "Oh, and your dress is coming along well. If I don't see you tomorrow night, I'll see you Friday?"

"Definitely."

Sally smiled and thanked me again before heading out into the hallway with the boxes of baked goods. I was about to follow after her when something along one wall of the gym caught my eye. Another table had been set up there, covered with a white cloth like all the others. Several photos were set up on the table, including two large ones—one of Easton and another of Yvonne. Smaller photos were set out around the large ones, but there were far more of Easton than of Yvonne.

The reporter was by herself in each of her pictures and all appeared to be professional headshots. I wondered if the organizers of the memorial had found them all on the Internet. The pictures of Easton were different. While he was alone in one of the smaller photographs—dressed in fishing gear and holding up a large salmon—in all the others he was with family or friends.

Rowena was in most of them. In one picture, Easton—looking no older than forty—was beaming with pride, his arm around his wife as she held up a trophy. I leaned in for a closer look before studying the rest of the display. Another photo showed Easton on the deck of his yacht, along with Rowena and Pippa. Some of the other photos on display included people I didn't recognize.

I stepped back from the display, sadness pressing at my heart. Easton would be missed by so many, but I had to wonder how many people would miss Yvonne. Her daughter probably would, but was there anyone else? I wasn't sure, and that brought me as much sadness as knowing how Easton's death had affected so many.

I decided not to linger in the gymnasium any longer. I didn't want to end up talking to Avery. She hadn't noticed me yet, but I didn't doubt that she would if I stuck around.

I made my way out of the school and around to the parking lot. The day was already heating up, but there was a pleasant, gentle breeze that I was sure The Flip Side's outdoor diners would appreciate. I unlocked my car and was about to climb into the driver's seat when a piercing scream shattered the quiet of the morning.

Slamming my car door shut, I ran in the direction of the alarming sound. It wasn't hard to figure out where it had come from, since a second scream followed the first.

I rounded the corner of the building and stopped so suddenly that I nearly lost my balance.

Avery stood outside an open door, her face pale and her eyes wide. As she let out a third scream, I saw the source of her distress.

My stomach churned.

Jay Henkel lay sprawled on his back, his camera on the ground beside him and an arrow piercing his heart.

Chapter Twenty-Nine

I whipped out my phone as Sally burst through the back door of the gymnasium.

"What on earth is—" Sally spotted Jay's body. She let out a gasp as her face paled.

"Don't get any closer," I cautioned. "I'm calling 911."

Sally's face still had a startling lack of color to it, but she seemed to absorb my words. She took Avery's arm and pulled her niece away from Jay, moving closer to me. Avery burst into sobs and buried her face in her aunt's shoulder. Sally held her and patted her back, but her stunned gaze remained fixed on Jay's body.

I didn't need to check Jay for a pulse to know he was beyond help. The gray tinge to his skin and the partially dried blood told me he'd been lying there awhile.

The gymnasium door opened again, and a middle-aged woman poked her head out. Her eyes nearly popped out of her head when she saw Jay.

"There's been a terrible accident," Sally said quickly. "Please keep this door shut and tell everyone to stay in the gymnasium."

Her wide eyes glazed with shock, the woman nodded and pulled back, shutting the door with a loud *click*.

After I called in the emergency, I tucked my phone into my pocket and stared at the gruesome sight before me. I tried to take in what I was seeing, but Avery's loud sobs distracted me.

"Maybe take her around the corner," I suggested to Sally, hoping Avery wouldn't be quite so distressed once she could no longer see the body every time she raised her head.

Sally nodded and led Avery away. As they disappeared from sight, I took a couple of steps backward. I wasn't too close to Jay, but I didn't want to contaminate the scene in any way. At the same time, I didn't want to go around the corner of the building with Sally and Avery. If I kept the body in sight, I could at least make sure nobody else approached the scene.

I could still hear Avery crying, but the sound wasn't so loud anymore. I returned my attention to Jay. The front of his T-shirt was soaked with drying blood. There was so much of it that I was barely able to tell that the shirt had once been gray. Blood had also pooled on the ground, especially to the left of his upper body.

That probably meant that he'd been killed here and not moved from somewhere else. But why would he have been behind the school gymnasium? And when did he die?

As I'd already noticed, the blood on his shirt was starting to dry, but some of it still looked wet. I doubted he'd been there all night, but possibly since early that morning. The strap of his camera was around his neck, the camera itself lying on its side next to his head, the lens cracked.

I took another step backward as sirens sounded in the distance. They grew louder, and I waved when the first sheriff's department cruiser turned into the parking lot. I gladly left Jay's body behind and walked quickly over to meet Ray as he climbed out of his vehicle.

"It's Jay Henkel," I told him. "The photographer." I nodded at Sally and Avery. "Avery—the younger woman—found him. I heard her screams."

Ray nodded as another cruiser turned into the parking lot. "Stay here."

I was more than happy to do as instructed. I had no desire to see Jay's bloodstained body again, and my legs suddenly didn't want to hold me any longer. As Deputy Devereaux got out of his cruiser and joined Ray, I sat down on a concrete barrier that separated the parking lot from a walkway that ran along the side of the building. Sally came over to join me, bringing Avery with her, holding her niece's hand. They both sat down. Avery had stopped crying, but she was still sniffling. Even though I didn't like her much, I felt sorry for her. She'd had the shock of a lifetime, one that would probably affect her for a long time to come.

Sally pulled out her cell phone. "I'm going to call your mom, okay, honey?" she said to her niece.

Avery nodded, staring at the ground.

A third cruiser arrived on the scene. Sally phoned Avery's mother and explained the situation to her, and then we all sat silently as we waited. Eventually, I had to stand up to stretch my legs. They were going numb from sitting on the concrete barrier for so long.

Finally, Deputy Devereaux approached us and spoke to us one at a time. It was late morning before I was allowed to leave the scene and return to The Flip Side. By then, everyone at the pancake house already knew that the sheriff and his deputies had been called to the elementary school. I told Leigh, Sienna, Ivan, and Tommy that Jay had been murdered, but The Flip Side was so busy that I didn't have a chance to provide them with any details.

When the last customers had left and I'd locked the front door, we all gathered in the kitchen.

Sienna spoke up first. "How was he killed?"

"He was shot with an arrow," I said. "Right through the heart."

Leigh's face took on a green tinge, and she sank down onto a nearby stool. "How awful."

I focused on Tommy. "And Avery found his body."

Shock registered on his face. "Is she okay?"

"Not really, but her aunt was there and her mom picked her up from the school."

He glanced down at the frying pan he'd been about to put away. "That's good she's got family with her."

Leigh and Sienna peppered me with questions, and I answered the few that I could while Ivan and Tommy listened.

"So the killer didn't steal his camera?" Sienna asked.

"You think someone would kill him just for the camera?" Leigh sounded surprised. "An arrow through the heart seems like a lot of effort for a thief to go to."

"I was thinking the killer might have been after what was *on* the camera," Sienna explained.

I nodded. "His photos."

Sienna and I told Leigh about Jay's habit of sneaking photos of people in their private moments.

"And you think that's why he was killed?" Leigh asked. "He had photos that the killer didn't want getting out?"

"It's definitely a possibility," I said. "But his camera wasn't taken."

Sienna bit down on her lower lip for a second. "And why kill Yvonne *and* Jay? I mean, it's most likely the same killer, right?"

"Probably," I said. "And I'm not sure why."

But I knew I wanted to find out. My plan to leave the investigation to Ray had gone up in smoke when I'd seen Jay's body.

The mystery had grown even more complicated, and I knew I could no longer leave it alone.

* * * *

Leigh and Sienna left the pancake house shortly after our discussion in the kitchen, but Ivan and Tommy kept working, doing some prep work for the next day and cleaning up. I was in the office, updating The Flip Side's social media, when Tommy appeared in the doorway.

"All done for the day?" I asked.

"Yep. See you tomorrow."

"Tommy," I said before he could turn away. "I know it's none of my business, but are you and Avery an item?"

Tommy shifted his weight, clearly uncomfortable. "She wanted us to be."

"But you didn't?"

He ran a hand through his hair, messing up his short faux-hawk. "I liked her at first, but then…" He shrugged. "We'd only known each other for about a week when she started getting all possessive. It kind of weirded me out, so I broke things off."

"To be honest, she unsettled me too," I said. "I had an odd encounter with her on the weekend. I was having a barbecue with Brett's family and realized she was watching us from the beach after it got dark. When I asked her what she was doing there, she said she was hoping you were at the barbecue. The whole thing was strange. I think you did the right thing by ending things before they went any further."

"Yeah." He didn't look very happy. "I feel really bad for her, though. Finding the body must have really freaked her out."

"It did, but her mom will look after her."

Her mother had taken Avery into her arms as soon as she'd arrived at the school, and Avery had seemed to take great comfort from her presence.

"That's good." Tommy took a step back into the hallway. "See you tomorrow, Marley."

"See you."

Ivan left shortly after Tommy. I'd finished up all the work I'd planned to do that day, but I stayed in the office, leaning back in my chair, feeling unsettled. Avery had mentioned that she was into archery. Could she be the killer? But what possible reason would she have to want Jay dead?

Chapter Thirty

"How much does Charlie know about tides and such?" I asked Brett the next morning as we got ready for the day.

Brett pulled a T-shirt from a drawer. "He's pretty knowledgeable, I think."

"Then I need to talk to him again."

Brett tugged the shirt on over his head. "About Yvonne's murder?"

I sat down on the edge of the bed. "We don't know where she was killed. I'm hoping Charlie might be able to help with that. Was she killed on land and pushed into the water from shore? Or did the killer take her out on a boat?"

"Not everyone has access to a boat," Brett said, following my line of thought.

"Exactly. So that could help narrow down the suspect list."

Brett took my hand as we headed downstairs. "Do you want me to come with you? I could meet up with you after work."

"I'll let you know. If I get a chance, I might pop over to the marina this morning."

We ate breakfast together and then went our separate ways. Brett took an excited Bentley to work with him, and I enjoyed my leisurely stroll along the beach. As soon as I arrived at The Flip Side, Tommy poked his head out the pass-through window from the kitchen.

"I've got news," he announced before disappearing.

I pushed through the kitchen's swinging door. "What kind of news?"

"About Jay's murder." Tommy stirred a large bowl of batter. "I talked to Rob from the *Wildwood Cove Weekly* again. According to him, the SD card was missing from Jay's camera."

"So the killer *was* after his photos." I filled the kettle with water and switched it on.

"Then there could be two killers," Ivan said as he cracked an egg into a bowl.

"I suppose." I fetched myself a mug and dropped a tea bag into it. "A second killer could have murdered Jay because they wanted to get rid of pictures he'd taken."

"Or," Tommy added, "Jay could have had photos of Yvonne's killer so the same person iced him."

"That's what I was thinking too." I sank down onto a stool, feeling defeated. "So we don't even know how many murderers are out there."

"How would the killer have known that Jay had photos of him?" Ivan asked. "Or her."

"Blackmail?" Tommy suggested.

"That was his style." The kettle had boiled, so I poured hot water over my tea bag. "Maybe Jay took photos of Yvonne's murder. Or photos of the killer and Yvonne together right around the time of her death. Even that could have been enough to worry the killer."

"All speculation," Ivan grumbled.

I fished my tea bag out of my mug. "You're right. I don't have much in the way of solid clues, but I'm hoping to get more information later today."

Ivan glared at me from across the kitchen. "One killer or two, you need to be careful."

"I will be." I slipped out of the kitchen before he could lecture me further.

Later on, after the breakfast rush, the stream of hungry customers slowed enough that I was able to leave the serving to Leigh and Sienna. I was excited to pick up my wedding dress from Sally's shop, but first I planned to swing by the marina to see if Charlie was there. I walked quickly, not wanting to be away from the pancake house for too long, and reached the marina in a matter of minutes.

The area hummed with activity. Several locals and tourists strolled along the streets near the marina while others came and went from the docks. A woman I didn't recognize was the only person in the small office, but she told me I'd find Charlie somewhere nearby. She was right; as I made my way down the steep ramp to the docks, I spotted him chatting with a teenage boy.

I slowed my steps, not wanting to interrupt their conversation, but when the boy hopped aboard a boat and Charlie turned my way, I picked up my pace again.

"Morning, Marley," he greeted. "Looking for a boat to rent?"

"Not today," I replied, although it was a tempting thought. Maybe Brett and I could spend a day out on the water soon. "I wanted to ask you a question about Yvonne Pritchard."

"I heard she was murdered. Crazy. I'm not sure if I'll be able to answer your question, but I'll try."

"She was found on the beach, toward the eastern end of the cove. For her body to end up there, where would she have entered the water? Along the shore somewhere? Here at the marina? Or would she have been out on a boat?"

Charlie rubbed the back of his neck. "Probably not here at the marina, but I can't rule it out for sure. And both of the other scenarios are possible."

That wasn't what I'd hoped to hear.

"Sorry to disappoint you," he said, reading my expression.

"No worries. I was hoping to narrow down where she was killed, but I guess that's not possible." I scanned the area around us. "Are there security cameras here?"

"One up at the top so we can see who comes and goes and two others down here."

"I'm guessing the sheriff already looked at the footage."

"Yep. He's got a copy."

"I don't suppose you saw it?"

"No, but Gillian did. She's up in the office. We can go talk to her if you want."

"That would be great."

I followed Charlie up the ramp and into the small building that housed the office. The same woman I'd spoken to earlier sat at one of the two desks, working on a computer.

"Hey, Gillian," Charlie said. "Marley here's looking into the death of that reporter, Yvonne..."

"Pritchard," I supplied.

"She has a question about the security footage."

"Are you a private detective?" Gillian asked with a note of excitement in her voice.

"No, nothing like that," I said. "I'm just... helping out a friend who knew Yvonne."

She seemed to accept that explanation. "What do you want to know?"

"Was Yvonne seen on the security footage around the time that she died? That would have been sometime Friday night."

"No. After I gave a copy of the footage to the sheriff, I looked through it myself, out of curiosity. I heard the victim was seen alive over at the park shortly before ten o'clock."

"We lock the gate at the top of the ramp at ten," Charlie said. "You need a key to get through until we open up again at six."

"Who all has keys?" I asked.

"The staff and anyone who rents a slip."

"Nobody came in or out between those hours who didn't belong," Gillian said. "There were only a few people, and I recognized all of them."

"So no Yvonne," I concluded.

"Nope."

"Okay, thank you," I said.

"Does that help at all?" Charlie asked as we left the office.

"A little."

Yvonne's killer couldn't have taken her out on a boat from the marina, and she also couldn't have been killed down on the docks. But I still had no idea where she *had* been killed.

I thanked Charlie for his help, wondering if I was wasting my time by trying to untangle this mystery. Despite my efforts, I didn't seem to be making much headway.

I left all those thoughts behind me when I entered Sally's shop. The reception area was empty, but when the bell tinkled over the door, Sally emerged from the back room. Her smile wasn't as bright as the other times I'd seen her, and her makeup job hadn't quite disguised the dark rings beneath her eyes.

"Marley, come on through."

"How are you today?" I asked as I followed her into the back room.

"I didn't sleep well last night, after all that happened. I wish I could wash the memory of seeing that man's body out of my mind, but I can't."

"I know what you mean." I'd had unsettling dreams during the night, one evolving into a full-out nightmare. "How's Avery doing?"

Sally let out a weary sigh. "Better than yesterday, but she's still very upset. Her mom's going to set her up with some counseling."

"That's a good idea," I said.

I couldn't help but wonder if Avery needed counseling for more than just the grisly discovery. If she'd killed Jay, she was far more troubled than her aunt realized. Maybe I should have kept quiet, but I couldn't rein in my curiosity enough to stop myself from asking my next question. "Why was Avery behind the gymnasium?"

"I asked her to go out there and see if there was a recycling bin. Of course, now I wish I'd never asked."

"You couldn't have known what she'd find," I said, thinking maybe Avery was innocent after all. She'd had a legitimate reason for being behind the gym, so she probably hadn't orchestrated her discovery of Jay's body, and her distress had seemed genuine. Of course, there was always a chance that she was a good actress.

"Anyway," Sally said, managing a tired smile, "I've got your dress here. If you'll try it on again, I'll make sure everything's just right."

A shiver of excitement ran up my spine as I slipped into the dress. Somehow wearing the gown made my upcoming marriage seem more real. The wedding was less than a month away and I didn't normally wish for summer to speed by quickly, but I was getting impatient for the day to arrive.

This time when I put the dress on, the bandeau top fit perfectly, and now that Sally had hemmed the skirt, the length was much better for walking through the sand. Since the wedding would be taking place on the beach, I'd decided to wear barefoot sandals—basically foot jewelry—rather than shoes or traditional sandals. I already had the silver-and-rhinestone jewelry at home, tucked away in a box along with the silver halo that would be fastened in my hair.

When I stepped out from behind the folding screen, Sally smiled, this time more brightly.

"Lovely," she said. "You chose well. The dress really suits you."

She buzzed around me, checking this and that, and stepping back now and then to assess her alterations with a critical eye. Soon, however, she declared herself satisfied and made sure that I was too. I was thrilled and had no complaints, so I changed back into my regular clothes and Sally carefully tucked the dress into a garment bag I'd decided to purchase from her.

After I'd paid my bill, I took the dress home and hung it in the closet of the guest bedroom. The garment bag was opaque, so Brett wouldn't see the dress even if he opened the closet, which I doubted he'd have any reason to do before the wedding.

I returned to The Flip Side in time for closing and cleaned up the restaurant before returning home again. As I spent some time playing with Flapjack, I considered going for a swim, but then I remembered that the Golden Oldies Games would come to a close that evening. Most of the events had already finished, but there were some track and field races still going on. I could always go for a swim later, so I decided to head over to the athletic field to take in the final events. Maybe—just maybe—the Golden Oldies Games would wrap up without any further drama.

Chapter Thirty-One

The starter's pistol fired right as I arrived at the athletic field. Half a dozen women charged away from the starting line. Felicia was among them, I noted as the women drew closer to me before rounding a bend in the track.

Tommy waved at me from nearby and came over to meet me, his camera and press pass around his neck.

"What race is this?" I asked.

"The final of the four hundred meters," he said. "The final for this age group, anyway. There are a couple more to go after this one. Then they'll have the men's races."

I shaded my eyes so I could see the runners. They'd reached the opposite side of the track. Felicia had a good lead on the rest of the pack at the moment. Clearly the theft of her best gear hadn't had a detrimental effect on her performance.

"I'm going to grab some shots of the finish," Tommy said before hurrying back over to the track.

I stayed put, deciding to watch the end of the race from where I was rather than trying to find a seat in the middle of the event. A moment later, Felicia crossed the finish line, several paces ahead of the next competitor. She raised her arms in victory, a triumphant smile stretched across her face. She waved to the crowd, basking in the applause and cheers. A couple of reporters hurried over to speak with her while Tommy and another photographer snapped several pictures.

I was about to head for the bleachers when Tommy returned to my side.

"I've been thinking about Jay's photos," he said.

"What about them?"

"The SD card might be gone, but he probably backed up all his photos. Maybe on his cloud, or a computer, or both."

"Good point." His photos were his livelihood, so it made sense that he'd make sure to have a backup. "So Ray might be able to see the pictures after all."

"There's a good chance," Tommy said. His gaze strayed back to the track, where the next group of competitors was lining up for the start of the race. "I need to get some more shots, but I'll see you later."

I almost turned away, intending to head for the bleachers, when I caught sight of Felicia's face. She stood only a few paces off, close enough to have overheard us. Several people stood near her, chatting excitedly, but she wasn't paying them any attention. Her gaze was fixed on me, though when she realized I was looking her way, she schooled her features and reengaged with the people next to her.

Strange, I thought as I found a seat halfway up the bleachers. I'd only had a brief glimpse of Felicia's face before she changed her expression, but I could have sworn that I'd seen stark fear in her eyes.

* * * *

Although I'd planned to watch the next race, I ended up watching Felicia instead. I wanted to see if she displayed any other strange behavior. She'd moved off to the side of the track and was speaking with some of her fellow competitors, doing nothing unusual. After missing an entire race while I studied Felicia, I gave up and turned my attention back to the track. Maybe I'd imagined the fear in her eyes.

Another race ended, and there was a lull before the next one. My attention wandered, and I spotted a familiar couple sitting three rows below me. As I watched, Bryce Harcourt stood up and climbed down from the bleachers, leaving an empty space next to Claudia. Before I had a chance to second-guess myself, I left my seat and slipped into the spot vacated by Bryce.

"Hi, Claudia. How are you enjoying the races?"

Her surprise at my sudden appearance lasted only a second or two.

"They're great," she said. "It's always nice to take in some of the other events after I'm done competing."

"Are you and Bryce going to the banquet tonight?"

"We are and I'm looking forward to it. It's one last chance to hang out with my fellow athletes before we disperse for another year."

"I hope you've enjoyed your stay in Wildwood Cove."

"Oh, for sure. There were some unfortunate events, of course, but the town is lovely and overall I had a great time."

"How about Bryce? How's he handling the death of his ex-wife?"

Claudia's face clouded slightly. "He's upset that his daughter has lost her mother, but he hadn't had anything to do with Yvonne for several years."

"So he didn't see her here in Wildwood Cove before she died?" I asked, trying to keep the question casual.

Claudia stiffened. "He wasn't in town then. He didn't arrive until after she died."

I was surprised she was trying to keep up with that lie now that the sheriff knew it wasn't the truth. Maybe she wanted to prevent rumors about Bryce's possible guilt from flying around.

I did my best not to sound too accusatory. "But I saw him at the park on the night of the opening ceremonies."

What I didn't bother to point out to Claudia was that Bryce's alibi relied on her being truthful. Since she was also on my suspect list, I didn't know whether to believe her or not.

Her eyes flashed. "Were you the one who told the cops Bryce was here?"

"I had to."

Claudia lowered her voice to a harsh whisper. "Your decision to be a tattletale caused nothing but grief for Bryce."

"It's not my fault he lied to the police." I knew I was venturing onto shaky ground, but I kept going. "And why would he do that if he didn't have something to hide?"

"He lied because he knew he'd be a suspect if he didn't. Yvonne was his ex-wife. Of course the cops were going to be suspicious of him! He was hoping to avoid all that."

"By lying, he just looks guiltier than ever."

"Well, he's not guilty. Bryce is a good man. He had no affection left for Yvonne, but he certainly didn't kill her."

"How can you be sure?"

"He was with me all that night. That's how I know. And the sheriff knows it too."

I spotted Bryce heading toward the bleachers, two drinks in hand.

"Then I guess he has nothing to worry about."

I got up and made a hurried departure from the bleachers before Bryce returned. No doubt Claudia would tell him I was the one who'd exposed his lie to Ray. I didn't want to wait around and find out how he'd react to that.

I decided to circle around behind the bleachers and find a seat at the opposite end from Bryce and Claudia, but I didn't make it far before I stopped in my tracks. Felicia was behind the bleachers, zipping up a blue sports bag. She glanced around as she hoisted the bag's strap up over her shoulder. Then she strode off at a quick pace.

My curiosity kicked back into high gear. First, I'd caught the glimpse of fear in Felicia's eyes when I was talking to Tommy, and now she was acting shifty, like she didn't want anyone to notice her leaving the field. Why would she care? Her race was over, and as far as I knew, the medal ceremony wouldn't take place for another hour.

It was pointless for me to sit down and watch the remaining races. There was no way I'd be able to concentrate. I wanted to know what was up with Felicia. Maybe if I found out where she was headed, I'd get some answers. I figured it was at least worth a shot.

I made sure to keep a good stretch of distance between us as I followed her off the field and along a residential street. We were heading to the west, and Felicia didn't change her course for several blocks. When we'd almost reached the Wildwood River, she took a left, onto a street where the houses on the southern side backed up against the forest.

Instead of continuing to follow the paved road, Felicia struck off along a dirt one that led into the woods. She slowed her pace and I ducked behind a tree as she glanced over her shoulder. I cautiously peeked around the trunk, hoping she hadn't spotted me. She'd resumed walking, so I figured I was safe.

I wasn't eager to follow one of my murder suspects into the woods, but I desperately wanted to know why Felicia was heading that way and why she was being so sneaky. It didn't surprise me when I gave in to my curiosity yet again, but I made sure I was aware of my surroundings and I moved as quietly as possible.

Ahead of me, Felicia rounded a bend in the road. I caught a glimpse of her through the trees and bushes, but then she disappeared from sight. As I approached the bend, I slowed my steps, not wanting to walk into any sort of sticky situation.

When I reached the curve in the road, I cozied up to a tree, sneaking a peek around the trunk. It was a good thing I'd decided to be cautious. Felicia had stopped mere feet beyond the bend in the road. If I'd kept walking out in the open, she would have spotted me right away.

I watched from my hiding place as Felicia dropped her bag on the ground and parted the bushes at the side of the road. I barely had a chance to wonder what the heck she was looking for when she yanked a plastic shopping bag out from behind a clump of ferns.

Something told me she wasn't there to collect garbage from the side of the woodland road. A second later, I knew for sure that she hadn't picked up trash.

Felicia opened the plastic bag and pulled out a pair of running shoes, followed by what looked like a spandex racing outfit. She stuffed the shoes, clothes, and the plastic bag into her sports bag and zipped it up.

I ducked behind the tree and shifted around it as quietly as possible as Felicia rushed past, the bag over her shoulder again. I held my breath, desperately hoping she wouldn't spot me. I didn't dare breathe again until she'd disappeared from sight.

I leaned against the tree for support, relief momentarily robbing of me of my strength. Felicia had passed within five feet of my hiding spot. I didn't even want to imagine how she might have reacted if she'd found me spying on her. She clearly hadn't wanted anyone to know what she was up to, and I could understand why. I was pretty darn sure she'd just retrieved the gear she'd claimed was stolen from her earlier in the games.

Why would she go to the trouble of stashing her gear in the forest and pretending someone had stolen it?

I didn't have a chance to mull that over. As I stepped out from behind the tree, my phone buzzed in my pocket.

Sienna had texted me, and her message sent me hustling out of the woods. *Need you at my place!* she'd written. *Hurry!*

Chapter Thirty-Two

I jogged all the way to the Driftwood B&B. By the time I arrived, I was tempted to keep going past the house and into the ocean to cool off. Instead, I slowed to a walk in the driveway as a sheriff's department cruiser pulled away from the house, heading for the road. Ray was behind the wheel, with Deputy Eva Mendoza sitting up front with him. I stopped short when I realized that Levi was sitting in the back seat of the cruiser.

I turned to watch as the vehicle left the driveway for the road and disappeared from view. Hurried footsteps pulled my attention back toward the house. Sienna ran down the front steps to meet me.

"Has Levi been arrested?" I asked.

Although he'd made it onto my suspect list, he hadn't been one of the top names on it.

"Not arrested," Sienna said. "But they're taking him in for questioning." She lowered her voice. "Maybe they'll arrest him after they interview him."

"Do you know why they're taking him in?"

"Same reason as before—the half-finished article the sheriff found on Yvonne's computer. Plus, it sounds like someone overheard Levi arguing with Yvonne about it." Sienna took my arm and pulled me toward the house. "Pippa's inside, crying her eyes out."

"Your text made me think you were in danger," I told her.

She winced. "Sorry about that. I didn't want you to miss the drama."

She put a finger to her lips and led the way into the foyer. In the living room to the right of the entryway, Pippa sat on a settee with Patricia next to her, trying to comfort her.

"How could everything go so wrong?" Pippa wailed as Patricia handed her a tissue. "None of this was supposed to happen."

"Is there anyone I can call for you?" Patricia asked.

Pippa wiped away her tears and sat up straighter, collecting herself. Her voice was much steadier when she next spoke. "No, thank you. I'll be fine." She stood up. "I appreciate your kindness. I think I'll go back to the suite and rest for a while."

Sienna and I hurried along the hall to the kitchen so it wouldn't look like we were gawking. A moment later, the front door closed and Patricia came down the hallway.

"Goodness," she said as she joined us in the kitchen. "I don't think we've ever seen such drama here at the B and B."

"We've never had a killer staying here before," Sienna said.

Patricia sank down into a kitchen chair, her face suddenly pale. "Surely Levi isn't really the killer. He seems like such a nice young man."

Sienna opened the fridge. "Isn't that what people often say about murderers?"

"I can't believe it," Patricia said.

I sat down at the table with her. "He might not be the killer, but clearly the sheriff thinks there's a chance he could be. Sienna said Ray mentioned something about a half-written article found on Yvonne's computer. Did you hear anything more about that?"

"A little bit. Sheriff Georgeson seemed to know Levi was aware that Yvonne was writing an article about him and Pippa at the time of her death. Apparently she'd referred to Pippa as a cougar and had speculated that the reason she kept a much younger man so close to her was because he was helping her cheat by providing her with drugs."

Sienna brought three glasses of iced tea over to the table. "Did Yvonne have any proof of that?" she asked after we'd thanked her for the drinks.

"I don't know," Patricia said.

"I don't think she cared about things like proof." I took a long drink of iced tea. The cold drink felt great going down after my jog out in the heat. "She seemed to like ruffling feathers. I'm not sure the truth really concerned her."

"And the paper she worked for would print her lies and gossip?" Patricia sounded shocked.

I shrugged. "Some of it, anyway. It's not exactly a well-respected publication."

"I don't know why some people enjoy tearing other people's lives apart. It's a shame that's what she spent her energy on."

"I'd have to agree," I said.

"So is Levi the killer or not?" Sienna had already downed half her drink.

"It's possible," I said. "He does seem very protective of Pippa and her reputation."

"And there's those photos Jay took of him and Pippa," Sienna added. "Maybe they pushed him over the edge."

She quickly explained to her mom about the clandestine pictures.

"Were they really that bad?" Patricia asked.

"Not the one that I saw," I said. "But who knows what other photos Jay took? Maybe he had evidence on his camera that Levi was Yvonne's killer. Or it could be that Jay was the one who overheard Levi's argument with Yvonne."

"Or maybe Levi's completely deranged and just likes killing," Sienna suggested.

"Let's hope not," her mother said. "That's even more unsettling than targeted murders."

"What did Levi say when the sheriff asked him about the article?" I asked Patricia.

"He admitted that he was mad at Yvonne about it, especially since she'd insinuated that Pippa was using drugs to cheat. He got so worked up while talking about it that Sherriff Georgeson had to tell him to calm down."

Sienna finished off her drink and set the empty glass down with a thud. "So he's definitely got a temper."

"If he murdered Yvonne, we'll probably find out soon enough," I said. "He could even be arrested before the day is over."

"I don't want it to be him," Patricia said. "But at the same time, it would be such a relief to have the killer identified and off the streets."

I couldn't argue with that.

I stayed and chatted for a while longer before going home. The iced tea had helped to soothe my parched throat, but I was still uncomfortably hot. After spending a few minutes with Flapjack, I changed into my swimsuit and plunged into the ocean. The cool water refreshed me immediately.

As I floated on my back and thought over the day, I had to fight back against the impatience threatening to tighten my muscles. I wanted to know if Ray had nabbed Yvonne and Jay's killer, but like everyone else in town, I'd have to wait to find out.

* * * *

After Brett arrived home and we'd eaten some dinner, we decided to head over to the park to take in the party that would wrap up the Golden Oldies Games.

"Hopefully there's no more drama," Brett said as we walked into town. "We've definitely had enough of that for a while."

That said, the drama had shown no signs of stopping so far.

"Stick close, okay?" Brett gave my hand a squeeze. "I don't want you getting hurt again."

His thoughts had wandered in the same direction as my own. There was a chance that whoever had shoved me onto the road would be at the park again that evening. As much as I didn't like that thought, I wasn't about to turn around and go home. I wasn't going to let anyone scare me into hiding myself away.

When we arrived at the park, a band was already playing on the stage and food trucks were parked along the street, doing brisk business. We bought a bag of mini donuts to share and found a spot on the grass to sit down and munch on our snack as we listened to the music. Although there was already a good crowd at the park, more people were arriving all the time. The banquet for the athletes had likely only wrapped up recently, so many of the people who'd attended that event were probably still on their way to the party.

I was surprised to see Pippa arrive a while later. There was no sign of Levi, so I wondered if he was still at the sheriff's office in Port Angeles. I'd expected Pippa to be too upset to come to the party, but I noted that she had Rowena with her. Maybe they'd both needed the distraction.

The women had drinks in hand, purchased from one of the nearby food trucks. Rowena waved to someone, and the two of them disappeared into the crowd.

The next person I recognized was Felicia. I pointed her out to Brett. I'd already told him about how I'd followed her earlier in the day.

"Maybe I should talk to her," I said. "See if I can get her to admit to lying about someone stealing her gear."

"And what if she's the killer?" Brett asked in a low voice. "You don't want to tick her off."

"True."

I made no move to get up. I didn't know why Felicia would kill Yvonne and Jay over a lie about a fake theft, but that didn't mean it hadn't happened. Brett was right—it was best not to antagonize her.

I ate another mini donut and focused on the music. Halfway through the next song, someone stumbled out in front of us, blocking our view of the stage. It was Rowena, I realized.

"Let's get you back to the yacht." Pippa put an arm around her.

Rowena's shoulders were sagging, and her head lolled slightly to one side. "I'm afraid I don't feel too well," she slurred.

They'd barely made it past us when Rowena's knees buckled. Pippa was unable to hold her up, so she slid to the ground in a heap.

Brett jumped to his feet, ready to help. He had first aid training so I left him to it and hung back. Rowena was now murmuring incoherently as she lay on the ground.

"I'm going to call an ambulance," Pippa said calmly, already dialing on her phone.

Claudia appeared at my side, staring at Rowena. "What's wrong with her? Is she sick?"

Pippa didn't answer, instead speaking to the person who answered her call.

A crowd was forming around us as people shifted their attention from the band to Rowena.

"Let's give her some space," Brett said to the people milling about.

I moved back as everyone else shuffled a few feet away, clearing a circle of space around Rowena, Pippa, and Brett.

Rowena's eyes had closed, and she was no longer mumbling. I noticed Pippa taking her pulse, and for a second fear almost brought my heart to a standstill. I worried that Rowena had stopped breathing, but then her chest rose and fell.

Whatever was wrong with her, at least she was still alive.

Chapter Thirty-Three

An ambulance arrived at the park and took Rowena away to the hospital in Port Angeles, Pippa riding along with her. After that, the crowd's attention quickly shifted back to the band that had resumed playing up on the stage. I couldn't refocus my attention so easily.

"Was she drunk?" I whispered to Brett, remembering the way Rowena had slurred her words.

"I didn't smell alcohol on her breath," Brett replied. "And Pippa said she'd only had half a glass of wine at the banquet."

I couldn't oust the worry that had taken up residence in my stomach. "Whatever's wrong with her, I hope she'll be okay."

"She's in good hands," Brett said.

I knew that was true, but she'd already been through so much. Her time in Wildwood Cove wasn't likely to leave her with any happy memories.

Despite my best efforts, I still couldn't focus on enjoying the music, and it didn't take long for Brett to pick up on the fact that I was restless. He was happy enough to leave the park, so we decided to call it a night even though it was still early.

We'd made it to the sidewalk when a sheriff's department cruiser parked down the street. As Ray climbed out of the vehicle, someone gasped behind me. I spun around in time to see Felicia dodge behind a tree.

I moved around the trunk until I could see her. "What are you doing?"

"Nothing!" She had her back pressed against the tree.

"Hiding from the sheriff?" I guessed, pretty sure I was right.

"Of course not!" She scowled at me, but I didn't buy her lie.

I glanced over my shoulder. Brett was talking to his uncle, just a stone's throw from where I stood. Now that I was right next to Felicia, I couldn't stop myself from prodding her with questions.

"Are you afraid he knows you faked the theft of your running gear?"

Fear flashed in her eyes, but anger quickly rushed in to replace it. "I don't know what you're talking about."

"I saw you in the woods," I said. "Maybe I should tell the sheriff how you hid your gear in the bushes."

Her anger disappeared, and her fear made a comeback. "No! He'll think I killed Jay."

"Jay knew?"

"He at least suspected. He insinuated that he had photos of me hiding my gear, but I don't know if it was true."

"If it *was* true, Sheriff Georgeson most likely already thinks you had a motive to kill Jay."

"That's what I'm afraid of." Felicia closed her eyes briefly. "What a mess."

"Did you kill Jay?" I figured I was safe enough asking the question with Brett and Ray only a few feet away.

"No! I'm not a killer. I'm not a criminal of any sort."

"You faked a theft," I reminded her. "You wasted police time. Why did you do that?"

"Because all the media cared about was Beryl Madgwick. Just because she's ancient!"

She was jealous of the attention Beryl had received? That seemed so petty, but it explained the evil look I'd seen her send Beryl's way before.

"Why hide your gear in the woods?" I asked. "Why not stash it in your hotel room?"

"I'm rooming with another athlete. I didn't want her to come across it."

I sensed a presence behind me at the same time as Felicia's eyes widened.

"Ms. Venner," Ray said. "I'd like to speak with you."

Her shoulders sagging with resignation, Felicia stepped away from the tree. "Fine. Let's get it over with."

Ray shot me a stern glance before returning his attention to Felicia. I took Brett's hand and walked away without looking back.

I wasn't sure if I believed what she'd said about not killing Jay, but I decided to leave that to Ray to figure out. If he arrested Felicia, the whole town would know about it soon enough.

* * * *

As soon as I thought Patricia would be awake the next morning, I texted her to ask if she had any news of Rowena or Levi through Pippa. She soon wrote back and told me that Pippa and Levi had returned to the B and B late the night before. Rowena had spent the night at the hospital, recovering.

When I asked if Patricia knew what Rowena was recovering from, she said she didn't. Pippa had simply said that she'd fallen ill at the park.

Now that the Golden Oldies Games had wrapped up, most of the coaches and athletes were packing up and leaving town. The Flip Side was still plenty busy, thanks to the many tourists, but the line out the door lasted only for a brief spell during the breakfast rush. After that, business became more manageable.

I felt so bad for Rowena and all that she'd been through lately that I decided to take her some flowers. Leigh and Sienna didn't mind me leaving the pancake house for a couple of hours, so I popped over to Blooms by the Beach and purchased a bright bouquet of gerbera daisies. I hurried home, where I picked up my car and then drove into Port Angeles.

I didn't have too much trouble finding a parking spot at the hospital, and I only had to pause briefly at the information desk to find out Rowena's room number. Once I was in the right part of the hospital, I slowed my steps, checking the room numbers as I passed by each door. When I found the right one, I stopped outside the open door and raised a hand to knock on the door frame. I pulled my hand back as I heard soft voices inside.

"It's the same drug that was found in Yvonne's body during her postmortem."

That was Pippa's voice, I realized.

"So someone was trying to kill me?" Rowena's voice held a note of panic.

"Let's not jump to conclusions," Pippa said calmly.

"Why else would someone drug me?"

"I don't know," Pippa admitted. "I'm going to call the sheriff. He needs to know this happened."

I didn't catch Rowena's next words.

Since I didn't want to get caught eavesdropping, I tapped on the door frame and stepped into the room. Rowena sat propped up in a hospital bed, Pippa in a chair at her side. They both looked up at my entrance.

"I hope this isn't a bad time," I said.

"Of course not." Rowena gave me a weak smile. "It's so nice of you to stop by, Marley."

"I wanted to bring you these," I said, indicating the bouquet of flowers, "and see how you're doing."

"The flowers are beautiful. Thank you."

Pippa stood up and reached for the bouquet. "I'll see if I can find a vase for them." She took the flowers and left the room.

"How are you feeling?" I asked Rowena.

"A bit embarrassed. I wish I hadn't made such a spectacle of myself at the park."

"I wouldn't worry about it," I said. "As long as you're okay, that's all that matters."

Rowena blinked back tears. "I can't believe someone slipped drugs into my drink at the banquet."

"Is that what happened?" I asked, not wanting to let on that I'd listened in on her conversation with Pippa.

"It has to be. I just found out I had drugs in my system last night. I can't think of any other explanation."

"Why would anyone want to hurt you?"

Before Rowena could reply, Pippa returned, with the flowers now in a vase of water.

"Marley and I should leave you to rest," she said as she set the flowers on the table next to Rowena's bed.

"I don't really want to be alone," Rowena confessed.

Pippa gave her an understanding smile. "Then I'll stay with you."

I took that as my cue to leave. As much as I wanted more information from Rowena, she appeared to be growing tired, and I had a hunch that Pippa wouldn't let me pepper her friend with questions.

After sharing a few parting words with the two women, I excused myself and left the hospital. On the way back to my car, I tried to figure out who would want Yvonne, Jay, and Rowena dead. By the time I returned to Wildwood Cove, I still didn't have a good answer.

* * * *

"How's Rowena doing?" Sienna asked the next day.

We hadn't had much chance to talk after my return from the hospital yesterday. Now that the lunch rush was over, we took the chance to linger outside the kitchen and catch up.

"She seems to be all right," I said, checking the coffeepot. It was still half full, so we had enough to get us through until closing, which was quickly approaching.

An elderly couple came up to the counter to pay for their meals. Sienna looked after them while I cleared their table and carried the dirty dishes into the kitchen. By the time I returned, the couple had left The Flip Side.

Leigh was wiping down the table I'd just cleared, so I stayed with Sienna, telling her quietly about what I'd overheard at the hospital.

"The same drug?"

I hushed Sienna when she spoke a little too loudly.

"Sorry," she whispered. "So the murderer tried to kill Rowena too?"

"Seems like it."

Sienna moved closer and lowered her voice further. "I think I know who did it."

"Who?" I asked.

"Levi."

I couldn't keep the skepticism out of my voice. "But Ray didn't arrest him after questioning him, and he doesn't have the strongest motive."

"I know, but—"

"Hold on," I said, noticing that a group of four was finishing up their meals of crêpes and Belgian waffles. "I'll be right back."

I grabbed the coffeepot and checked if anyone at the table needed a refill or wanted anything else. They all assured me they were fine. I stopped by another table before returning the coffeepot to its spot behind the counter. Sienna, in the meantime, cleaned up another recently vacated table before hurrying back to me.

"I searched his suite," she whispered.

"What? Levi's?"

She nodded.

"Sienna!" I glanced around and reminded myself to keep my voice low. "You said you wouldn't."

"I know, but I couldn't help it!"

I closed my eyes briefly. It was hard to be mad at her when I understood the magnetic tug of curiosity. Still, I couldn't let it go entirely.

"If you'd been caught, there could have been major consequences for your mom and her business. Not to mention that you could have become a target for the murderer."

"I was careful. I promise. I took a stack of clean towels with me so I'd have an excuse if anyone found me there." Before I could lecture her further, she hurried on. "Don't you want to know what I found?"

"Does Ivan make the best crêpes?"

Sienna grinned and pulled out her phone. After a couple of swipes at the screen, she showed me a picture of a pill bottle with Levi's name on it. The bottle appeared to be half full.

I read the drug name on the label. "Carisoprodol. Any idea what that is?"

"I looked it up online. It's a muscle relaxant. And guess what? It causes drowsiness."

I quickly scanned the restaurant, making sure no one needed our attention. "Okay, but we don't know if that's the drug the killer used on Yvonne and Rowena."

"We don't know that it's not," Sienna countered. "And if Levi *is* the killer..."

"He might go after Rowena again," I finished for her.

Sienna tapped away at her phone. "I'll ask my mom if Levi's still at the B and B. I think they're checking out today."

"I can't get it all to fit together in my head," I said as she sent the message. "Why would Levi want to kill Rowena? And why drug two victims and shoot the other with an arrow?"

"I don't know. Unless..." Sienna's eyes widened.

"What?"

"Maybe Rowena was having an affair with Levi and he wanted to end it but she didn't."

"Rowena and Levi?" Somehow I couldn't picture that.

"It's possible," Sienna said.

"I suppose." I still wasn't convinced.

Sienna's phone chimed. "Oh, no. Mom says Pippa and Levi packed up and left half an hour ago."

"So they're already on their way out of town," I guessed.

Sienna's attention remained on her phone. "Maybe not. I just asked my mom if they were leaving town right away. She says they were going to the marina to help Rowena pack up."

So there was still time, but time for what? I was as muddled as ever.

I noticed that Sienna was still texting with Patricia. "What else does your mom say?"

"She wanted to know why I was asking about Levi." She flashed an apologetic smile. "I told her you wanted to know."

"That's true enough," I said, unconcerned. "And she already knows I'm nosy."

"In the best possible way."

I smiled, but only for a fleeting moment. "I'm still not sure we've got it right, but if there's even a chance that Levi wants Rowena dead..."

Sienna's expression grew more serious. "Should we call the sheriff?"

"Maybe I should, just in case."

I hurried off to the office to make the phone call. The pancake house was almost empty of diners when I returned a couple of minutes later.

Sienna appeared at my side. "What did the sheriff say?"

"Nothing. I left a message for him. I told him about the drug Levi has, in case it's the same one used by the murderer."

"But Levi could kill Rowena before the sheriff gets the message."

I untied my apron, coming to a decision. "That's why I'm going to check on Rowena."

Chapter Thirty-Four

It didn't take long for me to get to the marina from The Flip Side. I jogged part of the way and then slowed to a walk as I made my way through the throngs of tourists on the streets of downtown Wildwood Cove. Next to the marina, the ice cream parlor was doing a roaring trade, and the fish and chips shop next door was busy as well.

I caught sight of Avery in the crowd as she headed toward Scoops Ice Cream. I didn't stop to say hello. My gut instinct told me that she'd been genuinely shocked when she found Jay's body, so I doubted she was the killer. Nevertheless, I didn't want to chat with her, and I also didn't want to waste any time. Pippa and Rowena could leave town at any moment, if they hadn't already.

When I spotted Levi, I realized I was still in luck. He likely wouldn't have been in town still if Pippa had already left. He was seated on a bench that looked out over the marina and was eating a take-out order of fish and chips. A mother and two young children occupied the other end of the bench, but they moved off as I approached, and I quickly took their spot.

"Hi, Levi."

He glanced up with surprise, chewing and swallowing before saying anything. "Hey."

He didn't sound too pleased to see me, but I didn't know if I should take it personally. Maybe he simply wasn't in a good mood after getting questioned by Ray.

"Things went all right with the sheriff?" I asked.

His blue eyes clouded. "You heard about that?"

"I was at the B and B when you drove off with him."

"Right." He crammed a French fry into his mouth and chewed hard.

"So are you in the clear now?"

"Of course," he said, still grouchy. "Everything's fine."

I wasn't sure I believed him. Ray obviously hadn't arrested him, but that didn't mean he'd been struck from the suspect list.

"I actually came to see Pippa and Rowena," I said. "Are they down on the yacht?"

"They don't need you bugging them."

I tried to keep my indignation in check. "I don't want to bother them. I just wanted to see how Rowena's doing." That wasn't quite true, but I didn't want him getting any angrier.

Levi swallowed down the last of his meal and crumpled up the paper wrapping. "She's fine. Or she will be once we get her home. I'll tell her you stopped by."

It was an obvious dismissal. Since I didn't want to antagonize him further, I thanked him as politely as I could and walked off. When I glanced back, he was watching me. If I headed down to the docks, I didn't doubt that he'd try to stop me, so instead I melted into the crowd of tourists outside the ice cream shop.

I circled back a minute later. Levi had left the bench and I wondered for a second if he'd gone down to the yacht, but then I spotted him heading across the street. He continued along Wildwood Road and disappeared into the Beach and Bean a moment later.

Taking advantage of his absence, I hurried back to the marina and down to the docks. I stopped at the bottom of the ramp, realizing that I didn't know which yacht belonged to Rowena. There were dozens of boats of various sizes moored at the docks. How was I supposed to figure out which one was the right one?

It turned out not to be too difficult. I decided to wander up and down the docks and within a couple of minutes I spotted Pippa sitting on the deck of a yacht called *Danny Boy*. I couldn't see Rowena anywhere. I hoped she was nearby.

"Hello," I called as I approached the yacht.

Pippa glanced up from something she held in her hands. "Hello, Marley."

I came to a stop next to the boat. "Is Rowena here?"

"She's down in the cabin with a visitor," Pippa said. "Why don't you come aboard?"

I climbed up onto the deck, wondering who was with Rowena. I wanted to ask, but I figured that might be too nosy, even for me.

"What have you got there?" I asked as I got closer to Pippa.

She held up a small stack of different-sized photographs. "The photos used for the memorial display at the banquet. The organizers got most of them from the Internet, but they thought Rowena might like to have them, just in case she doesn't have copies of some of them."

"That was thoughtful of them."

The photo on the top of the pile was one I'd seen while dropping off the sticky rolls and scones at the school. It showed Rowena holding a trophy while Easton stood with his arm around her, beaming with pride and happiness.

"They made a good couple," I said.

Pippa smiled sadly as she stared at the photo. "They really did."

"May I see that for a moment?" I asked.

I wasn't sure why I'd made the request, but something at the back of my mind was trying to get my attention—a thought or a memory I couldn't quite grasp.

As Pippa handed over the photo, I heard voices from somewhere nearby. A second later, Beryl Madgwick emerged from the cabin, Rowena following right behind her.

"I'm so glad I had a chance to stop by and see you," Beryl was saying to Rowena. "We'll have to get together in Seattle sometime."

"That would be lovely," Rowena said.

Beryl noticed me standing near Pippa. "Oh, hello."

"Marley," Rowena said, "what a nice surprise."

"I just came to say good-bye." I was surprised to find I sounded normal. My throat had gone so dry that it was hard to get any words out.

"I've got to run," Beryl said. "Take care, Rowena. See you soon, Pippa." She smiled at me before hopping down to the dock like she was fifty years younger than her actual age.

I wanted to leave with her, to get off the yacht, but I didn't want to let on that a light bulb had just illuminated in my head, so brightly that I couldn't think of much else. Despite my best intentions, my hand shook slightly as I handed the photo back to Pippa.

"I'd better get going too." I turned away, ready to leap down to the dock, but Rowena's next words froze me to the spot.

"I wish you hadn't looked at that photo."

I glanced back, and my heart nearly stumbled to a stop.

Rowena held a spear gun in her hands, pointed at me.

Chapter Thirty-Five

Pippa gasped. "Rowena, what are you doing?"

Slowly, I turned to face Rowena again, moving an inch closer to the edge of the deck as I did so.

"I was hoping *nobody* would look closely at that picture," Rowena said, never taking her eyes off of me.

"Because you won the trophy in an archery competition," I said, having noted the words inscribed on the prize. I'd missed that when I'd first seen the photo at the school, but this time I'd looked closer and had grasped the significance of the trophy right away.

Pippa sat slack-jawed in her chair. "Rowena?"

My mouth was so dry that my tongue didn't want to move anymore, but I forced it to loosen. "Why? Why did you kill them?"

"We don't have time for questions," Rowena said, her words clipped.

Pippa had recovered from the worst of her shock, but she was still aghast. "Put that down, Rowena. What in the world do you think you're doing?"

"I'm sorry, Pippa." Rowena sounded truly remorseful. "I never wanted you to know."

"No…" Pippa's hands gripped the armrests of her chair so tightly her knuckles turned white. "*No. You didn't.*"

A tear leaked out of the corner of Rowena's right eye and trickled down her cheek. She had her eyes focused on me, but I sensed the tear was more for Pippa.

"Untie the moorings," Rowena ordered me.

I didn't budge. My heart raced so fast that I thought I might pass out.

"Stop this!" Pippa moved to get out of her seat.

"I can't!" Another tear ran down Rowena's cheek.

Pippa had frozen, leaning forward in her chair, poised to stand up.

"I won't hurt you," Rowena said to her. She jabbed the wickedly sharp point of the spear gun in my direction. "But I *will* hurt her. If I have to."

"This is insane." Pippa's words were so weak I barely heard them.

"Help her untie the moorings."

I glanced Pippa's way, desperately hoping she'd do something to get me out of this predicament. She didn't move, still frozen in the same position. Her eyes shone with unshed tears. "Can we talk about this?"

"Not until we get away from here."

The panicked edge to Rowena's voice sent my heart tripping over itself. I didn't know how my legs were still holding me. I wished I could get my phone out of my pocket without Rowena noticing, but that was impossible.

"*Please*," Rowena begged her friend. "Help me get us out of here."

Pippa finally acquiesced, getting to her feet in one smooth motion. I didn't know how she could move so gracefully under our current circumstances. I was trembling like a leaf. But I was the one with the spear gun pointed at my heart.

"Do what she says," Pippa said to me.

Both her voice and expression had transformed, totally calm now. I recalled that she was a medical doctor. Maybe that training was kicking in, letting her stay unflustered in the face of jeopardy.

Pippa moved to the edge of the deck and began untying one of the moorings. I glanced from the spear gun to Rowena's face. The desperation in her eyes told me that what she'd said was true—she'd kill me if it would help her flee.

I convinced myself to move, mirroring Pippa's actions. I struggled with the knots, so she came over and helped me after she'd finished untying her line. The yacht drifted slowly away from the dock.

"Get us out of here," Rowena said to her friend.

Without a word or a glance my way, Pippa moved to the wheelhouse and started up the yacht's engine. The gap of water between the boat and the dock widened. I briefly considered jumping overboard, but Rowena could easily shoot me with the spear before I got off the boat.

I wished I was safely at home with Brett, but that was pointless. Although, thinking of Brett helped to clear the haze of fear from my mind. With or without Pippa's help, I had to keep Rowena from making me her next victim.

She nodded toward Pippa, the spear gun still leveled at my chest. "Move."

The movement of the yacht made my shaky legs even less steady. I tried my best to climb slowly and carefully up toward the wheelhouse, not wanting to startle Rowena with any sudden or jerky movements. The

small wheelhouse was crowded with three of us inside it. There was barely
enough room for Rowena to keep the spear gun pointed at me.

Pippa continued steering the boat. Although she kept her gaze fixed
straight ahead, I noticed tears trickling down her face.

"I can't believe you killed Easton," she said, barely above a whisper.

"I didn't!" Rowena sounded horrified by the accusation. She choked out
a sob. "I never could have hurt him. It was that awful woman!"

I broke the silence I'd kept for the past few minutes. "Yvonne? She
killed your husband?"

"Yes!" She glanced down at the weapon in her hands and seemed to
reconsider. "In a way."

"Tell me what happened." Despite her silent tears, Pippa's voice was
steady and not without compassion.

Rowena's gaze shifted her way before returning to me. "It all went
wrong." Her voice nearly broke. "Yvonne was supposed to be the only one
to die. She didn't deserve to live. Not after what she did to our Danny!"

I wanted to know who Danny was, but I didn't interrupt.

"We told her we had a great story to share with her," Rowena continued.
"One she could write about for the *Insider*. We invited her to the yacht for
cocktails and a chat. She never expected a ruse. It was easy to get some
sedatives. Easton wrote me a prescription for one he used a lot in his dental
practice, and we used the pills to spike Yvonne's drink. That was meant
to make it easy to kill her. She wasn't supposed to fight back."

"You planned the murders," I said, unable to hide my disgust.

Pippa shot me a warning glance, so brief I almost missed it.

"Only Yvonne's," Rowena protested, as if that made things less terrible.

"And you pushed me into the street." I knew that had to be true.

"That was a warning. I kept an eye on you after all those questions you
asked me at the coffee shop. If you hadn't been so nosy, we wouldn't be
in this mess!"

I thought she was more to blame than I was, but I didn't think it would
be wise to say so. Instead, I tried to keep her talking about the murders.

"Yvonne wasn't seen on the marina's security footage," I said,
remembering what Gillian had told me.

"Yes, she was," Rowena countered. "I went back to the yacht in the
afternoon and waited there. Yvonne arrived with Easton later that night.
Yvonne and I look fairly similar, so we were hoping she'd be mistaken for
me on the security footage, especially in the poor lighting and in Easton's
company."

That must have been what had happened.

"What about Jay?" I asked. "Why kill him?"

"He read too many of Yvonne's articles. He figured out we had a reason to want her dead. When he started insinuating that I was involved, I had to keep him quiet. So I set up a nighttime meeting with him at the school parking lot. I made him think I'd be willing to pay for his silence. He didn't even know what hit him. I've always been a good shot."

My stomach churned at that statement and I tried not to stare at the spear gun. "Did you take the drugs yourself the other night?"

"I wanted to make sure no one would suspect me. I figured the best way to do that was to make it look like I was meant to be another victim."

Pippa closed her eyes briefly. "What happened to Easton? He died in a fight with Yvonne?"

"We tried to push her overboard, but she started fighting with Easton. I had to make her stop, so I used the spear gun."

I had trouble swallowing as I stared at the weapon trained on me. It had already been used to commit one murder. Rowena wouldn't hesitate to use it again.

"I thought she'd die right away," Rowena continued. "But she didn't. I pulled out the spear and then we shoved her overboard, but she grabbed on to Easton and he went over with her. I don't know if he hit his head or what, but he never resurfaced."

A sob tore out of her body. The intense grief behind it would have affected me more if I hadn't known she was a killer.

"How am I supposed to go on without Easton?" Her body shook with sobs.

If I was going to make a move, this was my chance. I might not get another one.

I was about to throw myself toward the spear gun, hoping to knock it aside, when Pippa launched herself at Rowena. The spear gun clattered to the deck.

"Run!" Pippa yelled at me.

I scrambled over their bodies as they struggled in a heap. I clambered down to the deck below and then came to a halt. There was nowhere to run *to*.

I had to help Pippa subdue Rowena so we could take the yacht back to the marina. I spun around, planning to return to the wheelhouse, but then I saw Rowena's fist connect with Pippa's jaw.

"I'm sorry!" Rowena wailed.

Pippa slumped down to the deck. I backed up a step and hit the railing behind me. I tugged my phone from my pocket, hoping I'd have reception.

Rowena grabbed the spear gun.

I was too far away to fight her for it, and I didn't have time to use my phone.

As she raised the weapon, I dropped my phone on the deck and did the only thing I could think of.

I jumped overboard.

Chapter Thirty-Six

I gasped when I broke through to the surface, the chill of the water an unpleasant shock. The yacht was moving away from me, but it still wasn't far off. I spotted Rowena on the deck.

I sucked in as much air as I could and dove beneath the waves, terrified Rowena would try to shoot me with the spear. Kicking hard, I swam as far as possible before returning to the surface.

The yacht had moved farther away. I blinked water out of my eyes, trying to spot Rowena. I couldn't see anyone on the deck anymore. Maybe she'd given up on killing me.

That thought brought me some relief, but it didn't ease my anxiety entirely. I was out in the ocean, alone, and Rowena was getting away. I couldn't do much about her at the moment, so I focused on saving myself.

I was a decent swimmer, although my T-shirt and shorts hampered me more than a swimsuit would have. The shoreline wasn't too far off, so I swam in that direction, hoping it wasn't farther away than it appeared.

After a few strokes, I paused and checked over my shoulder as I bobbed up and down on the waves. The yacht continued to grow smaller. I hoped Pippa was okay. Rowena had hurt her after saying she wouldn't, but she'd seemed so distressed by punching her friend that I hoped she wouldn't do anything worse.

I resumed swimming, but I had to stop and rest after a few minutes, treading water while I tried not to panic. The shore didn't seem any closer than it had when I started swimming.

I thought of everyone I'd see when I reached land, especially Brett, Flapjack, and Bentley. I had to keep swimming if I wanted a chance to hug them all again.

That spurred me onward. I swam and swam, and then paused for another rest.

The low buzz of a motor reached my ears. I splashed around in a panic, thinking Rowena had turned the yacht this way and was coming to finish me off. But the sound came from a small speedboat zooming its way out from the marina.

Hope exploded in my chest. I waved my arms and yelled for help.

I feared the boat would speed right past me, but then the lone occupant steered my way and cut the motor.

Help had arrived.

* * * *

The heat of the summer sun had never been more welcome. Charlie had brought me a blanket from the marina's office to wrap around my shoulders, but the sun was proving to be the best antidote to the chill that had settled into my bones during my swim.

Sheriff's department cruisers lined the street by the office and curious onlookers had gathered on the sidewalk, trying to figure out what was going on. Brett was on his way, thanks to a phone call from Charlie. He'd made that call after contacting the Coast Guard and the sheriff's department.

Charlie was at the top of the ramp, looking out over the docks, when Rowena first pointed the spear gun at me. By the time the yacht had left the marina, he was already calling for help. Moments after my rescuer—a local fisherman—had hauled me from the water, the Coast Guard had closed in on Rowena and now its vessel was approaching the docks.

I jumped up from the bench where I'd been sitting, letting the blanket fall from my shoulders. Despite Deputy Rutowski's protests, I hurried down the ramp. By the time I reached the dock, a Coast Guard officer was handing a handcuffed Rowena over to Ray.

Without any conscious thought, I backed away as Ray walked her in my direction. I couldn't bear to get too close to her after everything that had transpired.

When she spotted me, her face crumpled. "I'm sorry," she said, her voice breaking.

By the time the words were out of her mouth, Ray was escorting her up the ramp.

My heart thudded so hard that it was almost painful, and only partly from coming so close to Rowena again.

I rushed along the dock toward the Coast Guard vessel. Before I got there, I drew to a stop, relief weakening my legs. Deputy Devereaux stood at the end of the dock, helping Pippa down from the vessel.

When she saw me, she rushed over and pulled me into a hug, unconcerned about the fact that I was soaking wet.

"Thank God you're all right!" she said.

I hugged her back. "I was about to say the same about you."

"I'm so sorry for everything."

"None of it was your fault," I said as I pulled back.

She didn't seem to hear me. "I should have known what was going on."

"How could you?"

She wiped a tear from her cheek. A bruise had already formed on her jaw where Rowena had struck her. "It was all about Rowena and Easton's son, Daniel. He died two years ago, drove off a bridge and into a river."

We walked slowly along the dock toward the ramp, where Rutowski stood, probably waiting for us.

"What did that have to do with Yvonne?" I asked.

"Daniel was a great tennis player," Pippa explained. "He had a bright career ahead of him, but then he got banned from the sport for a year after a positive drug test. It was a mistake—something he took when he had a bad case of the flu. Yvonne wrote an article about him, making it seem like something more sinister, like he'd been deliberately cheating, possibly for a long time. Some people believed what they read. It crushed Daniel. He stopped training and became depressed. Nobody knows for sure if he drove off the bridge on purpose or if it was an accident. It could have been either."

"That's terrible." I couldn't help but feel some compassion for Easton and Rowena, even after what they'd done. I knew all too well how painful it was to unexpectedly lose a loved one.

"Daniel's death left Rowena and Easton broken. I just never realized *how* broken. When they ran into Yvonne here in Wildwood Cove…"

"They decided to take revenge," I finished for her.

And now three people were dead and Rowena would go to prison, probably for the rest of her life.

My heart ached from all the devastation and sorrow.

When we reached the top of the ramp, I saw Brett climbing out of his truck.

Suddenly, my heart hurt a little less.

Chapter Thirty-Seven

Butterflies had fluttered in my stomach all morning, but now they flitted through my entire bloodstream. I was excited, not nervous. I'd awakened earlier than usual, and the last few hours had ticked by so slowly that I'd thought this moment might never arrive.

I smoothed down the skirt of my dress and checked my reflection in the bedroom's cheval mirror one last time. My mom stood next to me, carefully wiping a single tear from her cheek with a tissue.

"You're so beautiful, sweetheart."

"No crying," I said, although I couldn't make the words sound stern. I also couldn't stop smiling. "Not yet."

She smiled too, her eyes still watery. "No guarantees."

She gave me a hug before making sure that every curly lock of my hair was in place, the seed pearl halo circling my head in exactly the right way.

Lisa and Chloe had disappeared downstairs for a few minutes, but after a tap on the bedroom door, they both reappeared.

"Everyone's here," Chloe announced.

"It's time," Lisa added.

I could practically see their happiness and excitement shimmering in the air around them. It was probably a fraction of what I was radiating.

I gathered up my skirt so I wouldn't trip on the stairs and followed my friends out of the bedroom. My mom held my elbow as we descended the stairway, making sure I didn't lose my footing.

As we entered the family room, I caught sight of the antique ship's wheel on the wall and my smile brightened. Brett had loved his birthday present, and seeing it on display was a welcome reminder of the fact that this was *our* house now.

Flapjack sat on the windowsill, his tail twitching. He had his amber eyes fixed on the world outside the window, but at the sound of our footsteps he looked our way. I paused to run a hand over his fur, receiving a contented purr in return. He'd watch the festivities from here, but Bentley was down on the beach with everyone else.

Before stepping out through the French doors, I fingered the silver locket hanging around my neck. My mom had given it to me that morning. Inside the locket was a photo of my late stepsiblings. I'd almost broken my own rule about not crying when I'd seen it. I wished Charlotte and Dylan could have been there with me that day, but they were always in my heart.

I drew in a deep breath as my mom took my arm. The butterflies inside of me increased their fluttering. I couldn't wait any longer.

My mom and I followed Lisa and Chloe outside and down from the back porch. We drew to a stop beneath the arbor with its bright sunflowers and greenery. A second later, Lisa and Chloe began the slow procession down to the beach.

Everyone I loved most was present. Ahead of me, Brett waited in his suit and tie. When he saw me, the bright smile that lit up his face matched my own. Our eyes locked, and my butterflies gave one last whirl of excitement before settling, bringing me a sense of serenity.

My mom stayed at my side. She was going to walk me down the beach to Brett.

She squeezed my arm. "Ready, Marley?" she asked quietly.

"Ready," I said.

Then I took the first step toward the rest of my life.

Acknowledgments

I'd like to extend my sincere thanks to several people whose hard work and input made this book what it is today. I'm forever grateful to my agent, Jessica Faust, for helping me bring this series to life, and to my editors at Kensington, Martin Biro and Elizabeth May, for all their advice and guidance. I'm also grateful to Samantha McVeigh and the rest of the Kensington team for all their hard work. Thank you to Sarah Blair for always reading my early drafts and cheering me on, and to Jody Holford for providing feedback and being such an enthusiastic Marley and Brett fan. Last but not least, thank you to the Cozy Mystery Crew, my review crew, and all my wonderful friends in the writing community.

Recipes

Belgian Waffles with Strawberry Syrup

Strawberry Syrup

2 cups strawberries, diced
½ cup water
½ cup sugar
1 tablespoon lemon juice

Place the diced strawberries in a medium saucepan. Add the water, sugar, and lemon juice and bring to a boil over medium-high heat, stirring occasionally. Reduce to medium-low heat and simmer for approximately 10 minutes, until the strawberries are soft and the syrup has thickened. Refrigerate until ready to use.

Waffles

2 eggs
2 cups all-purpose flour
2 tablespoons sugar
3-1/2 teaspoons baking powder
1-3/4 cups milk
1/2 cup vegetable oil
1 teaspoon vanilla

Separate the egg yolks and egg whites into two mixing bowls. With a hand mixer, beat the egg whites until they form stiff peaks. Set aside.

Sift the dry ingredients into a large mixing bowl.

In a separate bowl, add the milk, oil, and vanilla to the egg yolks and mix well. Add this mixture to the dry ingredients and mix just until combined. Gently fold in the egg whites.

Cook according to waffle iron's instructions. Top with strawberry syrup and serve. Serves 4.

Apple Cinnamon Scones
with Maple Glaze

2 cups all-purpose flour
1/3 cup sugar
1 tablespoon baking powder
2 teaspoons cinnamon
6 tablespoons unsalted butter
1 cup apples, chopped (I use Granny Smith)
1 egg
1 cup cream
1 teaspoon vanilla

Preheat oven to 400°F.

In a large bowl, mix together the flour, sugar, baking powder, and cinnamon. Cut the butter into small pieces and cut it into the dry ingredients with a pastry cutter or fork until it resembles coarse oatmeal. Mix in the chopped apple.

In a separate bowl, whisk together the egg, cream, and vanilla. Stir into dry ingredients.

Line a baking sheet with parchment paper. Place the dough on a lightly floured surface. Knead lightly, about 8 to 10 times. Form dough into a ball and place on the baking sheet. Flatten the ball into a disc approximately 1 inch thick. Cut into 8 pieces but do not separate the pieces.

Bake at 400°F for approximately 18 minutes, until golden brown.

Maple Glaze

2 tablespoons pure maple syrup
½ cup icing sugar
2 teaspoons cream

In a small bowl, mix together glaze ingredients until smooth. Once the scones have cooled, drizzle with glaze and serve.

Banana Nut Pancakes

2 tablespoons butter, melted
1/3 cup pecans, toasted and finely chopped
1-1/2 cups all-purpose flour
2 tablespoons sugar
2 teaspoons baking powder
1/2 teaspoon baking soda
1/2 teaspoon cinnamon
1/2 teaspoon nutmeg
2 very ripe bananas
1 large egg
1-1/2 cups unsweetened almond milk

Melt the butter and set it aside to cool. Chop and lightly toast the pecans.

Mix together the flour, sugar, baking powder, baking soda, cinnamon, nutmeg, and pecans. In a separate bowl, mash the bananas. Add the egg, almond milk, and melted butter to the bananas and beat together. Make a well in the dry ingredients. Add the liquid ingredients to the dry ingredients and mix together.

Ladle the batter into a greased skillet and cook on medium heat until bubbles form on the top and don't disappear. Flip and cook second side until golden brown.

Serve with butter and maple syrup. Serves 4.

**If you love the Pancake House Mysteries, then
don't miss the new Literary Pub Mystery series by
USA Today Bestselling author Sarah Fox!**

AN ALE OF TWO CITIES

In this intoxicating mystery by USA Today *bestselling author Sarah
Fox, a winter carnival becomes a recipe for disaster when a Shady
Creek celebrity gets iced.*

The Winter Carnival always brings holiday cheer, Christmas joy—and
tourists with cash—to picturesque Shady Creek, Vermont. At the center
of the glittering decorations and twinkling lights is booklover and pub
owner Sadie Coleman, creating original cocktails, hosting a literary trivia
evening, and cheering on her loyal employee Melanie "Mel" Costas as
she competes in the ice carving competition.

But holiday cheer can't compete with former resident and renowned chef
Freddy Mancini, who arrives with his nose in the air, showing off his ice-
sculpting skills like a modern-day Michelangelo. During the artists' break
in the night-long contest, Mel's tools disappear . . . and Freddy is found
dead with her missing pick in his chest.

Although the police turn their attention to Mel, it seems everyone in
town had a grudge against Freddy, including his assistant, his mentor, his
former flame, and even his half-brother.

Faster than she can fling a Huckleberry Gin, Sadie finds herself racing to
make sure the police don't arrest the wrong suspect—all while sharing a
flirtation with local brewery owner Grayson Blake. Their chemistry leads
to a heated rivalry at the hockey rink—and to the hot pursuit of a killer.

Keep reading for a special excerpt...

Chapter One

The town of Shady Creek was a winter wonderland. The first snowfall of the season had hit Vermont several weeks ago, not long after the last of the leaves had fallen, and others had followed close on its heels. Now, in early December, the snow lay in a thick layer on rooftops, tree boughs, and the surrounding countryside. I wasn't completely sold on the chilly temperatures, but even Ebenezer Scrooge would have had to admit that the snow-blanketed town was beautiful.

I paused outside the red door of the old stone gristmill that housed my cozy apartment and my literary-themed pub, the Inkwell. Maybe I was biased, but I thought the mill was the prettiest building in town, especially now that nature had decorated it with a layer of snow. The red-trimmed windows and red waterwheel made the place look cheery, even festive, and I'd seen several tourists snapping photos of the building in recent days. I'd taken a few photos myself, and had uploaded them to the Inkwell's Web site and social media accounts.

The cold air bit at my cheeks as I fastened the top button of my blue, puffy, down jacket and pulled my matching scarf up over the bottom half of my face. No snow had fallen overnight, to my relief. That meant I didn't have to worry about shoveling the walkway before the pub opened at noon. And no shoveling meant I was free to head for the village green—much whiter than green at the moment—to check out the opening day festivities of Shady Creek's annual Winter Carnival.

I crossed the footbridge over the creek that had given the town its name. The water in the middle of the creek remained unfrozen and babbled its way between the snowy banks, sounding cheerful as usual. As I made my way across Creekside Road to the village green, I saw that plenty of people had arrived before me.

A welcoming fire burned in a metal fire pit near the bandstand, and several people had gathered around the flames, chatting and sipping drinks from take-out cups, most likely from the Village Bean, the local coffee shop. The bandstand had been tastefully decorated for the season. Several swags made from evergreen boughs tied with bright red bows hung on the outside of the structure, and multicolored lights had also been strung around it. The lights weren't on at the moment, but every night since Thanksgiving, they'd lit up the bandstand with a festive glow.

Directly within my line of sight was a large white canopy, beneath which a few men and women with clipboards had gathered. Several huge blocks of clear ice sat here and there around the green, waiting to be transformed into anything from an angel to a polar bear. The village green was the site of the ice sculpture competition, the first event of the Winter Carnival. I'd never attended an ice sculpture competition before, so I was excited to watch this one unfold, especially since one of my employees, Mel Costas, was among the competitors. Even though I knew Mel was a talented artist, it had surprised me to learn she was taking part in the event, but she'd told me she'd been competing for years.

Apparently she'd won the last two competitions, as well as one several years ago. I had my fingers crossed that she'd win this time as well. Every year there was a cash prize for the creator of the winning sculpture, but this year the stakes were higher. Not only would the winner receive a check for five thousand dollars, he or she would also be featured in *Collage*, a national arts magazine. If Mel won, the magazine coverage could give her and her art some valuable exposure. If more people knew about her work, she'd get more buyers, both online and when tourists visited Shady Creek, as many did, especially during leaf peeper season and special events like the Winter Carnival.

Although several people were milling about near the canopy, it wasn't hard for me to pick out Mel from the crowd. At nearly five foot ten, she was on the tall side, and her blond and electric blue hair drew my eye easily.

I wasn't sure how she could stand to have her head uncovered in this weather, but it did make her easier to spot.

"Morning," I said after I made my way around two men to reach Mel's side. "How are things going?"

"Hey, Sadie," Mel greeted. "So far so good. The competition will be getting underway in a few minutes."

"Are you nervous?" She didn't appear to be, but she didn't often show what she was feeling.

"Nah," she replied. "More pumped than anything. I love this event."

"I can't wait to see your sculpture." I glanced around. "Where's Zoe?"

Zoe Trimble was the twin sister of one of my new employees—Teagan, one of the Inkwell's chefs. When I'd bought the pub, it was without a cook. It took me a few months to find the right candidates to take over in the kitchen, but I was glad I'd held out until Teagan and Booker, the other chef I'd hired, had come along.

Like Mel, Zoe was an artist. She was interested in ice sculpting, so she planned to hang around and learn whatever she could from watching the competitors. Mel had promised to explain the various steps and techniques as she worked.

"She's gone to get coffees from the Village Bean," Mel replied. "She'll be back soon."

I tugged my knitted hat down over my ears and eyed Mel's uncovered head. "Don't you want a hat? It's freezing out here."

She laughed. "It's not so bad, and I'll warm up once I get to work. I'll probably need one tonight, though."

The competitors had thirty hours to create their sculptures from several blocks of ice. At least some of the entrants would work through the night to get finished in time. I shivered just thinking about it. It was cold enough for me at the moment, with the sun peeking through the gray clouds overhead. I'd probably turn into an ice statue myself if I stayed outdoors all night.

"There's Alma," I said, waving to a woman with long, graying hair.

She smiled and waved back before consulting a clipboard.

I'd first met Alma Potts at the Inkwell, where she'd become a regular customer. She loved reading, like I did, and when she'd found out I was planning to host book clubs at the pub, she'd been eager to get involved. The last time we'd spoken, she mentioned that she was the head organizer of the ice sculpture competition.

"May I have your attention, please?" Alma's voice rang out over the snow-covered green. A sound system had been set up for the event, with speakers and a microphone beneath the canopy. "All competitors please go to your assigned stations. We'll be starting shortly."

I walked with Mel toward her carving station near the bandstand. Even before the carnival preparations had begun on the green, the snow had been packed down by people walking here and there and by kids playing. That made it easy to get around, and the carnival's organizers had cleared pathways through any areas that had escaped the trampling of booted feet over the past few weeks.

As we reached Mel's blocks of ice, Zoe jogged up behind us, a take-out cup clutched in each gloved hand.

"Just in time," I remarked as she handed one of the two cups to Mel.

Zoe's breath puffed out in a cloud. "There was a long line. Everyone seems to want coffee this morning."

I could have used one myself. I'd had coffee with my breakfast less than an hour ago, but a hot drink would have hit the spot right then, especially since I could feel my toes going numb inside my boots.

Zoe was dressed more warmly than Mel, with a hat pulled down over her wavy, dark blond hair, but she still wasn't as bundled up as I was with my scarf, hat, mittens, and puffy, knee-length jacket. Apparently I was more susceptible to the cold than my Vermont-born counterparts. I'd spent a few years of my life in Boston and Minneapolis, but I was from Knoxville and I'd never really been able to get used to cold winters.

As Mel did a final check of all her tools, I studied her competition, the carvers spread out around the green. I recognized a few faces, but there were also some I'd never seen before. People traveled from other towns and even other states to compete, I'd been told, so that explained the unfamiliar faces. Not that I necessarily would have recognized everyone anyway. I'd only lived in Shady Creek for about six months. I'd met a lot of people at the Inkwell during that time, but there were still plenty of townsfolk I didn't know.

A commotion at the eastern end of the green drew my attention. A tall man with his dark hair slicked back strode past the canopy. Something about the way he held himself gave me the impression that he thought he owned the entire village green. Maybe it was the way he kept his nose in the air and ignored everyone around him, even though several people had formed a small crowd, scurrying to keep up with his long strides.

"Darn," Zoe said when she noticed the new arrival. "I was hoping he wouldn't show up."

Mel turned around to see whom she was talking about. "Ignore him," she advised.

"Who is he?" I asked.

The man had arrived at the last unoccupied carving station and now faced his followers, his chest puffing out as he radiated self-importance.

"Federico Mancini," Mel replied. "Better known around here as Freddy."

"He's a local?" I said with surprise, wondering why he was completely unfamiliar to me when he seemed to want everyone to notice him.

"He grew up here in Shady Creek," Mel said. "He moved away when he was about nineteen or so. I don't think he's been back since. Not until today. From what I've heard, he thinks this town is beneath him now."

Freddy appeared to be in his midthirties, a few years older than me, so he must have been gone for well over a decade.

"Why the sudden reappearance?" I asked.

Mel returned her attention to her tools. "Probably so he can rub his success in our faces."

"He's a chef in Boston now," Zoe explained. "And he owns a restaurant. A pretty fancy one, I think. I've never been there myself, but I've heard people talk about it from time to time."

I'd lived in Boston for over two years before coming to Shady Creek when my life in the big city fell to pieces, but I'd never heard of Freddy Mancini. That wasn't surprising, though. As much as I loved good food, I'd never been part of the foodie scene in Boston or anywhere else, and I'd never had the budget to eat out at expensive restaurants.

I continued to watch Freddy as he spoke to the small crowd around him, clearly enjoying the attention. A couple of people held out their smartphones to record what he was saying. I noticed Joey Fontana of the *Shady Creek Tribune* among those gathered around the chef. If the others were reporters as well, which at least some of them seemed to be, I didn't know which newspapers they worked for. Joey and his father owned the *Tribune*, the only local paper, and I knew both of their part-time coworkers by sight. I'd never seen the other reporters before.

"Are there journalists here from out of town to cover the event?" I asked.

"Looks like it," Zoe said before taking a sip of her coffee.

"Is that usual?"

"Not really," Mel replied. "It's typically just the local paper that covers the Winter Carnival, but other reporters have shown up once or twice when somebody high profile has come to compete. Not in recent years, though. At least, not that I recall. Freddy's won a handful of competitions around the country and even a couple around the world, so I guess he's attracted some additional interest."

"Hopefully that's good for the town," I said. If more people knew about Shady Creek, maybe more would come to visit.

"*He* sure isn't," a male voice muttered close by.

The owner of the voice was walking past us. More like stomping past, actually. Black hair stuck out from beneath his dark green wool hat and his stormy eyes were nearly black as well. With his hands stuffed into the pockets of his jeans, he positively glowered at the world around him as he headed across the green, away from Freddy and the gaggle of reporters.

"What's with him?" I asked once the man was out of earshot.

"That's Leo Mancini," Zoe said in a low voice.

"Freddy's half-brother," Mel added.

"It doesn't sound like there's much brotherly love between them," I said. Mel shrugged. "There never really was."

That was sad. I wondered what was behind their animosity, but I didn't dwell on it for long. Any thoughts of Leo and Freddy fluttered out of my mind as Alma's voice rang out through the cold air again.

"Welcome, everyone, to the thirty-first annual Shady Creek Winter Carnival!"

I clapped my mitted hands along with everyone else. A few people in the crowd added whistles and cheers.

"Before the ice-sculpting competition gets started, I'd like to give a shout out to the people and businesses that made this event possible."

As Alma went on to thank the sponsors and all of the volunteers who'd organized the competition, a striking woman with long dark hair detached herself from the crowd still gathered around Freddy. She was texting on her smartphone, but she glanced up as she passed by. She did a double take, recognition and surprise registering on her face.

"Jade!" Freddy bellowed.

The woman nearly jumped and then quickly backtracked toward the chef.

I glanced Mel's way and caught a quick glimpse of surprise and recognition on her face as well before a neutral expression took over.

I was about to ask her who Jade was when Alma called out, "Let the sculpting begin!"

Mel set aside her coffee and picked up her tools.

The competition was underway.

Printed in the United States
by Baker & Taylor Publisher Services